# Teresa in the Middle

Edward Stringer

Erika
Best Wishes
keeping it local:
Edward

For more information contact

edwardstringer64@gmail.com

First paperback edition September 2024

'The Knoll' Front Cover Image by Bob Prince

Front Cover Formatting by Cathy Hundt

ISBN 978-1-7384485-4-8 (Paperback)

ISBN 978-1-7384485-5-5 (E-Book)

# Introduction

Teresa in the Middle, a warm feel-good nostalgic rom com…something of a departure from my first two novels; the more peaceful amongst you will be pleased to know this story has a body count of zero. I have always loved gentle comedy, BBC sitcoms in particular in all their guises, from my earliest memories to more recent offerings too numerous to mention. Films including Four Weddings, Love Actually, Notting Hill and of course just where would we be without our Bridgit? So I hatched an idea to write a rom-com novel, not only set where I spent my formative years but at the same time period…*those seventies*, 1978 to be exact.

Although born in Kent, I spent ten very happy years growing up in the Vale of Berkeley in rural Gloucestershire. I moved away when I was 21, however I have lived very nearby for many years, I can easily go and get my 'GL13 (the local postcode) fix', which I do…frequently.

So with the location and the year decided, I thought I'd challenge myself further. What if I wrote the story in the first person present with a female lead? It quickly evolved into something almost interactive; where you, the reader follow our heroine! the irrepressible, often dizzy Teresa through six, at times chaotic and testing months.

I've had such a fantastic time writing this story, so many great memories flooding back; I truly hope you enjoy reading it.

I extend my grateful thanks to my beta readers (the literary world's equivalent of crash test dummies) for their encouraging, enthusiastic feedback, one of them even going so far as to say, 'You wear the skirt well, reading the manuscript I often had to remind myself the author is male!' High praise indeed.
Thanks also go to Mr Bob Prince, who listened to my ideas…I really mean ramblings about how I'd like the cover image to look and made it happen.
I extend a big, big warm thank you across the Atlantic…Brooklyn, New York to be precise to Cathy Hundt for formatting the cover with her usual precise, unruffled professionalism.

Dedicated to my Mother

Who as well as being a great mum, in the mid 1970's took the bold step of leaving behind the ever increasing concrete of Kent for the green fields of Gloucestershire.

# Chapter 1

## *A Lovely Day in May, 1978*

*Primrose Cottage, Brookhayes, Gloucestershire.*

He's singing in the bathroom, that husband of mine, just along the landing. Da-da-da-ing really, a broken chorus of cheerful utterances, no tune, no words. It must be early, my radio alarm clock thingy-me-bob hasn't crackled into life yet. Perhaps I didn't set it last night, that wouldn't surprise me, but it must be early. He hasn't shaken me yet with a 'T, don't forget to pick up my suit from the dry cleaners', or 'T, go to the garage to tell them my car needs a service next week'. On top of that I'm still breathing fresh air, not asphyxiating from *that* aftershave.

In my head, giggling, I picture myself amid a scene of mild panic inside an imaginary hospital ward.

"Doctor Mendham, Doctor Mendham, how will she ever survive; she's turned blue, she's not breathing, whatever could it be?"

"Well Nurse Killum, it's very grave, oh it's the worst case I've ever seen. Hideous aftershave inhalation if I'm not very much mistaken. There is little medical science can do for her; a fatal intoxication, probably a result of her husband's secretary buying him aftershave for Christmas."

"Her husband caused this? the brute."

"Nurse, you are on the right lines, but I rather think it's Blue Stratos not Brut that's the noxious substance in question.

Her only hope…a kiss from a prince, but finding one in this parish at such short notice? I'm afraid there is little hope for her."

The radio alarm crackles into life, jolting me from my reverie.

'*Lovely day'*...ah that's a nice song, '*lovely day,*' very easy to sing along with.

So, I did set it, I can remain hibernating, snuggled under the continental quilt for another ten minutes, enjoying some jolly music, bliss.

'*Lovely day...lovely d–* ' With a crackle the poor radio alarm is brusquely silenced, replaced by a huff and a tut.

"What an infernal racket, right I'm off now T, see you tonight," he says.

My forehead receives its routine perfunctory 'muah', a harbinger, the invisible but pungent Blue Stratos haze is about to engulf me like a plume of mustard gas. All done at lightning speed, I can't possibly respond. He delivers his parting gift to me as he breezes out the door.

"Don't forget we are at the Pitman's tonight." And he's gone, 'trap, trap, trap,' down the stairs, the jangle of keys, the backdoor shutting, his car pulling away...and...he's really gone. Ohh, God, no, the Pitman's.

At least now I can turn the 'infernal racket' back on.

Crackle...hum...hum, the song has finished, replaced by the cheerily droll disc jockey, advising us which horse to back, his 'winner', today's hot racing tip from Haydock Park with his soft chirpy singy-songy Irish brogue.

"Oh and by the way listener, that last song was...as if it wasn't already obvious enough, for goodness sake the eejit forgot the words half way through, trying to pull the wool over our eyes, repeating the title over and over, anyway it was of course, 'Lovely Day' and looking out from the bowels of Broadcasting House you have to agree with the fella, it's a lovely May morning."

Hmmmmph, well, 'lovely day', that's very easy for you to say Mr Wogan, you and the current Mrs Wogan don't have to go to the Pitman's for a dinner party tonight.

Anyway I suppose I'd better get up. Let me introduce myself, I'm Teresa...not T, definitely not T, that really grinds my gears, and it's never Terri...grrrr, it's Teresa. The only permitted exception to the rule is from my God-daughter Alice, she calls me 'Arrnty Treezurr'. She's only four and lives on a farm so I turn a blind eye; in fact I love it when she calls me that.

Teresa Sheen...Sheen being my married name, funnily enough before I was married my surname, my maiden name was Green...Green to Sheen...are you paying attention, are you thinking was it? I am just checking to see if you are reading carefully. Of course it wasn't Green, even my mother wasn't *that* daft, no, it was Taylor.

Now, if you'd like to wait downstairs I will get out of bed and get dressed...after all we've only just met, a little privacy please. Then we'll go outside, I'll show you around Brookhayes. It won't take long, there are only four houses here, and two of those are unoccupied!

Brookhayes', population...four. A hamlet? just four cottages and a derelict chapel lining one side of the lane leading from the small village of Newell Cross to the main Bristol to Gloucester trunk road. From Brookhayes one cannot see any other dwellings whatsoever, just the strange spire thing on top of the local school; the school surrounded by woods and fields, my school. Our cottage is named 'Primrose Cottage', isn't it lovely? Oh, I see what you mean...trust me, it's beautiful.

~ooo~

I'd better go and ask Yvonne about tonight's arrangements, that's Mrs Pitman, it's not far, next door but one, see what time she'd like us to come around tonight...the dinner party. It's always seven o'clock, but well, good manners cost nothing. Ignore the vid-vid-vid sound as I walk by the way, it's my cords, I love them, so comfy and snug, a lovely bright orange. Raymond, my husband, *him,* him with the Blue Stratos, he detests them, my cords, whether it's the noise they make or the colour I don't know, probably both. The thing with Raymond is that we've aged differently, he gets older by the day.

Isn't it a beautiful morning? I love the spring, my favourite time of year, my roses haven't come into bloom yet and the daffodils and tulips have gone over but it's still lovely.

Right, this cottage is next door to mine, 'Ivy Cottage', Jack lived here, it's empty at the moment, he died six months ago. He was in his mid-seventies; he died suddenly and peacefully at home. He was the sweetest kindest man I've ever known, he got me through my darkest times; with my best friend Kim in a supporting role the two of them helped me through. I'll tell you about that a bit later, but I don't know how I would have got through it without Jack. His house is 'For Let' now, it makes me giggle a bit, 'Luc Panes and Co', the estate agent's name written on the yellow and black sign knocked into Jack's little bit of lawn at the front, it makes me think the windows are going to rattle and fall out on a windy night.

The last house in Brookhayes or the first...depends on which direction you are coming from...obviously. This is 'Rosebank Cottage', home to Ralph and Yvonne Pitman. Ralph is a clone of my husband in so many ways, they are actually great friends, unlike Yvonne and myself...we have always been friends by proxy, our husbands expect us to be friends, at best you'd call it an uneasy alliance, imagine Tom and Jerry when that big bulldog is about, 'Butch' I think he's called, enough of that for now.

Ralph and Raymond work in the same department in the same building for the district council, members of the same golf club, the same rotary club, they dress very similarly, similar age, oh, there is one thing, a yawning chasm that separates them. It's their Ford Cortinas, Ralph's is dark blue and Raymond's? well Raymond's is that same sort of insipid beige colour they use to make hearing aids look less conspicuous. It looks absolutely revolting, what on earth possessed him to willingly choose that colour?

Yvonne has a fabulous old brass door knocker, a fox's head, I can never resist the urge to shout 'boom, boom' in my best Basil Brush voice...probably a little too loudly every time I knock on it.

'Good morning Yvonne, what time tonight, seven o'clock?'

I can feel her eyes scanning me up and down as a sergeant major inspects a nervous squaddie on the parade ground. Odd socks, T-shirt back to front or inside out,...you laugh but...then there's age inappropriate clothing, melted chocolate on my trousers. The melted chocolate incident, well that really wasn't my fault. It was *that* noisy motorbike, roaring past my car so fast and close. The blessed thing made me jump out of my skin, just as I was about to pop a few Maltesers into my mouth from the box on the passenger seat whilst driving home from work. They rolled along the grooves in my Mini's seat, under my thighs and beyond! A warm day the chocolate coating comprehensively melted. If only Yvonne hadn't invited me in for a coffee immediately I'd arrived home, if only Yvonne's sofa hadn't been white.

"Yes Teresa, seven o'clock, and *no*...you don't need to bring anything, only yourselves," with a glib ha, ha, her eyes are suddenly drawn to the left. A car has pulled up outside Jack's, Yvonne stares but she quickly loses interest.

"Oh, it's just the letting agent, perhaps there is a potential tenant coming for a viewing."

'See you this evening then', as I turn to leave she casts a dismissive and disinterested 'mmm' my way.

Outside Jack's cottage another car has just pulled up, a black Range Rover, the driver getting down ungracefully from the seat of the quite tall vehicle just as I vid-vid-vid past, heading home.

'Good morning, lovely day', I greet him with a friendly smile, he nods back, incoherently mumbling something. I think his mind is elsewhere. He looks rather like a bank manager or something like that, he must be sixty if he's a day, round, shorter than me with ginger hair, what little there is of it. If he is to be our new neighbour at least I got to say hello before Yvonne did...little victories.

It's going to be a busy day for me. 'Vikki's', the hairdressers in Comberley at eleven o'clock, then I have to work from twelve until four. I have a little part-time job in the town's library. Raymond doesn't much like me working, I'm sure he feels it to be an affront to his manly responsibility of doing 'all' the providing, a slight on the primal 'inner caveman' in him. I think the inner or indeed the outer caveman has long since deserted him. It's been years since he's worn a leopard print loin cloth and carrying a wooden club dragged me by my hair into his cave to have 'his way' with me, sorry, I often go off on a tangent, you'll get used to it.

He may not like me working but we have an agreement, he is just about okay with me working part-time, you see I like to get out and meet people and earn a little bit of money, my Mini doesn't run or repair itself. I'll just wash the breakfast things before I go to Comberley.

Oh, how adorable, 'You are such a handsome chap, how did you end up in my kitchen sink, eh? you furry little castaway'.

A beautiful caterpillar, luxuriant jet black and vivid tan, an abundant covering of lengthy gossamer fine white hairs...he'll be a beautiful tiger moth by July. I'll pop him...or her outside in the garden, my buddleia bush, he'll be in good company there, amongst friends. All nature's wonderful creatures deserve a life don't they...even earwigs.

Right, let's get the car keys and head off to the salon.

~ooo~

*Vikki's Hair Salon, Comberley, Gloucestershire.*

"What are we doing today Teresa?" Tracy the hairdresser casts a critical eye over my hair, she's plonked me down in the chair nearest to the door and enveloped me with a huge white plasticky cape. Standing behind me, with both hands she scoops up my hair running her fingers through it, she's mentally measuring it, I can see her in the mirror, she's been willing it to grow.

Tracy is young but experienced enough, I trust her, she is also imaginative and creative. I have the feeling she's been itching to try something on me. I've noticed her, giving my hair a tiny trim every few weeks, trimming it a bit less than it's grown since the last visit. It's gradually descended to shoulder length. I think she thinks I haven't noticed, but I have. Patiently planning something, she tentatively tells me in her own subtle way it's time.

"Why don't we try something new, it's very fashionable and stylish, not to mention glamourous, it'll really suit you." So, with a little flattery aimed my way...always welcome, she's ready to unleash her creative idea, but clearly her self-confidence needs a little backup.

"I'll just get Vikki's opinion, won't be a tick." She breezes away to the far end of the long narrow shop.

I'll just have a nice little relax then, close my eyes. Sitting in my comfy chair next to the three driers on chrome plated stands in a row, partially enclosing the heads of the purple rinse brigade reading Woman's Realm, appearing almost comatose whilst gumming rich tea biscuits to death. The three driers' motors humming hypnotically. I'm drifting...drifting...drifting...*jolted!*

A thought, crashing into my head, the library; I have to be there in an hour, how long will Tracy's masterpiece take? Immediately I leap up and shuffle quietly along the shop, feeling ghostlike with the huge white nylon bib billowing around me. I patiently wait behind Tracy as she talks with Vikki the salon's owner who's engrossed in washing her sister's hair, face down in a sink, her head somewhere underneath a mass of frothy shampoo suds. Vikki is concentrating jets of water over the back of her sister's head from a rubber shower hose attachment pushed over the sink's taps.

Vikki and her sister Sharon are...er...robust women. Horsey...not the snooty hunting set type, the robust out in all weathers, up to their eyes in horse poo type. Endemic to this district, you'd almost think they'd be more suited to clipping the coats of Welsh cobs or Thelwell-esque ponies for gymkhanas than skilfully styling the manes of the town's womenfolk.

Robust opinions, robust humour, robust thighs...

As Tracy begins asking Vikki and her virtually submerged hairdresser sister their thoughts about her cutting loose with her creative genius it occurs to me that over the noise of the driers at the far end of the shop, coupled with the fact I have crept up rather quietly not wishing to be a nuisance, the three hairdressers have absolutely no idea I am standing just a yard or two away.

"Vikki, I got Teresa in the shop, I was thinking about giving her a 'shag'," Tracy says.

Not really unexpected, the coarse snorting and shrieking laughter that follows, along with a spluttery comment from Sharon beneath the froth.

"Whatever floats your boat darling, it's 1978 after all."

"Mmmm, which Teresa?" Vikki questioning, "Only we got two Teresas that come in here, darkening our doorway."

As Tracy hesitates, Vikki quickly moves to clarify things.

"There's that Teresa from the haberdashers...with the horrible long dank black hair, smells of mothballs, the one that looks like the bride of Dracula." From under the cascade of water, gurgling laughter from Sharon.

"Then there's that blond Teresa."

Oh, that must be me, blond Teresa, that's nice isn't it? But Vikki hasn't quite finished.

"The dappy blond from the library, you know, the one with the red Mini that backed over the Lyons Maid sign outside the sweet shop last time she was here." More gurgling laughter.

Well...I think rather indignantly, that really wasn't my fault. It was the window cleaner's fault, he must have put the blessed sign behind my car, it certainly wasn't there when I went into the hairdressers. Vikki still hasn't finished.

"The dozy mare drove off with the sign still jammed under her car, they found what was left of it, the mangled remains were on the pavement by the bench outside the town hall." Both Vikki and Sharon, like a pair of hyenas were now uncontrollably convulsing with laughter...robust humour.

Tracy though, to her immense credit remains professional and courteous. "It's blond Teresa from the library, what do you think, her hair is shoulder length, will a shag suit her?"

Vikki has now calmed down a little, her wheezing cackle subsiding as she gets her breath back.

"Oh...aaah...ahh, oh my God...I love working here...we have such a laugh don't we?" Now able to speak clearly again she continues giving her no nonsense advice to her younger colleague.

"Yes Trace, a shag will be fine, just don't go cutting the fringe short, not on an older woman, they get wrinkly foreheads. Keep the fringe long, only, I did a shag on an older woman last week, *her*, her from the hardware shop...you know the one...mutton dressed as lamb. Well I cut the fringe a bit too short, she went out the shop looking like one of they hideous aliens off star trek...what's it called, is it a Klingon?"

Tracy decides she'd hazard a guess at my age.

"Teresa, blond Teresa isn't that old, probably thirty-five or something, she don't look wrinkly."

Thank you Tracy. I'm actually forty-one and you have unwittingly just made me very happy.

"Whatever Trace, just keep the fringe quite long, trim it just short enough so she can see to drive properly, we don't want the daft mare to demolish anymore signs."

As Sharon and Vikki resume tittering at my expense while dishing out sage wisdom to Tracy, it dawns on me that Tracy is going to turn around at any moment. I decide it would be best all round if I slip invisibly back to the chair...Have you ever seen a cat when it realises it can't possibly win a fight?...how it slinks backwards incredibly slowly...as if trying to make itself invisible...that's me now...slinking backwards slowly unseen. The 'dappy, dozy, daft, blond, mare' with the wrinkly forehead.

Tracy does a fantastic job, I am thrilled, she looked a little worried now and then but with five minutes to spare I am outside the shop checking for ice cream signs hidden behind my car feeling like Farrah Fawcett.

~ooo~

*The Pitman's , Rosebank Cottage, Brookhayes.*

"Evening, evening come on in, how was the journey? ha, ha, ha, ha." Ralph is a little jolly, a little *too* jolly.

He always makes that remark, as if worried we'd encounter problems on the less than seventy-five yard walk between our cottages.

'Hi Ralph, I think someone has been lurking around the cocktail cabinet'. I greet him with a fleeting peck on the cheek, we get on quite well, Ralph and I. He mimics a mocking worried expression.

"Yvonne is in full flight, I'm keeping my head down, keeping out of the firing line." Giving me a theatrical wink. He turns to Raymond.

"Raymondo, the usual?" As if Ralph needs to ask. It's fair to say my husband is rather predictable.

"Yes Ralph, that would be nice."

"And Teresa, Teresa, Teresa...Cinzano Bianco, ice and a slice?" Ralph rubs his hands together briskly as he hovers close to the trolley laden with an assorted selection of different size and colour bottles.

"You look different Teresa," turning from the drinks trolley he casts an interrogatory glance my way. Singularly unimpressed by my loose-fitting skirt and blouse he raises his gaze upwards.

"Your hair, it's your hair, a new hairdo, I like it, very snazzy."

Yvonne blusters into the lounge from the kitchen, greeting us with a cursory glance.

"Good evening Raymond, T." grrrr.

"Yvonne darling, doesn't Teresa's hair look nice? very 'with-it', perhaps you should have yours done something a bit like that, eh? give the old pudding basin a bit of a rest." Ooops, Ralph has wasted no time in getting the evening off to a flying start, Dutch courage? I feel a little uncomfortable about it, but don't overly worry yourself about Yvonne, she is one of life's natural born survivors.

As hardened and resilient as an armour plated cockroach in a pleated dress and a pageboy. Tutting she quickly counters Ralph's sniping comment.

"It doesn't suit older women, Amanda wears her hair like that at the moment, but it suits her so much better, her hair is thicker, and she is a far more appropriate age." Well, that's told me, fancy turning up to a dinner party after a visit to the hair salon with entirely age inappropriate although undeniably glamorous locks, whatever was Tracy the hairdresser thinking?

Amanda? Just who is Amanda, I can hear you asking. Well, Amanda is the Pitman's daughter. I don't entirely blame her, she never really stood a chance, she is the only child of an only child, Yvonne. Amanda is *Yvonne's* daughter, Ralph is her despairing father, her natural father but Amanda is undoubtedly *Yvonne's* daughter, I think you know what I mean. Indulged, praised, spoilt, and placed on a pedestal similar in height to Nelson's Column. Princess Amanda is the most intelligent, beautiful, stylish, best at everything young lady in the Northern Hemisphere and probably the Southern one too. Except she really isn't,  and her father Ralph will happily tell you that too...provided a certain someone is out of earshot. I'm not going to say anything spiteful about her because as you get to know me you'll find out it's not in my nature.

Yvonne gives Ralph the sort of withering scowl that suggests later Ralph may...no...will regret his amusing but ill-judged pudding basin quip.

"Come through, come through, the food is ready." Yvonne, nonchalant and breezy, beckons us towards the dining room where the starters await.

'Ooops-a-daisy', I proffer my apologies, blushing with embarrassment as I retrieve my starter from my lap and place it back in the little glass  bowl on the table, now encircled by a spreading slick of oily dressing.

'What did you say it was called again Yvonne? it's rather tricky to get your spoon in; I've never seen one before.'

"An avocado pear." A little superior, she tries not to look bemused, Ralph and Raymond openly laughing wasn't helping, not even attempting to stifle their  laughter as I fought and lost the battle with the rock-hard vinaigrette filled avocado half.

After clearing the starter wreckage from the table Yvonne produces a large casserole dish. Placing it with pride in the centre of the table with a flourish.

"Coq-au-vin, it's Amanda's favourite.'" she proclaims in that 'ta-dah' sort of way. The men  make some tittering childish remarks *obviously,* something about a Ford Transit and a mattress, not entirely unexpected. With the third bottle of Blue Nun nearly empty, their volume and courage are increasing with every passing empty goblet. Yvonne's dish is a triumph, very tasty I thought, I never hesitate to tell her when she cooks something wonderful.

Over a goblet of brandy and a few 'After Eights', signalling that the end of the evening is drawing near, Yvonne holds court enthusiastically describing her 'new bathroom suite', going into excruciating detail, the tiles, the bath, basin, and bidet; even the precise colour of the grout hadn't escaped scrutiny at this early planning stage. Oh and don't forget the heated towel rail, Yvonne informing us that Amanda can't use a cold towel when she comes home from university where she is studying law brilliantly. Apparently it brings her out in a rash, she has such sensitive skin.

"Ralph, darling... go and bring the brochure, it's in the bathroom." She drags out the word brochure to sound as if it had several u's.

As Ralph heads out of the dining room, I seize the opportunity I've been waiting for.

'I'll just pop to the loo Yvonne.' No, steady on, it's not what you are thinking, I'm not hoping to catch Ralph alone, in of all places the bathroom, quite the opposite in fact.

The Pitman's have a compact 'cloakroom', by the backdoor, well that's what Yvonne calls it, bafflingly free of cloaks not even a hook to hang one on, it does however have a lavatory, a wash basin, and the piece de resistance...a tacky knitted Spanish lady doll covering the spare toilet roll.

The thing is...the thing is Ralph has this habit of giving my behind a hearty slap when circumstances allow, i.e when Yvonne or Raymond aren't looking. He is only playing, it doesn't hurt, but I don't much like it; at the same time I don't want to cause a fuss. That's why I wear my gypsy skirt or something similar when I come to the Pitman's. Never tight cords or heaven forbid, '*those Levis*' as my best friend Kim calls them. I reason that if it's safely camouflaged under the loose layers of cheesecloth then he won't see it, think about it, and so be tempted to slap it.

My master plan works. Returning to the dining room, the three are all discussing quite heatedly the finer details about which builders should be trusted to install the upstairs bathroom. It would seem local builders especially Mr Watkins polarise opinion; both Ralph and Raymond with almost partisan passion were disparaging about their lack of skill and timekeeping. Even going so far as branding Mr Watkins a cowboy, Raymond adding that he should at the very least have the common decency to wear a mask like 'The Lone Ranger' when the unreliable layabout presented one with his bill.

Unnoticed I slip back to the table, satisfied, sitting on an unslapped bottom next to my husband.

Yvonne passes the bathroom sales brochure to me.

"Would you care to take a look, Teresa?"

She really isn't asking, it's more a command. Half interestedly I flick through the pages, she was taking great pride and delight in telling me her grand design she'd devised for modernising the 'upstairs' bathroom.

'Oooh, look.' I notice something of interest on one of the pages and become quite excited. On the back page, a colour chart, six squares showing the various colours the bathroom suites are available in. One in particular caught my eye, highlighted with a bright red star excitedly pronouncing, 'Available Spring 78'.

'Look at that, avocado, as in avocado pear?' Pointing excitedly, I'm a little quizzical and awestruck, before this evening I'd never heard of, seen, or tasted an avocado. Yet now I'd temporarily worn one on my lap, still bearing the vinaigrette stains to prove it and my mind was racing and not necessarily in a positive way at the prospect of lying naked in a giant enamel avocado half, filled with warm water and bubbles. Yvonne nods patronisingly as I prod the red starred colour sample.

"Yes, Teresa, that is how it's spel—" in my excitement I abruptly butt in.

'Oh, that's ghastly, whoever on earth would want a green bathroom suite? And *that* pink, yuk, alright if you happen to be Barbara Cartland I suppose. The baby blue looks lovely though doesn't it?"

Raymond reaches under the table and takes my hand, squeezing it rather firmly.

"Right folks," he says, "we'd best be making tracks, thanks for a very nice evening," promptly he stands up.

Well, that was quite sudden I think, as I sip the last of my brandy.

"You're welcome, thank you for your company, your place next time." Yvonne has that relieved look as if a great weight has been lifted from her shoulders...the pressure is on me now.

~ooo~

*Primrose Cottage. Brookhayes.*

"Absolute bull's eye." Raymond laughs heartily as we enter our cottage.

'Bull's eye?' I questioningly ask putting the kettle on. Still howling with laughter Raymond wipes a little tear from the corner of his eye.

"When you'd nipped to the loo, Yvonne said what colour bathroom suite she'd ordered." He was off again, giggling inanely like a schoolboy.

"Yvonne told me she was going to order it in the pink, but Princess Amanda had talked her out of it, 'go for something more sophisticated Mummy, choose the avocado'."

# Chapter 2

## ***A Saturday in May***

*Primrose Cottage, Brookhayes.*

"You well and truly put your foot in it last night T, calling Yvonne's bathroom suite, what was it you said?"

Raymond seems slightly cross, odd, he'd thought it hilarious last night, but he is sober now, probably sporting a bit of a hangover too I shouldn't wonder.

'Oh don't remind me, ghastly, I said I thought a green bathroom suite would look ghastly'

"I was so embarrassed, you should think before you blurt out your opinions," sighing and huffing the way he often does.

"I have to go into the office for a few hours this morning T. Not sure how long I'll be, I have to have the April accounts finalised by next week or they'll have my guts for garters."

That's unusual, Raymond working on a Saturday, never mind, I can take some flowers to the churchyard and take a walk to my 'knoll' this afternoon. It's my special place, we all have a special place don't we? the 'knoll' as I call it is mine.

'It's not like Paula to get behind with the accounts is it?'

Paula is Raymond's secretary...Blue Stratos...she is superhuman, looking out at the world through huge thick framed glasses, a rarely smiling automaton, she is organised, efficient and punctual.

She dresses in the same manner...efficient, continuing the theme, her hair...a sort of 'bob', efficient and maintenance free. Everything it seems in Paula's world is geared towards ruthless efficiency, outwardly devoid of emotion, she's like a plump Swiss watch in a crimplene dress.

"She is trying to juggle looking after her mother, move home, divorce her useless lump of a husband and hold down her job, so I have to make allowances."

'Move home?'

"She is moving in to her mother's house, the old girl has recently gone into a care home, she'll probably never come out, well not upright anyhow, so it's empty. Paula will be left it anyway, it makes sense, but it needs a devil of a lot of work." Raymond slides out of bed and heads for the bathroom. "I'll go to my club and play a round of 18 tomorrow instead, there'll be less people out tomorrow anyway."

Golf...Raymond and Ralph's diversion from their otherwise humdrum lives. Yvonne, and *her* daughter Amanda, when she's not at university being brilliant that is, often make up a foursome. Raymond has tried a few times to show me how to play...With all the different clubs, handicaps, terminology, and etiquette you can imagine how that turned out. No, golf is definitely not for me I'm afraid. I like to swim, always have, I go most weeks.

There is one of those new-fangled 'leisure centres' in Stroud with a very nice pool. Stroud, that's about ten miles away. Kim and I swim there for an hour once a week and afterwards we put the world to rights over a drink at the 'Fox and Goose' at the end of our lane.

~ooo~

Excuse me a moment, the phone is ringing.

'Comberley 419'

"Teresa, Yvonne, don't look now but the 'to let' sign has come down on 'Ivy Cottage' and that odd little man with the ginger hair has just parked on the drive."

I am awkwardly cringing, but hopeful, her excitement suggests last night's bathroom suite faux pas isn't high on her list of priorities...By the way when Yvonne says 'don't look now' it means drop whatever you are doing this instant and look right now.

'Ah well Yvonne, I suppose at least he looks mature, he will probably be quiet.'

"Mmm, yes I suppose, it's just, he looks so...so...oh what is the word I'm looking for?" I offer her a suggestion; not sure it's an actual word.

'Bank managery-ish?'

Yvonne punctuates her pause with a few mmm's.

"Actually Teresa I was just going to go straight in with boring but yes, bank managery-ish." Another momentary silence, my fingers tightly crossed that she's not mithering about last night, I want to say how much I liked her 'coq-au-vin' but feel compelled to maintain strict 'dinner party silence' hoping it blows over.

"Right, I just thought I'd let you know about 'Ivy Cottage' I have to go, bowls club committee meeting this morning ciao." With a sigh of relief I hear the clunk and the rapid continuous burr tone as the receiver is replaced Yvonne's end.

Fiddlesticks, now that's annoying. In next door's back garden, some carnations are just starting to bloom, I was going to take some to the churchyard; if a tenant has moved in that puts an entirely different complexion on it. There is nothing in bloom in my borders at the moment. Imagine what the 'odd little man' would think, quite the introduction to the woman next door, her wandering about his garden helping herself to his flowers.

Wait...Wait, hold on just a tick, there is no car there now, he must have gone out. Fortune favours the brave. Slippers on feet..., scissors in hand, let's go next door, I'm sure he'll not notice a few missing flowers.

~ooo~

*Ivy Cottage, Brookhayes.*

Jack was a fantastic gardener, I could never aspire to reach his level of green fingeriness but over the years I learnt a thing or two from him. His carnations are...were always beautiful, he'd supply me with a limitless amount of flowers, the florist in the town would never get fat from me. Right, let's just cut a couple more, a couple more and...

"The inventory failed to mention the cottage came with a gardener."

For a moment I freeze, motionless, now I must have imagined that, somebody saying something. A swift glance over my shoulder says otherwise. Smartly dressed in his dark suit peering through small, round, brass-framed spectacles, the 'odd little man' is regarding me, looking rather amused.

'Oh, hello, I was just...er...um...deadheading, yes that's it, deadheading these carnations; you really need to cut out the early blooms to encourage bushing.' Scrambling in the back of my mind, success...that sounded convincing didn't it? I manage somehow to recite one of Jack's oft' quoted gardening pearls of wisdom. He rubs his chin whilst looking at the cut blooms in my hand.

"Speaking as someone who possesses very little or in fact next to no gardening knowledge whatsoever, carrying out this, ahem...essential maintenance is best done in one's nightwear is it?"

'Oh absolutely, yes, the earlier in the day the better, early worms and birds you know.' My blushes from being caught red-handed are slowly subsiding.

"I see, well thank you very much for your diligence. The name's Lionel by the way and you are?"

'I'm Teresa, I live next door, I've been looking after Jack's garden as best I can since he passed away; I imagine that you'll be keen to put your own mark on it now Lionel.' I'm thinking to myself you are extricating yourself out of this well Teresa. Now the gate...focus on the gate...head to the gate. He smirks at me and lightly titters.

"No, I won't be living here, I'm simply making the necessary arrangements, the tenant who'll be living here is expected to move in next week. Meanwhile feel free to carry on tending the garden and pinching...I mean pinching out the flowers until then." Turning on his heels, whistling he heads back towards the cottage.

~ooo~

*St Winnifred's Church, Comberley, Gloucestershire.*

This is our church, it's where Raymond and I got married all those years ago, it has played host to the two happiest days of my life...and the worst.

Over here, here, just here. This is the grave of my little baby son, Anthony, Anthony James Sheen. Our dear little child. He was taken from us when he was just six months old. Meningitis, a cruel disease that doesn't discriminate, it doesn't care who it takes. It came on so suddenly, we rushed him into the hospital here in the town in the middle of the night, I handed him over to the nurses, within half an hour they had the onerous task of telling Raymond and me that our beautiful baby boy had died.

What followed for me can only be described as a total breakdown, I could barely hold myself together leading up to Anthony's funeral. The aftermath was absolute collapse.

Raymond and I coped and grieved in different ways. Initially we grieved together, united, comforting each other but soon his stiff upper lip and pull yourself together maxims alienated us. We became increasingly distant as his frustrations bubbled over. It left me feeling isolated...alone.

Enter Jack next door, we were very close friends before Anthony was born, after Anthony's death he stepped up, really stepped up. I'd fallen so far into an abyss of depression I couldn't eat or sleep; everything, even washing myself was a huge, almost insurmountable hurdle, the longer it went on the weaker I became.

During those first few weeks I could barely cry, I don't know why but I couldn't weep for my child, and that made me feel guilty. I constantly told myself I was a bad mother, neglectful, I loathed myself, if I was a better mother I would have noticed Anthony was sick earlier and he might have lived. After countless offers to help me and receiving countless, 'no I am okay's' as an answer he'd had enough, he could see I was broken, badly broken.

One afternoon Jack came around to my cottage, he literally scooped me up and took me next door to his house. He made me a cup of tea that I just let go cold. He sat down beside me on the settee and just put his arm around me. Some old black and white western was on the telly. He just sat beside me, saying nothing, lightly stroking my hair while we watched the posse chase the bandits.

It was just that simple warm closeness to another warm human being that did it, within a few minutes I was bawling my eyes out. I cried floods and floods of tears while the Indians chased the stagecoach. The shoulder of his green and white checked shirt was soaked.

After two hours constant weeping I fell asleep, the sheriff had rescued the squaw; for the first time in several weeks I fell asleep. The film had finished, another film had started but Jack dare not move, I was asleep, and he wasn't going to allow anything to disturb that.

Raymond came around to Jack's after work and saw me fast asleep on Jack's shoulder, thanked Jack and went back home. Jackanory, Z cars, World in Action, Softly Softly, The Money Programme, The Nine o'clock News, and the Sky at Night, Jack endured it all, all the more amazing he didn't like the telly much. Jack was an outdoor man, but he didn't move a muscle for seven hours that first day while I slept. When I awoke it was dark outside and Jack was absolutely bursting for a pee, he'd remained totally still while I slept on his shoulder. This went on for weeks and weeks, I could only sleep during the day on Jack's sodden shoulder, he didn't complain, not once.

At least now I was sleeping but still not eating, weight was falling off me, weight I could ill-afford to lose. I was a bag of bones, Jack started cooking  dishes in the early morning before I, on his insistence went around to him. Entering his house a tantalising smell would be hanging in the air, he'd make extra so Raymond had a meal to heat up when he got home. Delicious food, at first I couldn't face it, then one small mouthful, the following day a little more and so on. Jack had to tend to his garden and do his groundsman's work at the local cricket ground at ridiculous times of day.

He was becoming exhausted, I was asleep on his tear-soaked shoulder most of the day. My long term best friend Kim really stepped up during this period too, as much as anything taking care of Jack who'd selflessly devoted himself to caring for me while Raymond worked.

Jack and Kim, like a pair of crutches to a legless person; The two of them kept me upright through those very darkest of times. I couldn't and wouldn't have survived without them.

After around six months I was on the road to recovery. I could eat small meals, sleep in my own bed at night and had just about enough energy to at least get through half of the day. Nowadays, even after nearly ten years I still have wobbles; I still shed a little tear once or twice most days.

Just give me a few moments alone with Anthony, I'll put Jack's beautiful carnations on his little grave while I tell him my news, then we'll go. I have to pop in the butchers.

~ooo~

*Castle Street Butchers, Comberley.*

"Morning Twiggy, what would you like today darling?"

'I don't know, what do you recommend?'

His lips pursed, he casts a slow gaze across the counter towards the shop window display. Trays and trays of meat separated by funny little green plastic hedges. Mince, liver, beef joints, faggots, and chops. Hanging from their hind legs gazing down on the neatly displayed meat selection, two large, very dead rabbits. Wide-eyed and startled looking, staring as if in surprised disbelief.

I am often startled, staring in surprised disbelief too when I'm in the butchers...the prices.

The butcher raises his arm, one finger outstretched, a eureka moment. He whispers to me in a fairly hushed tone, as if divulging a closely guarded secret, worried someone was going to overhear him in his otherwise empty shop in the deserted street.

"We got venison sausages Twiggy, the deer come from the estate fresh this morning, how about four of they, they'm big and rich mind, will that do you and your old man?"

Venison sausages from the estate, fresh this morning, big and rich, how could I possibly refuse?

'Yes please, that would be perfect.'

He yells towards the door leading into the backroom of the shop over the noise of persistent chopping sounds and Roger's very hearty rendition of 'Figaro'.

"Roger, fetch I four venison sausages for Twiggy will ya?"

The Castle Street butchers, Roger and Nicholas, considerably overweight, they look uncannily alike to each other. Ruddy, shiny, perma-smiling faces topped with gingery blond colour straw-like hair.

You'd swear blind they were brothers or at the very least cousins. They swear blind they are not related in any way, although I'm not entirely convinced. In this district among the rural community there seem to exist dynasties of families and I would imagine that bloodlines are not always quite as exact and pure as they'd have you believe. But it doesn't matter, Roger and Nicholas are genuinely nice men if not a little macabre looking with their dark blue aprons worn over their white shop coats, always looking as if they have carried out multiple brutal murders with their cleavers.

Twiggy? well I haven't told you this yet, but I was born in Deptford in London two years before the war. My dad went off to fight in France when war broke out and was never seen again. When the bombs started raining down on London my mother, brother and I were sort of self-evacuated to Lydney in Gloucestershire. My uncle and aunty lived there, they'd moved from London a few years previously, so the three of us lived with them. I was two years old at the time, we lived there for many years before moving over the other side of the River Severn to Comberley.

When I was twenty-one I met and fell in love with Raymond. He showed up one evening at a dance at the new-fangled 'motel' on the Bristol to Gloucester trunk road. Romantic but sensible, mature but fun, he was eleven years my senior. With that lovely cheeky twinkle in his eye and his dark curly hair he swept me off my feet. Meanwhile my brother who had been born, bred, and disillusioned in England decided he'd emigrate to Australia for a tenner taking my mother with him.

Although I've lived in Gloucestershire for virtually all my life, growing up with my mother who's always retained her very strong London accent it was bound to rub off on me. So I suppose it was inevitable. Given the butchers penchant for dubbing some of their customers with nicknames, a skinny blond woman with a mild but still detectable London accent it was always going to be 'Twiggy'.

'How are Caroline and Zoe?' I ask as Nicholas wraps up the sausages.

"They're fine Twig, our Zoe is seven months old now, sleeping through the night, everything is good."

Caroline is Nicholas' wife, I got to sort of know her last year, the day of the Queen's silver jubilee. There was a big party in the castle meadows, I went with Kim. Raymond had a Rotary Club engagement so couldn't make it. There was a hog roast, a little fun fair for the town's children, a carnival parade, that sort of thing, oh yes and it was fancy dress, no particular theme although Queen based dressing up and union jack flags were encouraged.

Well, there was an...an...incident. The carnival parade consisted of tractors pulling trailers behind them around the meadows with the fancily dressed brownies and sea-scouts, young farmers, football team etc, perched on hay bales on the beds of the trailers, it was all going swimmingly. That was until the tractor pulling the Leighbury on Severn District Silver Band and Wurzel Gummage turned sharply in error through a gate into the very bumpy and rutted adjoining field which rose up steeply, well a good deal more steeply than the tractor driver had at first anticipated. The band members dressed as olden day soldiers remained seated as did waving Wurzel and Aunt Sally, however the bales didn't remain. They all slid with considerable speed from the back of the trailer depositing the twelve band members holding their somewhat bulky instruments, Wurzel, and Aunt Sally along with a number of hay bales in the fortunately dry field entrance.

The reaction from the considerable crowd assembled nearby was mixed. A few gasps of surprised horror; predominantly the incident met with unbridled cider fuelled roars of laughter. The gateway to the field looked as if a giant toddler in a tantrum had angrily upturned their toy box in it, tossing a good few generous pitchfork's worth of hay over the prostrate figures for good measure. Kim...ever cool Kim, I can count the number of times I've heard her swear, properly swear on one hand, but she did swear that day.

"Fucking hell Teresa, Caroline is pregnant," as we precariously tottered towards the carnage over the ridiculously rough ground in our ridiculously high heels.

'What?' I had no idea who Caroline was.

"Aunt Sally, Aunt Sally is pregnant." Kim shouted as we picked the best route through. For me the whole thing just became surreal. A pregnant Aunt Sally buried under a platoon of groaning old-fashioned soldiers with trumpets in a field. The hazy air thick with a heady combination of sizzling hot dogs, candy floss and wood smoke, all the while my ears were ringing from the steam organ's overly speedy, overly loud and tinny rendition of 'It's a long way to Tipperary'.

The St John's Ambulance woman was helpful, cheerful, and seemed knowledgeable. Caroline swore she was feeling fine, but that was never going to be enough for Kim.

"Teresa, we're going to take her to Gloucester to get her checked over." Aunt Sally protested but once Kim has made up her mind...resistance is futile.

Half an hour later, my little red Mini screeched to a halt outside the casualty department in Gloucester's massive hospital and we cajoled a still complaining about all the unnecessary fuss and bother Caroline inside to be checked over.

The staff and patients in the large, packed waiting room couldn't entirely hide their amusement as a limping, grumbling Aunt Sally entered. On either side, supporting her, teetering on the very edge of stability in their ridiculously high heeled boots and shiny silver skin-tight jumpsuits, none other than Annifrid and Agnetha of Abba fame, in reality Kim and yours truly.

As we sat in the waiting area while Aunt Sally was being checked over for structural damage, me in my tight blue knitted hat and ostentatious bright blue eye shadow we received numerous requests to 'sing us a song', it seemed 'Dancing Queen' or 'that, that, what's it called Fernando' were the most requested. Although tempted, Kim and I hadn't drunk anything like enough cider. We reluctantly agreed with heartfelt compassion for the assorted injured and wounded assembled in the casualty department that they had probably suffered enough.

Caroline was fine, a small cut on one of her fingers and a massive bruise on her bum but otherwise fine.
Five months later she gave birth to a…I'm not going to say bouncing…baby girl…Zoe.

# Chapter 3

## *A New Face in Brookhayes*

*Primrose Cottage, Brookhayes.*

'Comberley 419'

"A motorbike Teresa, it seems the odd little man has a motorbike."

'But the 'odd little man', Lionel isn't the new tenant Yvonne, he told me that he is just arranging things.' Yawning, I smile to myself, little victories, I'd known for a week now, ever since Lionel had caught me pinching carnations in my nightie. I knew that he wasn't going to be the tenant, deviously I'd neglected to tell Yvonne, that sounds a bit mean but it's unusual for someone to know something before she does so it's to be savoured...little victories.

I can sense her indignation as she exhales loudly, a dissatisfied huff.

"Yellow it is, with lots of shiny silver pipes, I bet it will be noisy.

'I haven't heard anything', I tell her...except paranoid gossip I think to myself.

"Well, that's because it arrived in a van with lots of boxes, what can you see from your upstairs? I haven't seen any people yet, just some boxes and that noisy motorbike.”

‘No, same here, nothing, if I see anything of interest I’ll make sure I report it, I’ll call you back, bye Yvonne.’

Yvonne’s obsession with wanting to know the ins and outs and the comings and goings is bordering on paranoia at times. Neighbourhood watch is one thing, but Yvonne can be almost ‘Orwellian’ in her ‘Big Sister’ vigilance to safeguard Brookhayes from those she judges to be unruly or nefarious.

Cow muck!...The lanes around our district offer several advantages over chaotic crowded city streets. They are always quiet, no jams, traffic lights, roundabouts, zebra crossings and they are winding and bendy to make driving fun. They do however suffer a few drawbacks. Not being gritted in the winter when it snows, making driving become way, way *too* much fun. During the summer when the farmers are harvesting there are tractors and harvesters everywhere. And then there’s the cow muck, a slimy green carpet covering the roads when the herds of Friesians move along the road from field to field.

Look at my poor little car, its sides and wheels covered in cow muck, it’s high time I give it a spruce up. I’ll just get the hose, sponge and my washing up bowl. No, are you quite mad? that’s revolting, not the one from the kitchen, I kept my old one for cleaning my car.

It's so fiddly washing the hub caps and bumpers. Look at the poor back bumper, it wasn’t always that funny shape, people park so close don’t they? Oh and that pesky ice cream sign didn't help. The oft' replaced back bumper of my car is frequently the butt of wisecracks at my expense during our dinner parties.

Well that's it done, all red again, no cow muck, time for a good old rinse with the hose.

My favourite part...it's such a lovely day, the sun is shining, the birds are singing and I'm going to join them.

I love this song, it's new, all about a Russian monk, he sounds like a bit of a rascal by all accounts, by the way, I like to make up my own words.

*'Ra, ra, see it gleam...Teresa's car is nice and clean',*

The Fairy Liquid suds! I always use too much, are slowly sliding down the windows like little icebergs as I hose my baby down in the same style I'm singing...with gusto, joy, energy...discord!

*'Ra, ra, squeaky clean...very nice job Mrs Sheen.'*

My own take on the lyrics, how did you like that?

*'Ra, ra, squeaky cl–,'*

Turning around I freeze in my tracks in shocked surprise; the words of my very improvised song fall onto the wet foam splattered concrete. A man...a man just a few yards away, looking at me, standing still, on the edge of the drive. Where did he come from? a stranger. I cringe, he must have heard me strangling that song. I might have said I *like* to sing, but I don't think I said that I actually *could* ...there is a difference. I can feel myself turning red, I wish the earth would swallow me whole.

Gosh though, he's rather handsome, nicely dressed too, pull yourself together Teresa I tell myself.

'Hello,' I'm trying to sound confident and failing.

"Good afternoon, I've just moved in next door, I wonder if I may ask you a small favour, if it's not too much trouble, but please finish rinsing your car first." He smiled a sort of sideways smile. Is it possible for a voice to mesmerize you instantly in just one sentence as if you are hypnotised? He spoke with the smoothest Scottish accent I've ever heard, it was like soft silky satin.

'I've finished rinsing it', self-assured.

He points to underneath the front bumper, it was still covered in soapy froth.

'Oh yes, oops I missed a bit.'

Trying to look composed and collected, as much as one can when washing a car, nonchalantly pulling on the hosepipe pointing it at the bubbles, nothing. The blasted hose has a kink and it's become trapped under one of the rear wheels cutting off the water to the sprayer. Trying to act cool and unruffled in front of this man with *that* voice, my attempt to dislodge the hose with a wild flick of my arm is met with success.

It's quite astonishing just how much water can come out of a thin hosepipe so quickly with so much force. In the full gaze of this handsome stranger, in my effort to look blasé as my left hand flicked the hose free from under the car wheel my right hand holding the sprayer had wandered unnoticed by me. The hose now free of its restrictive kink unleashed a torrent on a biblical scale barely more than a few inches from the side of my face. I recoil from the blast and the shock of the cold water as the deluge splats me, staggering to the left, like a puppy skidding about on a wet floor my foot plants itself on the rim of the washing up bowl, still three quarters full of soapy, cow muck infested water it violently overturns swamping my white soon to be green canvas shoes.

I can do nothing but just look at the ground for a moment as the water steadily drips from my face and hair. Oh well, so much for looking graceful.

'Hi, I'm Teresa, you were saying you wanted to ask a favour.'

A gentleman, he resists the urge to smirk at me making a very soggy ninny of myself, he just casually glances down at his feet briefly then looks at me with that cute half smile. It is the sort of smile that isn't sneering or smug, it has a sincere warmth, giving the impression its owner is a happy confident soul.

"Perhaps you may like to get a towel first?" he suggests. I could only giggle now, any attempt at elegance and dignity had joined the soapy green water languidly flowing down the drive towards the drain. I squelch towards the tap to turn off the hose.

'Would you like a cup of tea...er...erm?'

"Callum, Callum Gilchrist." Well of course it is, even his name is fabulous, I'm in serious need of pulling myself together, I'm definitely swooning.

"A cup of tea would be lovely Teresa although I really don't want to be a nuisance."

'It's no problem, come into the kitchen and sit down, I'll just go and change while the kettle boils, I'm soaked right through, right through to my knick–, er...yes...come in, follow me.'

In dry clothes, my hair no longer dripping, over a cup of tea I have so many questions, they have formed a muddled stuttery log jam.

His smile increases and one of his eye brows lifts.

"I met the lady next door...Yvonne, earlier."

Gently blowing over the surface of his tea he takes a little sip.

"She was very, what's the word, very...welcoming." His expressive eyes implying that he'd probably been a little overwhelmed by Yvonne's zeal.

'She has a heart of gold really, she often comes across as blunt and patronising, but she is a good soul.'

What? come on she is, deep down she is, I know we have our moments...frequently, but she's a good sort, what I like about Yvonne is that she can take it as well as she dishes it out and she doesn't harbour grudges.

'Where are you from Callum?'

"Edinburgh...but I work all over the place, I'm in shipping."

'Edinburgh, I've never been to Scotland, I'd like to visit one day, the Highlands look very beautiful, I had a biscuit tin with a scene from the Highlands with a stag on it once.'

I can't believe I just said that...biscuit tin, what was I thinking?

"You should, may I suggest going to–." The phone begins ringing in the wall alcove by the front door.

Callum gestures to answer with a sweep of his flat hand towards it.

'Comberley 419.'

'Oh, hello Yvonne'.

'Yes, I have.' I look across the four feet to the table where Callum is seated.

'I know, he seems very nice.' He gazes towards me.

'Yes, he said, Edinburgh apparently.' He smiles as he listens to one half of a conversation about him.

'We are just having a cup of tea.'

'Ha ha-ha, I think that's probably just a silly rumour, Yvonne really I can't ask him that, I've only just met him, they must wear pants, it gets very cold in Scotland.' Relaxed, I have known him less than half an hour, yet I feel so comfortable, although I'm still in full swoon mode, especially when he speaks.

'I haven't seen it, A *red* Cortina you say, how racy.'

'Okay, take care Yvonne, speak later.' Putting the receiver down I return to my chair, lifting my tea cup.

'That was Yvonne, warning me all about this mysterious man going around charming all the fair maidens of the parish into making him a cup of tea.'

"Teresa, that's very good, uncanny, do you recall I wanted to ask a favour? well I was wondering if you might possibly have a spare tea cup I could borrow, just until tomorrow, mine has got broken in the move."

'You've only got one tea cup?' I'm surprised.

"I've only got one mouth." Mmmm, yes you have, and it's a nice shaped one I think as I titter at his quip.

'And is Sir a mug man or are you more a china cup and saucer type?'

"I prefer a china cup and saucer, but a mug will do."

Fishing about in my crockery cupboard, there is an old, blue willow pattern china cup with a matching saucer. I'd won it as a prize a few years ago at the annual fun fair in the castle meadows, shooting tin cans from a shelf with a little air rifle. Raymond was furious that he couldn't win one, especially as I'd succeeded at the first attempt. Unbeknown to Raymond, my brother had taught me how to shoot his airgun when I was a young girl. No matter how hard Raymond tried, with increasing frustration he missed every time. I had to stifle my titters, that male pride...his inner caveman. Seething, he spent a small fortune trying, in the end, out of ten pence pieces, he angrily accused the stall holder of tampering with the little gun's sights. Sorry I got side tracked, but I still laugh about it...Raymond's face.

Anyway back to the cup in the cupboard, it is miraculously free of chips, embarrassingly it's full of that light fluffy type of dust that gets everywhere and a little dead spider. I manage to hustle it into the sink unnoticed as he's finishing his tea and give it a swift rinse and dry. Handing it to him as he stands up from the table he takes it. The bright sunlight streaming in through the large kitchen window enables me to see his dark eyes clearly for the first time, tawny with a reddish tinge of henna, they have a warm friendly shine. Soft lines and dark circles under them, perhaps the house move might have been stressful.

"The racy red Cortina is my company car by the way. My car is in Felixstowe at the moment, Lionel is going to have it brought here in a few weeks." He looks at the unbranded underside's of the cup and saucer. I think to myself if you are hoping for Royal Doulton or Wedgewood then prepare for disappointment but he seems satisfied.

"Much obliged Mrs Sheen, I'll return it tomorrow, can I buy cups in Comberley?"

'Cups, you said cups, you want more than one?'

"Well, you were kind enough to offer me a cup of tea, I thought I should return the favour once I've settled in, it would be bad form to expect you to bring your own cup and saucer."

'I see, thank you and Mrs Sheen, how do you know my surname?" He grinned, pausing, I think he was carefully choosing his words, balancing what he'd like to say against what he thought he probably ought to say.

"I couldn't help but overhear when you were ...erm...serenading Rasputin, you were congratulating yourself on cleaning your car."

Oh, his voice, I'm beguiled, even when he's mildly mocking me it's intoxicating.

'Cups...you'd probably be better off going to Macsley or better still there's a Woollies in Stroud, don't make a special trip just for a cup though, you can hang on to mine for as long as you like, I have plenty.'

"You are very kind, thank you, I'll leave you in peace," reaching the back door, at length he smiles towards me.

"It's been very nice meeting you Teresa, Comberley is such a beautiful area I think I'm going to enjoy living here."

Wow, my heart is sort of fluttering, a weird sensation, he is gorgeous. Stop it, don't think that, I'm married. I made a promise all those years ago; I have never even come close to breaking my vows. Sometimes temptation has lurked around the corner, but I have always managed to turn around and walk the other way...I think that figuratively speaking, looking at the goods on display in the shop window but not touching is perfectly acceptable, and swooning, well we have no control over swooning do we?

# Chapter 4

## *Kim*

*The Fox and Goose Inn, Newell Cross.*

While she has gone to the bar to get the after-swimming cider I'll tell you about Kim.

She is my best friend...no question...I don't have to even think about it, she *is* my best friend. Jack next door, he would have been joint best friend, he was my best friend in a different way. The father I never had, the best father you could ever hope for; he passed away last year, I still miss him painfully every single day. Margaret at the library is a friend but a work colleague type friend.

I suppose...I...could nominate Yvonne at Rosebank Cottage in a supporting role, a bit like in the Oscars but really is she a great friend? Quite frankly after her comments about me when I was wearing my boob tube in the back garden last week I don't feel inclined to award her any type of 'friend Oscar'. Shall I tell you about that now? I'm meant to be telling you all about my rock, Kim aren't I? and as usual I'm heading off on a tangent.

No, I'm still seething about the boob tube, so I'll get it off my chest now, *chest,* I don't believe I just said that. Talking about chests I'll just briefly mention that I'm not overly blessed up top, just about enough to feel confident about myself. Let's just say they don't stop the traffic but on the upside they are not unruly when I dash about. But my boob tube doesn't do me any favours in that department, firmly compressing my meagre allocation. It's like wearing a geriatric but determined python, it's not got enough strength to totally squeeze the life out of you, but it will still have a damn good try.

Well, last week I was looking after Kim's youngest daughter, Alice, my God daughter. We were entertaining ourselves with a little game of badminton in the back garden, a lovely warm sunny afternoon. Little Alice bless her, she struggles to hit the shuttlecock but when she does, she hits it like she's the bionic woman, with a delighted squeal, she hit it...oh did she hit it...it sailed over my lawn, bounced off the roof of Jack's greenhouse and disappeared.

We have a little gate between our gardens, so Jack and I could easily water each other's plants when holidays were an annual source of joy for Jack and his wife, and in recent years loomed woeful for me. Two weeks with the 'new old' Raymond. Nowadays often somewhere dreadful, somewhere where there are golf courses, old battlefields or art museums, culture is okay, sure, but two weeks? For me it's two weeks solid of Raymond, the 'new old' Raymond twenty-four hours a day, no dancing, no Kim, no Mini, sorry, tangent again.

Anyway, safe in the knowledge my handsome new neighbour Callum was at work I went next door to retrieve the shuttlecock. In my flip-flops, little white denim shorts which Raymond detests and purple boob tube which he detests even more. You can imagine my horror when while I'm grubbing around in Jack's lengthy, long since mown lawn, Yvonne and her two cronies from the bowls club appeared in her garden for an illicit ciggy. They just appeared, no warning, as if they'd just been beamed down from the Starship Enterprise.

Yvonne takes on quite a different persona when she finds herself in the company of her cronies. A superior aloofness, whether those cronies hail from bowls club, the WI or the '45' club, where the indignant over 45-year-old has-beens of the Round Table end up. Yvonne was incandescent when she was told a special dispensation wouldn't be extended to her as a 'special' case and was uncompromisingly invited to either join her fellow over 45's in the '45' club or face the indignation and shame of being cast out like a leper...a pariah in a Pringle twinset. Anyway I digress, sorry, back to Yvonne and her cronies in the garden.

They'd clearly unscrewed the cap on the plonk and had had a couple, Lambrusco I'd guess, it's the usual culprit. Seeing me in the next-door garden the three of them stopped and stared.

"Teresa" she said, in that slightly posher Yvonne nasal tone. "Have you lost something?"

I swear I heard them muttering amongst themselves, not quite inaudible, it was as if there were three menopausal ventriloquists minus their dummies looking over the fence, their mouths barely moved but I heard them, all had differing opinions on just what it was they'd thought I'd lost.

Dignity...dress sense...mind.

I was mortified, like a chameleon I could feel my face becoming as purple as my boob tube.

'The shuttlecock, it must be here somewhere.' I said batting through the lengthy grass with the tip of my racquet. Yvonne hadn't finished, asking me as she exhaled a thin stream of smoke upwards.

"Is that...umm...'garment' entirely suitable for playing badminton during daylight hours, it's rather minimal isn't it, is it a new trendy sports fashion that we slightly...just very slightly more mature ladies haven't been privy to, what is it called?"

To be fair, she had a point, I was dressed as if I were going to a disco rather than playing with a four-year-old in the back garden.

'A boob tube,' I said, the very moment I uttered the words I regretted them. Why, why, didn't I just say I don't know? I wanted the earth to swallow me whole, that very instant.

Well they tried to stifle their titters, and they mostly succeeded, mostly. I could see the cogs in their minds whirring around, a little hesitant, they are suffering from 'Lambrusco lag' I thought. Immediately declaring the shuttlecock forever lost I beat a hasty retreat. Now I don't know, either my hearing rather like Alice's badminton swing is bionic or far more likely Yvonne's mouth's volume control switch malfunctions when swamped with Lambrusco but as I reached the sanctity of the gate and freedom beyond I distinctly heard her.

"Boob tube, did you hear that? boob tube she said, poor deluded woman, I think the word she was looking for was tube...just tube., I didn't see any boobs."

Well, the cackling and shrieking that succeeded Yvonne's observation by the bowling club coven was worthy of any production of Shakespeare's famous Scottish tragedy that cannot be named, namely the scene with the cauldron.

Anyway back to Kim. I first met Kim that very first day I arrived mid-way through the first term of the first year of big school, a school virtually surrounded by fields and woods.

"Kim, show the new girl around will you please?"

Mrs Gibbons, our form tutor, as was the case with most of her actions she was simply looking for the path of least resistance, she hadn't *really* framed it as a question, more an order. Looking back it's easy to see why Kim would be her first choice for diligently and responsibly discharging such duties.

I shadowed Kim those first few days while she showed me the ropes. They became those first few weeks, months, and years. We formed an unlikely duo, the unlikeliest duo, I'd love to say like Batman and Robin but in reality...much more like Jekyll and Hyde, Kim being Doctor Jekyll to my somewhat frantic crazy Mr Hyde obviously, but our friendship blossomed and endured.

She dealt with school in a way you had to admire. Keeping her head below the parapet she shrugged it off like water off a duck's back. One of her secrets was she seemed invisible, keeping herself pretty much to herself, bullies didn't even notice her. The teachers uninterested as they mostly were in their charges granted her a smooth passage, probably because in reality she was hardworking and smart without making a song and dance about it, no one noticed her.

In the five years we were together at school she didn't get so much as one telling off, one detention or one single smack from Mrs Gibbons' infamous 'dap', a large white and green tennis shoe hanging menacingly on the coat rack as a constant reminder to behave. It was her sidekick, 'the canvas enforcer', whose sole purpose, God, a sole pun, sorry, try again, whose only purpose was to preserve law and order in the classroom.

I, on the other hand was quite regularly extended an invitation to enjoy an extra hour in the classroom after the four o'clock bell and during one particularly fractious term after a lengthy run of 'dapable' indiscretions, apparently setting a new class record, Mrs Gibbons in her exasperation implored me.

"Teresa, you really should strive to improve your errant behaviour," as I rubbed the cheeks of my glowing behind, she said in that straight-talking no-nonsense tone, the pitch never rising...never dropping.

"Young lady, I'd like you to imagine that should by some miracle you ever get married, on your wedding night the embarrassment you'll feel when you have to explain to your new husband...whoever the poor, unwitting creature may be, upon first sight of your skinny unclothed carcass just why it is you have the Dunlop logo indelibly imprinted on your bottom." It wasn't that I was really naughty, perhaps you may say high-spirited, but frequently my mouth would engage before my brain had the chance to counsel it.

'Invisible' Kim surprised everyone although probably not herself by cleaning up in her 'O' levels, staying on for sixth form, more success in those oh so difficult 'A' levels leading to her becoming one of the rarest elite of alumni from our big school virtually surrounded by fields and woods. She went to university in Exeter to study law, while the majority of us had been 'processed' by the secondary modern system and left to our fates at barely sixteen.

There is no sour cheese on my part, she fully deserved her success. Kim had simply made the most of what scant opportunity was on offer and through sheer hard work had got her young adult life off to a flying start. My rock, Kim. I've always been so proud of her, admire her, and love her immensely.

This pub we are sat in the beer garden of, it is our 'local', the 'Fox and Goose'. It's always been our local, the current landlord and his wife, Ernie and Lisa have been here a few years now, they are a very nice couple. He is amusingly dry, never flustered, he just gets on efficiently with the job of licencee. Lisa has taken up the 'pub-grub' several notches since she took up residence.

Before Lisa the hungry patron of the pub was limited to crisps and packs of peanuts or cashew nuts pushed into a cardboard sheet featuring a colour picture of an attractive, scantily clad, or topless, very much overly endowed young lady, the more packs of peanuts that were sold, the more flesh is revealed, oh, and there were little jars of tiny vinegary cockles that nobody ever bought, pickled clitorises Kim dubbed them. Now with Lisa in the kitchen there's a whole host of mainly deep-fried hot foods served in baskets which I usually avoid but she serves some fabulous Cromer crab sandwiches, homemade lasagne, chicken Madras curry, and my absolute favourite, Wiltshire ham, egg and chips.

Ssssh, act innocent and whistle, it's Kim, here she comes with the drinks.

Kim pops down two pints of cider on the picnic style table nearest to the front door of the pub handing me the two 50p coins I requested. It's a nice evening and we like to sit in the huge beer garden when we can. One moment, I'm just going to pop over to the ciggy machine in the lobby. I know I shouldn't but after swimming, over a drink with Kim a B&H is the icing on the cake.

"Does Raymond know you still smoke?" She asks as I sit down.

'No, he thinks I've given up, but I enjoy one a few times a week.'

She shakes her head, "Where do you hide them, so he doesn't catch you out?"

'Oh, there are several places Raymond never looks and would never ever think to look, my heart...my soul...my knickers.'

Kim titters, a little guardedly because she knows well enough, we talk so candidly, there is a streak of truth in my flippant quip.

Kim with her usual professionalism and integrity, changing names and exact details she regales some of the juiciest snippets from the daily life of a popular, busy and very well respected Macsley solicitor; she is really much more interested in the new arrival next door...Callum.

"How is the handsome new neighbour?" I'm put under Kim's microscope now, she has this way of looking at you with an intensity that is unnerving, like a cat.

'Callum? Oh yes he's alright, he's been busy at work, he works strange hours, he says it depends on the tide times.'

In the few weeks since Callum has moved in we have spent time together on a few occasions over a cuppa and a biscuit. He told me he works at the docks in Leighbury-on-Severn, a mile away.

'We are going for a stroll to the knoll next week. He said he enjoys walking in the countryside so I thought I'd show him my special place.'

Kim, raises one eyebrow with a muted titter, "That's nice, he should feel very honoured, you don't go showing your *special* place to just anyone do you?" Kim always delivers her innuendos so gently.

Changing subject I ask Kim the font of knowledge about something else.

'Kim, what's the best thing for getting paint off the cuff of a shirt?'

"What kind of paint?" now she's getting technical.

'I don't know, it's a sort of maroon colour paint, there's a smear of it I want to get off the cuff of one of Raymond's shirts.'

She laughs a particular laugh, she has a library of different laughs tailored to the occasion. This one, quite frequently used, it's the Teresa is being dense laugh. "Not the flipping colour, the type, emulsion, enamel, oil?"

'He says a workman left a tin of paint on his desk in the office when it was being repainted, when he moved it there was a trace of wet paint on the rim that marked his cuff. Raymond smelt of paint when he came home that day, it was unusual, he went to work on a Saturday a few weeks ago.' Kim takes a sip of her cider, she's thinking carefully, I'm surprised as she deliberates at length.

"Is it one of those God-awful nylon shirts he wears nowadays, the ones that reek of stale sweat by the end of the day and give you an electric shock when you iron it?"

'Yes, it is, I don't know why he buys those instead of cotton ones.'

"My best advice is do nothing, just throw the flipping thing in the bin where it belongs; you could try giving it a gentle rub with some turps, although don't be surprised if the bloody thing melts before your eyes as you rub it."

'How is Mark?' Kim's eyes light up, Mark is her husband. Like many things about Kim it was a big surprise when they started courting and after a few years they married. Sixteen years and three children later they have the most fantastic life and marriage. The only thing they had in common is farming. Kim's father had a poultry farm, which he left to Kim. Free range chickens and turkeys was his business, hundreds and hundreds of them. Mark was the son of a dairy farmer a mere quarter of a mile away. So, nowadays he looks after the chicken farm while Kim is a partner in the solicitors firm in Macsley.

Mark was in our class at school, but Kim and Mark had no interest in each other back then, it wasn't until she returned from university that the spark of romance first flared between them, those wild young farmer evenings. At school I thought Mark was a hunk, he, unsurprisingly showed absolutely no interest in me or come to think of it any of the few obviously pretty 'it' girls who often tried and failed to win Mark's affections.

Once a week throughout the autumn and winter at school we had 'games', we girls played hockey on the 'Redgra', a grainy red all-weather sports pitch. As I was useless at hockey I was always 'put' in goal. In our team we had several gifted hockey players particularly Kim, meaning the opposing team's goalie was kept gainfully employed for the fifty minutes of the game repeatedly taking the ball out of the back of her net. I on the other hand was basically unemployed. I am still haunted by the ghostly howling of the bitter January wind gusting through the nearby trees to this day. Stood still for fifty eternally long minutes on the exposed pitch in nothing but a thin shirt and short skirt. The harsh biting cold, wind, and rain would whip across my bare skinny legs, transforming them from their usual very light pink to blotchy red by half time. By full time I was a painfully numb purple, knowing the worst was still to come. The uncomfortably hot almost scolding water from the showers agonisingly thawing my icy, goose bumped flesh back to a more normal temperature...heinous torture.

The only distraction I had, I mean, I didn't have to worry much about the other team's players coming towards me, was that the boys played rugby on the grass pitch close to the Redgra.

Mark was at least a head taller and considerably wider than any of the other basically wimpy adolescent boys. He was at fourteen years old taller and equally as stocky as Mr Thompson the P.E. Teacher. The rugby matches in common with our hockey matches were generally a foregone conclusion. The boys from our form in their red jerseys simply had to pass the ball to Mark. He just had to run towards the other teams goal line, the opposing team's more foolhardy players attempting to tackle him would be left in a trail of destruction in Mark's wake. The smarter ones, through previous painful experience would despite being cajoled and jeered by Mr Thompson just let Mark run unhindered to the H-shape goal and score.

The odd thing about Mark was that he didn't grow much more after being around fourteen, he remained more or less the same size and the other kids caught him up. Kim often jokes that Mark's mum forgot to pack him off to start school until he was nine or ten years old.  He is though, at forty-one or possibly forty-five or six still a hunk.

# Chapter 5

## ***The Knoll***

*Ivy Cottage, Brookhayes.*

'Wow, that's a big one Callum.' I titter rather childishly as he answers the door with his I suppose impressive looking camera in his hand, smiling back.

"It's a telephoto lens, it's great for zooming in." He fishes an O.S map out of his pocket and opening it places it on the boot of his red Cortina backed up on the drive.

"Can you point out where this 'knoll' of yours is on the map Teresa?"

'It's about here, close to the canal and the river'. I point rather casually at the map whilst he looks at it studiously. I thought it a bit odd, Callum doesn't strike me as someone who'd get overly hung up with boring mappy detail, more a devil-may-care and go-with-the-flow type of rambler. Although I don't blame him, honestly would you go for a reasonably long walk in the countryside with me leading the way without a map?...well really, you don't have to say *no* quite so avidly.

'We don't need a map, I know where it is.' I beam, with for once justifiable confidence.

"Och, I'm sure you do, it's just out of interest." Nearly four weeks on and I'm still swooning when he speaks. He looks smart as usual, even dressed to go for a stroll in the countryside he looks more Savile Row than scarecrow. I've noticed that about him, he takes care with how he dresses, never flamboyant or pretentious, just stylish.

The 'knoll' is about three quarters of an hour's walk away. A few fields of barley and corn succeeded by a mile along an old stony ankle twisting coach road. Next a trail through shady, broadleaf woodlands. Finally climbing up the steep grassy bank to the peak of the hill; the highest point for miles around. The top of the hill is round, five mighty horse chestnut trees stand proudly in a circle. The view is magnificent, Mayhill in the distant north, the spans of the elegant Severn Bridge to the south. In the near distance the ship canal bordering the tidal estuary of the River Severn and beyond to the Forest of Dean. This is the first time I have sat on the top of *my* hill with my back resting against the trunk of one of the conker trees in the company of someone else. Callum has taken his camera out and his shutter is clicking away in the direction of the docks, I am surprised that he is so interested in the tall grey grain silos, wharves, and couple of rust-stained coasters, surely he got to see them close up when he was at work.

While he is faffing about with his camera, preoccupied, I gaze at him, intently but not quite staring. I suppose it's because I'm wondering how old he is, I would guess somewhere between a well 'lived-in' thirty and a low-mileage, one-careful owner forty.

Actually I remember now, on one occasion when I was sitting up here far away in my own world, the farmer whose land I was 'trespassing' on approached from behind me. I had no idea he was there. I was having a 'bad day', and with the waterworks in full flow it was easy for him to sneak up unbeknownst to me. He asked me, quite politely I might add, what I was doing on his private land. I jumped out of my skin in shocked surprise, quickly I offered him an apology saying through my sobs that I didn't mean any harm I just wanted to sit and cry somewhere peaceful and beautiful. As I made to go, I suppose he empathised with the distress I was in, he beckoned me to sit back down, he joined me, this friendly looking if not weather-beaten old chap. I told him about my son Anthony and how I somehow find some sort of solace in this almost enchanted spot. He laughed a little as he explained he does exactly the same thing...comes here to this exact spot to remember the long life he'd had here with his wife Doris, who'd died a few years previously, they had worked this land together since they were first married. He held my hand, sitting together quietly in silence we both had a little weep. As we parted he told me I was welcome to come here whenever I wanted. People can be so kind can't they?

'You can get your photos developed in the chemists in Comberley', I look across to Callum, he's put his camera away, his eyes closed, looking very relaxed, that slight smile that seems permanently etched on his face. Trying to be surreptitious but failing miserably I keep finding myself just staring at him as he dozes, well he is rather easy on the eye.

"Thanks, I'll bear that in mind, I usually send them off in the post." He produces a foot long round plastic tube from his rucksack with the word 'Canon' printed on the end. I feel a little disappointed, I was hoping, maybe...no, definitely a little selfishly that dragging him, to this lovely quiet place that I would be able to 'have him all for myself' so we could talk, we could get to know each other, I hadn't factored in that he would indulge himself fiddling with his equipment in one of those 'hobbies' that men seem so fond of. My experience of men and their 'interests' is Raymond and Ralph spending an indecent amount of both time and money on ludicrously expensive erm...'components' I think that's what they call them for their 'Hi-FI' record players. Amps, tuners, deck, then they just sit passively, listening to classical music seeing if they can hear any crackles while talking in a strange language about feedback, tweeters, woofers, and gain.

For me, the world of music reproduction is a far more active, far simpler affair. Portable radio cassette player...check, T-rex tape...check, all furniture in the vicinity pushed to the side...check, volume knob to max, push play...I love to boogie.

Wait...hold on, it might not be as bad as I feared, Callum has unscrewed the lid of his boring massive camera lens tube and produced two wine glasses. Oh...and...it gets better. A small bottle of wine wrapped in a bag of ice.

"Frascati, I thought it suitable, light, fruity, easy on the alcohol." As he pulls the cork with a plop.

Oh my God...he is so suave, it's almost as if James Bond has moved next door. His eyes twinkle as he hands me the glass, the ice has worked wonders, the wine is refreshingly chilled.

"To friends Teresa, cheers."

'Cheers Callum, to friends.' He looks away gazing across the river. "It seems that I owe you an apology."

'Oh really, and why is that?' I really have no idea.

"Lionel brought a lawnmower to the cottage for me, when I mowed the grass with Yvonne in attendance over the fence to supervise me...it would appear that I, quite unintentionally you understand have brutally murdered a badminton shuttlecock." I Laugh and then begin blushing as I remember Yvonne's boob tube jibe, hoping she was discreet.

"When the unfortunate shuttlecock appeared somewhat desiccated from under the mower, Yvonne said that it was yours." Dare I ask?

'Did she mention anything about me looking for it in the jungle?'

"No, she just mentioned that you'd lost it a few weeks ago."

I want to ask Callum about his family, his story. He comes across as a little reserved, shy even, it will wait, if he wants to tell me things then I'll just have to be patient, I don't want to pry. He is a good listener, patiently paying attention as I flit excitedly from subject to subject in no particular order or with any reasonable logic. Telling him where's the best place to buy fresh fish locally, my Uncle

James in London, my favourite music, Anthony, Jack, the library.
Walking back home my head is pleasantly dizzy, perhaps spinning a little from the wine, or perhaps it's the company, I've really enjoyed the day.

# Chapter 6

## ***The Library***

*Comberley Public Library.*

'Margaret, have we got any books on Edinburgh?'

"Hmmm, well you could try the travel section."

Margaret is my colleague, she isn't in the mould of an archetypal librarian. Very gentle, bohemian, flouncy and...err...purple, her knowledge of all things literary is encyclopaedic...*sorry*!

Dragging a trolley load of returned books to the reference section she is replacing them back on the shelves with an enviable nonchalance, it's her many years' experience.

"Are you perhaps thinking of a trip to Scotland Teresa?"

'Perhaps.' Sweeping the floor, a hair clip, a sweet wrapper, and a small green toy soldier accompanying me with the fluff as I move along fiction and romance. A slow rhythmic sharp tapping sound is emanating from the next aisle.

"Nothing to do with a certain new neighbour?" Margaret replies quite loudly through the bookshelves separating us. I can't help but smile, small town gossip.

"Kim and the kids were in earlier, she told me that you– oh afternoon Mrs Barnett, how's the leg?"

Rounding the edge of fiction I can see Margaret has been approached by Mrs Barnett, a weekly regular to the library, she is very much a no fuss and nonsense woman, but her bark is worse than her bite. It always falls to Margaret to see to her.

She can never be bothered with walking up and down the aisles choosing her book for the week, she simply asks Margaret to pick one for her. Discerning Mrs Barnett will give her earnest, often scathing opinion of Margaret's selection the following week. Criticising the plot or the ending as if Margaret had some bearing on it, as if she were the author herself. We joke about it sometimes when Mrs Barnett has left the library, making suggestions about how Margaret could rewrite and improve some literary masterpieces, 'Stig of Green Gables' and 'The Lion, the Witch and the Mockingbird' were some reworked classics we thought more to Mrs Barnett's taste.

"Margaret, *he* wants a new book this week, what have you got to keep the silly beggar quiet and out from under my feet." Mrs Barnett has a loud piercing voice, not exactly library friendly.

The 'silly beggar' in question is her browbeaten husband Alf. He used to come to the library every couple of weeks, quickly choose a book, it seemed any book, then go to the reading table with the comfy chairs and nearly instantly fall asleep. By the time his wife had sorted her book out and chatted to Margaret for ten minutes he was in a near coma, it was a devil of a job to wake him up. Nowadays Mrs Barnett leaves him asleep at home and comes alone.

Margaret casts her eye over the return trolley, picking up a well-read dog-eared paperback.

"How about this, it's called 'Cider with Rosie' it's set in Stroud." Mrs Barnett brusquely snatches it, holding it a mere couple of inches to her eyes, screwing up her face straining to look at the cover.

"I've not got me right glasses, 'Cider with Rosie' you say, what's it about? It sounds like it's got women and drinking in it." Margaret is about to give the squinting old woman an idea of the story, but Mrs Barnett impatiently dismisses Margaret's choice out of hand before she can begin, with a pained expression and a loud complaining voice.

"Look it's no good giving him anything that might stir up his urges, giving him ideas, not at his time of life."

Sniggering...not quietly enough it would seem at her remark as my broom glides over the floor by the natural history section, Mrs Barnett catches me with a bemused glare from beneath her maroon cloche hat.

"I don't know what you are sniggering about blondie, you'll be laughing on the other side of your face when your husband's eighty years old and he gets unnatural urges, waving his *thing* at you in the middle of the night."

"Mrs Barnett," Margaret is becoming assertive now, wanting to get her returns trolley finished so we can have our three-o-clock coffee and biccie. She's known Mrs Barnett for many years and knows how to handle her. Like a skilful fisherman playing a lively fish, she lets her have her say, ignoring her scathing remarks then coaxes her into the landing net. Or more accurately Margaret will stamp her library ticket, point to the door and in the most delicate, flouncy, purple way imaginable usher her through it.

"Mrs Barnett, this book, 'Cider with Rosie' is a gentle tale of Laurie Lee's early life growing up in Stroud, I can assure you that it won't enflame Alf's ardour, you'll be able to sleep safely in your bed."

As I'm passing listening to their conversation with my broom, fluff, paperclip, and soldier I casually mention to Margaret that there is a passage in the book where the author and the eponymous 'Rosie' have a youthful cider fuelled lusty encounter under a hay wagon. Margaret quietly shoos me away with a wave of one hand whilst the other she holds upright with her forefinger outstretched by her mouth.

I have rounded the bend on the home straight to the children's section and the steaming kettle beyond, I can snigger in peace now. The tiny green soldier has made a break for it and disappeared somewhere, but the grey fluff ball has increased in mass and the hair slide is entangled with the bristles of the broom, squeaking on the lino tiled floor.

Mrs Barnett limbers out of the library, her walking stick sharply tapping as she goes.

Right, I'll make the coffee, the library is nice isn't it? A posh new building with a revolving door and wheelchair access, no expense spared in Comberley 'don't-cha-know'. The revolving door often causes confusion when more than one member of our more mature patronage attempt entry and exit simultaneously. There is no predicting what the outcome will be, who will be ejected, who will despite their best effort be unable to leave, or sometimes just an impasse, two tweed clad geriatrics locked in a determined grim-faced gladiatorial struggle until Margaret or I can go and mediate, while trying to remain straight faced.

Our town's lovely new library, it's pleasantly airy and light inside; the ends of the building are nearly all made of lightly tinted glass. It's two years old, before it was built we had a large but cramped terrapin building, we froze in winter, baked in summer and it just plain old leaked whenever it rained during the rest of the year.

Additionally the district council had a small lorry converted into a mobile library, we drove to the outlying areas of the district twice a week when the temperamental beast's engine condescended to start. Years of unseen rust though, caused by the cow muck strewn country lanes condemned it to the scrap heap.

Margaret although very petite was good at driving the lorry and one afternoon we'd gone right down to Newdine-on-Severn around seven miles away, braving all the narrow twisty lanes. When we arrived back at the library we discovered a quite large area of the metal floor of the lorry had literally disappeared along with a few dozen books from the now overturned shelves. Dashing to our cars demented, we launched a hurried rescue mission, thank God it was a dry day. We managed to recover most, we think, not absolutely sure, a few were damaged irreparably, a few had to receive some first aid with Sellotape.

Mr Stamp the mechanic from the garage in the town took a look and pronounced the entire floor of the mobile lorry to be as 'rotten as a medlar, it's the cow-muck see, and what with the weight of all they books on the floor it was bound to give way sooner or later, good job it was just a load of old books that fell out on the lane and not one of you two gorgeous ladies.' Mr Stamp, hardly silver-tongued, he is nonetheless a thoughtful, oil-stained charmer. The council took the lorry away and said it wasn't going to be repaired or replaced, cut backs apparently although the massive cost of the new library wasn't a problem. The thing is, in this district it's difficult or impossible for a few people to leave the house...keep this quiet...I can trust you...Margaret and I operate our own unofficial mobile library with our cars, just for the few folks that are really housebound. If you look carefully among the books on the shelves in the new library you'll see some lane scuffed veterans of the mobile library.

# Chapter 7

## ***Daredevil***

*Primrose Cottage, Brookhayes.*

"In front of a packed crowd here at Arrnty Treesur's kitchen...I mean stadium, attempting a new world record, Evel Knievel is going to jump over two smelly girls and a–"

"Hey, we don't smell William, you do, *you* smell, you smell of poo."

'Alright Alice, alright, none of you smell.' Trying to maintain the peace, my kitchen is like a zoo. William continues mimicking with considerable skill I might add an excitable sports commentator.

"Never attempted before, a remarkable death-defying stunt, he's going to jump over two smell...two girls, a loaf of bread and a grown-up."

As I say, my kitchen is chaos, Kim unusually flustered had banged on my door a while ago.

"Sorry Teresa, I'm in a bind can you look after th–"

'You don't have to ask, bring them in.'

"I have the dogs too, I'll be back in an hour. We all have to be at the pictures in Gloucester by six, Sara's birthday treat...'The Little Mermaid', be good kids." And she left. It was already quarter past four, don't worry, it's Kim, she'll be there in time, relax.

William, her seven-year-old son has brought his toy stunt motorbike with him; my kitchen is to be the venue for the little plastic daredevil to attempt his latest stunt. The three of us ladies have been ordered to lie down side by side, for some inexplicable reason William insists that the loaf be added for Mr Knievel to leap over along with us terrified girls. As he's building the ramp from my chopping board and washing up bowl, my face is being enthusiastically 'cleaned' by Kim's two large boisterous black Labradors, comprehensively damp with slobber, they lick me with the same boisterous enthusiasm they do everything.

William was whipping up the crowd...us...into a frenzy as he noisily winds up the friction motor of the toy motorbike, pulling it repeatedly backwards on the floor, harshly whirring ...then he let it go.

"Here he comes up the ramp, he can't chicken out now, it's too late," William's commentator alter-ego has reached fever pitch.

Flying over the top of the chopping board the toy soars over Alice and Sara with ease then begins dipping sharply as gravity moves to thwart Evel. Skimming the top of the Sunblest packet it descends to floor level, still moving at a goodly lick it comes to a very sudden abrupt stop when it collides with the back of my head, all the time my face is still being zealously licked by the panting excited dogs while their loud near-constant booming barks echo around the kitchen.

Amidst the barking and squeals of giggling Kim's Land Rover's horn sounds repeatedly outside. I'm surprised as like well drilled automatons, leaving all their bits and pieces behind the three children and two dogs hurriedly head for the front door quickly filing out, Alice shrieking.

"Bye Arrrnty Treeshurr, thanks for having us."

A wave from Kim sitting in her car, the multiple clunking of car doors and they are gone, just a haze of smoke at the bottom of the drive. Well that was quite sudden.

The silence is eerily deafening, the top half of my stable style front door is shut, the bottom half wide open, gently swinging. My ears are ringing, and I reek of dog slobber. The past hour has been enormous fun, I love having the kids. The dogs unbeknown to me at the time had eaten most of the sliced bread, there's probably just enough left for Raymond's sandwiches in the morning if I give the few remaining unbitten slices a bit of a wipe. I'll tidy up later, I just need to pop next door, I have a problem, I need to see Callum.

~ooo~

*Ivy Cottage, Brookhayes.*

"Teresa."

'Hi Callum, I wonder may I come in? I need you and it just can't wait.'

His eyes narrow with intrigue.

"You'd better come inside then." Following him along the hallway we enter the lounge, his tape deck is playing in the background, a song I recognise, Dusty's hauntingly beautiful voice, 'The Look of Love'. In the centre of the room he turns to face me, I move closer to him, on the brink of being too close, barely a dozen inches apart. I turn to face away from him and he moves towards me, closer still. He is so close behind me I can faintly detect the scent of his cologne...feel his breath on my neck...gently he lifts my hair from my shoulders in his hands, running his fingers through it. I feel shivers running down my spine like electricity as he stands close, so very close. No words are spoken, the only sound is Dusty, her beguiling sultry tones. Finally after what seems an eternity, like soft satin he whispers in my ear, his velvety tone caressing my senses.

"Teresa...you seem to have a small plastic motorbike stuck in your hair."

'Yes, I know, I thought you'd be the best person to ask, you know all about motorbikes.'

He laughs loudly, the first time I've heard him laugh out loud, this loud. During our lovely lively chats when he hears about some of my antics he titters or chuckles in a reserved way, but he is laughing heartily now.

'Can you get it out?' Gently he lifts the toy and looks very carefully.

"I don't think so, there is a lot of your hair wound around the rear wheel, it's got tangled in the motor. It's jammed, the wheel will only turn backwards, that is just making things worse."

I feel frustrated, 'Oh, just cut my hair, get it out please Callum.' He hasn't moved away from me, remaining very close, thank God I remembered to wash the dog drool from my face before coming around. The light tingling sensation running up and down my spine is increasing with his proximity and touch, his touch on my hair and neck is giving me chills, my head feels fuzzy, Dusty really isn't helping!

"I'm not going to cut your hair Teresa, it will ruin it, your hair is so beautiful, I'll get it out another way, I won't be a moment."

He moves past me towards the front door followed shortly by a tinny drumming sound as the garage door is being lifted. Shaking my head from side to side I can feel the blessed motorbike touching the back of my neck, pulling on my hair as I move. Callum returns moments later with a pair of pliers and a large screwdriver.

Horrified, 'What are you going to do? please don't break William's motorbike, he loves it.'

"I have to break it apart." Before I can protest further I hear a crack, followed by a sharp snapping sound, a few pieces of white plastic fall to the floor by my feet. Firmly holding my hair in one of his hands to prevent it hurting, unravelling it gently from the workings, I'm free.

'Thank you Callum.' On the table William's beloved toy lies snapped in half, I feel mortified, I'm going to have to tell William what happened to it, it was an accident but still, I don't like seeing children upset.

Picking up the tiny broken pieces of white plastic from Jack...I mean Callum's floor there is a light thump on the table.

'I didn't know you wore glasses Callum.'

"Aye, for reading tiny writing, I need glasses." He is thumbing through the yellow pages.

"Which town has the biggest toy shop Teresa...Gloucester, Cheltenham, Bristol?"

'Bristol I would imagine, but I have to work tomorrow I don't have time–' He cuts me off.

"I'm not working until four tomorrow," he glances at his watch with an irritated sigh, "Och, it's already gone five. I'll have to ring around in the morning first thing, as soon as I find one I'll go and collect it, your wee man William will be none the wiser, I think in this case a little deception is okay."

'Thank you Callum, that's so kind, tell me how much it costs when you get it.'

"Would you like a glass of wine or a cup of tea?"

A glass of wine? I'd love to, but feeling a little fearful I decline, maybe it would further weaken my already crumbling resistance. I was already feeling heady, safer for me to go home. This...this whatever this is, it's in real danger of escalating.

'Thank you but I'd better go, Raymond will be home soon, I need to get his meal ready.'

"Right, right, I'll bring William's new motorbike around tomorrow as soon as I have it."

'Would you like a stroll to the knoll on Thursday morning if you are free?'

"I'd love to Teresa, have a good evening." Callum opens the front door for me, passing him, I'm fiddling nervously with Evel, the sweaty little now unemployed plastic daredevil is in my hands, pausing in the doorway I glance fleetingly into Callum's eyes and plant a light kiss on his cheek, before drawing away quickly.

'Thank you for everything Callum, see you tomorrow.'

Walking the fifty yards back to my cottage, *I kissed him, I kissed him*, what was I thinking, but it was just a brief peck, a kiss on his cheek, as you would kiss a friend or relative, calm down. I am walking away...away from temptation; I could have stayed for a glass of wine, but I didn't. It's for the best, that way the only fingers doing any kind of walking will be Callum's, flicking through the yellow pages.

~ooo~

*Primrose Cottage, Brookhayes.*

At my door, my emotions are in a maelstrom, churning over uneasily, holding Evel up close to my face, 'It's okay for you'.

Peering at him, obscured behind his silver helmet visor,

'You just have to jump over packets of bread and girls.' Noticing his legs have myriad deep pock marks and the red and white paint is chipped, 'Oh, yes fair enough, you occasionally have to endure being chewed by a Labrador, but you should try riding your little motorbike for a mile in my shoes.' Tittering a little, my mind flits back to Callum's table, Teresa, that was mean, poor Evel hasn't got a motorbike anymore.

# Chapter 8

## *A Wednesday in June*

*Primrose Cottage, Brookhayes.*

Raymond has just arrived home, his revolting beige Cortina is backing onto the drive. I'll pour him a drink.

In the kitchen, as he removes his jacket I greet him with a peck on his cheek and ask him about his day.

"Oh, just the same old day." He seems tired, he comes home a little later nowadays, ever more work and ever fewer staff he tells me as he gulps his drink in one mouthful.

'Has that dreadful smell of paint gone from your office now?'

"Yes," he pours another generous measure of whisky into the tumbler.

"Have you met the new neighbour at Ivy Cottage T?" grrr.

'Yes, I have, a few times. His name is Callum, he seems very nice. He is from Scotland, he works at the docks.'

"Ralph mentioned he was a Jock, Yvonne invited him around to join them one evening last week for drinks and nibbles." Taking a sip of his whisky then kicking off his shoes.

"He doesn't play golf, with all the courses they have up there you'd think he would...Philistine."

'Raymond, I was thinking would you like me to book a table for Saturday evening at the 'Comberley Arms' to celebrate our wedding anniversary.'

"If you like."

'Do you remember how many years it is, our wedding anniversary?' I wonder, let's find out.

"Errrm, seventeen?" He's not too far out, just one year.

'No, sixteen, we got married on the sixteenth of June 1962.'

"Ahh, yes you're right, sorry."

'We don't have to go there, we can go somewhere else if you'd prefer, it's just that I know you like those big steaks they serve there.'

"Wherever you think best T," grrrr.

'I have bought some lamb chops, I'll grill them, would you prefer mashed or boiled potatoes?'

"Whichever is easiest." He must be tired, years ago you know he would have answered that question with a bright twinkle in his eye, something like and said in good humour, 'whichever has the *least* risk of you burning the house down.' Or 'Mash T, then I can put a dollop on the end of your nose and lick it off.' Well, I'm going to do mash, I'm taking an executive decision, let that be an end to the matter.

'Have you given any thought about a holiday later in the summer? I could get some brochures, we *could* go to Spain again but what about Corfu? I watched the holiday 78 show on the telly last week, they went to Corfu, it looks lovely. Cliff Mitchelmore had a whale of a time, smashing plates and getting hammered on retsina.'

Alright you got me, I might just have made up the bit about the BBC presenter getting hammered on retsina. As if such a consummate professional would get drunk on cheap wine...no, it was ouzo.

"Yeh, get a brochure, but I haven't thought about a holiday."

'Okay I'll go to the travel agents in Macsley, Corfu does look nice, it's in Greece Raym–',

"I *bloody well know* where Corfu is, not everyone messed around at school like you did." Oooh, he's touchy.

"I'm sorry T, I didn't mean to snap, I'm tired and just want some peace and quiet. Look I'll tell you what, I have to go to Nuneaton next month for a work thing, a boring conference, once that is out of the way we can have a look for a holiday. By the way I thought I'd stay over for the weekend in Nuneaton after the conference; there are two supposedly fantastic golf courses in the area, I'd like to play a couple of rounds. I'll come home on Sunday evening."

'That's fine, what a good idea, if you're in the area why not? Raymond while I'm doing the dinner perhaps you'd like to go and have a relaxing soak in the tub with some bubbles and your drink.'

"Mmm, yes, perhaps I will."

Nowadays, baths are a solo affair, we'd often jump in the tub together years ago, but nowadays...

You know two years ago there was a drought. They call it 'The long hot summer of 76'. It was funny...funny unusual rather than funny ha-ha, there were public service announcements on telly. Most evenings a dreadfully stuffy man with a dreadfully stuffy voice would tell us, 'save water...don't wash your car...save water...don't water your garden with a hose pipe...save water...don't flush the toilet unnecessarily and put a brick in the toilet cistern.'

Well how was I supposed to know what part the cistern is? As I asked Raymond won't the brick get awfully, you know sort of pooey, I remember he laughed, kissed me on top of my head and said, 'don't ever change T'...grrrr.

That hot summer, and it *was* hot, despite the stuffy man's dire warnings, Raymond and I feeling terribly naughty would once a week throw his gloomy predictions about the end of civilisation to the wind and frolic together in a cool bath on those long, balmy evenings...it was only two years ago.

Holidays...they were such enjoyable fun in our younger days, not long married we had little money but big appetites for fun. We'd just take off in Raymond's temperamental Austin saloon car and our rickety old tent. We'd just look at the map, point to a place on the coast in Devon or Dorset and say that sounds like a pretty place and go. The journey would usually take longer than we'd planned; in our tent when it rained we usually had to take 'special measures' to stop our things getting wet. But for two weeks in the unpredictable English summer, in our car that frequently broke down, and in our tent that always leaked we had simple fun, it was pure joy.

After Anthony there were no holidays for a couple of years. In hindsight it might have been beneficial to travel somewhere far away. The harsh reality at that time though, my state of mind and physical health compelled me to remain at home, close to Kim and Jack, and to be near to Anthony's grave.

When we were ready to start having a summer holiday again, things had changed. I cried when I found out that Raymond had got rid of our old leaky tent. We had more money now and with the advent of affordable package holidays we began going further afield, Spain usually. Beautiful locations, usually chosen by Raymond for the golf courses in the area, leaving me alone to spend the day on a sun lounger by the pool reading and trying to dodge the frequent unsolicited attention of the ubiquitous Pacos or Pepes, a small army of young, seemingly sex starved waiters employed in the vast soulless hotels that had been recently thrown up along the seafront in Benidorm and Torremolinos. These annual cheap package holidays offered reasonably good food and virtually guaranteed pleasant weather, quite idyllic as long as the hotel had been finished being built.

But for me, that spark, the quintessential spark of fun was missing. We were low budget adventurers in our younger years, our bold pioneering explorer spirit was no longer necessary.

A short flight on a Dan-Dare plane followed by a coach transfer accompanied by repeated choruses of 'Viva Espana' to the hotel. Two weeks by a crowded pool on a plastic sun-lounger, then a return coach to the airport accompanied by hordes of straw donkeys, another flight on another Dan-Dare plane, bang before we knew it we were home. In those early days getting home even from Torquay or Bournemouth wasn't a same day certainty by any means. Getting lost or Raymond's car having a tantrum were everyday happenings on our annual two-week odyssey but that didn't detract, quite the opposite in fact, when we eventually arrived home we felt as if we'd conquered the world.

# Chapter 9

## ***Revelations***

*The knoll.*

"Those tall slender red and white poles, at either end of the bridge, do you see them?"

'Yes, I can.'

"Well, those are the secret, the captain lines the bow of the ship up with those and the ship goes through the swing bridge albeit with the tiniest gap either side."

Callum and I are sitting together on top of the knoll, the mist is gradually lifting from the lower lying ground surrounding the river and canal. A lovely warm summer morning. Sitting very close behind me, he is holding his big camera up to my face. His arms reaching around me as I peer through the view finder towards the swing bridge at the seemingly impossibly big ship squeezing through the seemingly impossibly narrow canal bridge.

"It's a tanker, taking fuel to a depot on the outskirts of Gloucester, the skipper will have to go through around another dozen bridges like that one before he gets there, they are highly skilled, they have to be, if the ship hits the swing bridge it'll knock it into the canal."

'You know a lot about the canal for someone whose been here for so little time, I can only imagine what would happen if they let me drive the ship.'

A skylark is somewhere, high above us merrily tweeting endlessly. Callum is now snapping away with his camera towards the docks.

"It's my business, shipping. By the way, my mum and dad are coming to visit next week, they are taking the train from Edinburgh."

'Oh how lovely, I bet you're thrilled about that.'

"Aye, they are good folks, I've no complaints about the way they raised me."

Excuse me one moment, I just need to breathe out deeply and slowly, I'm swooning again, it's all Callum's fault, him and that voice of his.

'Thanks again for getting William a new daredevil toy, thanks to you we got away with it, he didn't notice, I swopped the Evel's though, so he got the one with the dog-chewed legs, just to complete the well-meaning deception, tell me how much I owe you.'

"It was nae bother, my pleasure." His camera back in his bag; he produces a compact thermos flask...tartan pattern...obviously, along with two small white china cups. Pouring the coffee, the rich aroma is pronounced, tantalisingly strong. It's proper coffee, ground coffee, I suppose I shouldn't be surprised.

'The coffee is fantastic Callum, is that a Bay City Rollers Thermos, are you in their fan club?'

"Aye, it is," his smile broadens, "I have all their records."

It's so peaceful this morning, not a cloud in the sky, not a breath of breeze on top of the knoll.

"Teresa, can I ask you a question? if you don't want to talk about it then tell me to mind my own business, I won't be offended in the least." Carefully examining a long stalk of ryegrass he has pulled from the ground, running his fingers over the row of seeds huddled tightly together at its tip, he begins swishing it gently in his hand as if conducting an orchestra.

'Go on.'

"If it's painful then please tell me you don't want to discuss it."

'Okay, I will, now what is it?'

Deliberating, Callum is like this, measured, succinct, he's not one who blurts out things without thinking. Maybe...definitely I could learn something from him!

"After Anthony...did you not want to have another child?"

That's a tough one, awkward and complicated for one reason or another. I wouldn't usually want to talk about that.

But, with Callum...well, I feel that we have developed a connection, he's gentle and caring. I feel I can trust him to respect my thoughts, not dismiss them out of hand as if they are nonsense simply because they don't coincide with his. We have talked together candidly over the short time we've known each other, he carefully processes and in turn seems to value what I say. I suppose in short what I'm saying is that he listens to what I say, rather than just hearing it, that makes a really big difference.

'Yes, after I had recovered, mentally and physically, perhaps around eighteen months to two years after Anthony died.' I feel quite comfortable talking about it, I have only ever been able to talk freely about Anthony with Jack and Kim before.

'Raymond didn't want us to have another child, he worried that if it happened again, the new baby died, I wouldn't be able to cope. He told me he was just thinking about me but I'm not sure his reasoning was entirely selfless. He said he thought we were too old, I was thirty-one when Anthony died. Raymond thought it to be nature's way, it wasn't meant to be.' He is listening to me with intense concentration, as I pause he briefly compresses his lips.

"Tell me to mind my own business, but when you felt you were ready, that maybe *you* wanted another child did you and Raymond–"

I can see Callum is feeling awkward, his face becoming a little red, I anticipate the question. Feeling sufficiently at ease in his company to answer this rather searching intimate question.

'Hardly ever, Raymond lost interest, he'd make excuses, he was tired, he had a headache, the rare occasions that we did make love often he'd stop, saying he'd finished but I knew it was a lie, it was patently obvious, a woman can fake it, but a man...well.'

"How did that make you feel?"

'Worthless, unfulfilled, a failure as a woman if you want the truth, and the truth is all I'm going to tell you Callum.

The only thing I ever really wanted was to have a child with my husband. A child we could love, watch grow up, to call us Mummy and Daddy, see it take its first steps, the simple little things most parents take for granted, the things we never got to share with Anthony, that's all I ever wanted.'

Little tears are trickling down my cheeks, Callum hands me a cotton hankie from his pocket...he's so thoughtful.

"I'm sorry Teresa."

'No, no it's quite alright, it's good to talk about it.' Wiping my eyes, my nose is running a little, the combination of sobbing and the excessive pollen in the air at this time of year.

'How about you Callum, would you like children in the future?' As soon as I ask I wonder have I overstepped, I had told myself before to just be patient; if he wants to tell me about his past it had to come from him. He looks away, far into the distance.

"Yes I dreamt of having children, *we* dreamt of having children, on our wedding night Linda and I joked about how many bairns we'd have, we thought four would be nice."

'Are you married Callum?' He lightly shakes his head.

'Divorced?' I'm urging myself to stop prying, to stop questioning him but seem to be powerless.

He moves closer to me, my back is resting upright against the huge gnarled trunk of one of the conker trees. Deftly turning without saying anything he leans back into me resting the back of his head against my chest.

Reaching behind him and taking my hands he wraps my arms around him, placing my hands on his stomach.

"Don't think me over familiar Teresa, I just want to be close to you; I promise you I'm not going to try anything improper." He is acting a little strange, but I don't mind him leaning against me, in fact it's quite nice and I trust him implicitly.

"Linda and I met at school, we dated for years and years. We married five years ago, a fairy-tale wedding, it was a beautiful day, late spring, rather like today." He pauses, I can feel him nervously fidgeting, short, rapid trembling rocking movements back and forth, involuntarily I find my arms tightening around him.

"One November afternoon she went to visit her mother, the same as she did most days when I was at work. It was a short walk, maybe five minutes. She left her mother's house to come home at the usual time, twenty past five. She was always at home waiting for me with a cup of tea when I got in from work. That particular evening it was raining quite heavily as Linda made her way home under her umbrella. She walked across the zebra crossing outside our house, she'd walked across it countless times before.

That particular evening the driver approaching dinnae see her. Maybe because it was dark or maybe because it was raining we'll never know for sure, but it was probably because he was three times over the drink driving limit...Linda...my beautiful Linda was killed instantly...she also happened to be five months pregnant. We were expecting our first child. Two lives snuffed out just like...like that." His trembling increases in intensity as he becomes overwhelmed.

Trying to soothe him, feeling hopelessly inadequate. I have never had a fully grown man in my arms weeping uncontrollably, so grief stricken before. It's humbling and heartbreaking, this strong, confident man totally tearing down the walls of his emotions. I feel such pity for him, I feel his hurt; for the second time this morning I'm sobbing freely. Callum turning around faces me, overcome with anguish, embracing me very forcefully, squeezing me so tightly, his face on my shoulder. All I can do, all I can think of to do is to put my hand on the back of his head and let him cry, while I run my fingers through his hair, softly humming, rocking gently trying to soothe him.

The merry skylark has been joined by a few equally chirpy friends, the recently arrived for the summer swallows are twisting, soaring, tumbling and jinking with indecent speed and grace, displaying their aerial mastery as they skim over the tall buttercups growing randomly amongst the coarse ryegrass that covers the knoll.

Just sitting still, like Jack did for me, Callum can stay where he is as long as he likes. It's such a simple thing, saying nothing, doing nothing, just sitting together, embracing and holding hands with someone you care about, I know the true value of it. There is no hint of impropriety, we are simply it now appears kindred souls offering solace, compassion, and warmth to one another. While Callum is lying in my arms I just have to look at the beautiful view, watching the swallows chasing and feasting on unseen insects on the wing instead of watching the cowboys chasing the Indians as Jack had as I slept on his shoulder.

Callum remains perfectly still as if asleep with his face resting sideways on me. Around a half an hour passes before I can feel him becoming a little restless.

"I'm sorry Teresa."

'Don't be silly.' I talk softly, trying to empathise.

"I don't talk about it usually, I've only ever spoken to my family about what happened, they have always been very supportive to me, you are the only person outside my family I've told, I feel comfortable talking with you, particularly because we have both experienced how unspeakably cruel life can be, the horrific twists of fate it can inflict."

I feel that to be a fine sentiment, an honour that he's opened his heart to me, that he trusts me with it.

"Sorry for cuddling you, I don't wan–"

'Shush, it's fine, it's fine, it's nice we can support and comfort each other.'

"Do you have a pound note in your pocket Teresa?"

Odd, not quite what I expected, Callum has let me go and is sitting up. Reaching in the pocket of my jeans, my ordinary jeans not *those* jeans I pull out a fifty pence piece and a couple of coppers, holding them out in my palm.

"That's only enough for one." With a comical mock sulky pout and a wink he smiles. His usual colour is returning to his face. I'm still none the wiser.

"There is a wee shop down by the swing bridge, do you like cornettoes? The little old shopkeeper has all three flavours."

'I don't mind them, more of a raspberry Mivvi girl but a cornetto would be nice.'

"Well if we're having Mivvis then we can have one each, so we dinnae have to share."

# Chapter 10

## *A Thursday in July*

*Primrose Cottage, Brookhayes.*

It's swimming night, Kim is picking me up in ten minutes, we take it in turns to drive.

I have had to buy myself a new swimsuit today, my old one has very nearly given up the ghost, the seams are just about ready to let go. My new one...mmm...a racy, bright red, low back, hi-leg number. Yvonne would of course be horrified if she were to see it, I can hear her in my mind. 'Teresa you really should grow old with more grace and dignity, you really should wear more age-appropriate clothing.' But I think I can pull it off.

Luckily, I never put on any weight, the couple of pounds put on over Christmas are lost during the summer months. I suppose I should be thankful, a genetic gift from my mother? She was always slim, still is as far as I know, I haven't seen her in around sixteen years. We talk every few weeks on the telephone whilst Raymond hovers around me animatedly tapping his watch face with an outstretched finger mouthing something to me about the phone bill, sotto voce.

Maybe it's because I don't eat a great deal or perhaps it's because I swim and walk regularly. Raymond says it's because I'm always prancing about and fidgeting, he calls it nervous energy...whatever that is. As a teenager I was painfully skinny and teased mercilessly about it. 'Belsen Teresa' was one of the more hurtful taunts from loud mouth classroom bully Mandy Jones. The funny thing is that I saw her coming out of the toy shop in Macsley a few years ago with her huge tribe of whining, mucus covered kids; she was wearing a scruffy grey tracksuit. It would be fair to say she has put on weight since I last saw her...quite a bit. I gasped when I caught sight of her behind... it looked to me as if she were trying to smuggle a couple of space hoppers from the toy shop hidden down the back of her trousers. Exchanging pleasantries she seemed to have totally lost her appetite for ridiculing my body.

I filled out during my late teens and early twenties to a shape I have always been more or less happy with and over the ensuing twenty years stayed more or less the same size. Although I may just buy a push-up bra from time to time; overall, I'm content with my lot, or in my case...little. Sorry I've gone off on a tangent, back to the swimsuit.

The thing is that there wasn't a great deal of choice in the shop in Macsley; believe me I needed a swimsuit for tonight as a matter of some urgency. I can picture it now, being escorted blushing out of the pool, my old swimsuit languishing on the bottom of the pool in two tattered pieces whilst I am being covered with a towel by the disapproving lifeguard as he ushers me like an apprehended streaker at a football match towards the changing room, being given a stern invitation not to come to the pool ever again.

Three to be precise, just three choices of ladies swimwear. There was a miniscule bikini that looked more like a ball of string than an actual garment one actually wears. Next up, there was a style-starved pink number with a sort of short white frilly skirt around the waist, even the size ten was seemingly huge, most unflattering, a true passion killer. It was enough to turn any silver screen sex-siren into a pink Disney cartoon hippo in one fell swoop. The neckline was literally a few inches below the chin. I thought perhaps I'd get one to wear as a 'Paco repellent' should we go back to Torremolinos this summer.

That just left this bright red low back one piece affair. It looked nice, the only feasible option, so I bought it. I tried it on upstairs earlier, still have it on in fact. It feels strange wearing a swimsuit in the kitchen, like being on holiday but at home. It fits snugly and it's very comfortable although I have to say it's cut high and quite narrow, very narrow in fact around the crotch. I just need to pop in the bathroom for a moment, make a few...err...last minute adjustments. Sometimes a lady needs a little privacy. Would you mind waiting in the lobby by the back door for a few moments?

Right, I'll just leave the front door ajar so Kim can come straight in, it's drizzling outside. See you in a moment.

A knock on the front door, ah, here's Kim, bang on time as usual.

'Come in, it's open.' I yell towards the kitchen from the bathroom.

'Won't be a mo.' I shout to her footsteps scuffling on the doormat inside the kitchen. 'I had to buy a new swimsuit and it's really narrow around the crotch, I'm just having a quick scrape with Raymond's razor, honestly, I look like a yeti.'

Satisfied with my handiwork, leaving the bathroom I excitedly bustle towards the kitchen in my little red swimsuit, in *my* mind like a magician's glamourous assistant, with a big jump, arms outstretched I leap into the kitchen from the lobby.

'Ta-da... what do you think Kim?'

"It looks very nice Mrs Sheen." Compressing his lips with his hand on his chin, nodding in mild approval.

Oh, oops, it's Bob...the milkman, well this is rather embarrassing; out of the corner of my eye I see Kim's Land-Rover pulling up outside.

'But it's Thursday Bob, I erm...I...err...thought that–' It's not just my swimsuit that's bright red now.

"Yes, I know, I do normally come around for the milk money of a Friday but I'm taking Doreen away for a weekend in Minehead to celebrate our fortieth wedding anniversary, I *did* leave a note in your little crate to say I'd be round Thursday."

A note he says, well I didn't see *that*, maybe those pesky blue tits in the garden took it, flew off with it...they have form...well known for being light-fingered...or light-beaked in their cases, regularly pecking through the silver foil bottle caps and plundering the top of my milk, the creamy bit I enjoy the most.

'Two ticks Bob, I'll just get my purse.'

Kim's face is a picture as she enters the kitchen. Bob the milkman smiling at her, I notice them cheekily wink at each other as they pass one another close to the door.

"Quite the den of inequity is Brookhayes isn't it?" Kim is highly amused at my embarrassment.

I laugh, 'It's not what you think.'

"It never is, when you've handled as many divorce cases as I have nothing surprises me. It's often the milkman, caught by the suspicious husband, but in most instances the bored housewife is usually caught wearing a negligee or sexy lingerie rather than swimwear." Kim grins back.

"Nice swimsuit by the way, shall we get going?"

~ooo~

*The Fox and Goose Inn, Newell Cross.*

The little pub is packed as we head to the bar for our after-swimming cider. The persistent grey drizzle forcing us inside, fruitlessly looking around for a table Kim's arm is nudged by Stan, one of who Kim and I call with great affection the 'Three Stooges' to who for many years the Fox and Goose has become their second home.

"We'll shove up a bit, you and Teresa can sit by us." It's quite an honour, the Three Stooges who now unfortunately only number two, Stan and Herbert; the third now sadly absent stooge was Jack, my lovely long-term next-door neighbour, confidante, and father by proxy. Stan and Herbert have the bench seat and wonky rectangular table in the corner, close to the bar and conveniently close to the fireplace. The pub's clientele accept it, it's *theirs*, their table, no question. For Kim and me to be invited to join them is a lofty hallmark of acceptance...that we belong.

"Your hair looks wet Teresa, have you been out in all that blinking drizzle?"

'No Herbert, we've been swimming, that new pool in Stroud with the big diving boards.' He looks vacant, turning his gaze to the few playing cards in his hand.

"I haven't been swimming in years, I can't remember the last time."

"Dunkirk." Stan chips in from over the rim of his pewter tankard.

"Eh?" Herbert lays down a couple of cards saying something about a pair, a five, and a knob.

"Dunkirk, you deaf old buggar; Dunkirk that was the last time you went swimming." Stan titters, "Mind we didn't have diving boards to play with there though."

Herbert starts laughing, "No, just bloody Stukas."

"I heard new people moved into Jack's place." Stan emitting a light huff throws down his few cards onto the table, bemused as Herbert sniggers while he hops his matchstick several holes further along the well-worn wooden crib board.

'It's just one person, a man from Scotland, he's a very nice chap.'

Stan taps Kim's arm then takes her hand. "I'm glad I've got you sat down here Kim, I want to rejiggle my will. Only I got a few more grandchildren now and I want to see that everything's shared out fairly, not that there's much mind. Only our Derek's missus is a shifty mare, I don't want her getting her greedy paws on anything more than Derek's fair share."

Herbert grabs Kim's other hand, "She will an all, try and get more, Stan's right, she's...a right shifty mare."

Kim is mildly amused as her hands are being held and repeatedly lifted up and down gently as if she were a puppet while the two old men conclude their character assassination of 'Derek's missus...the shifty mare'.

"Just ring me at my office Stan and we'll make you an appointment or would you like me to come to your house, if it's easier?"

Stan smiles at this, "That's service that is isn't it Herbert? proper service, not like the rest of the bloody country, gone to the dogs it has. What with strikes, unemployment and you haven't heard the half of it, I heard on the news which was read by a woman that we may even end up with a woman Prime Minister, God help us."

"Eh, what?" Herbert lifts his tankard looking ruefully into the bottom of it.

"A woman, a woman Prime Minister, you deaf beggar."

"Ah, well I suppose she can't make any more of a mess of the country than that clown we've got at the moment can she eh?"

Stan and Herbert finishing their beer, they push their tankards together on the corner of the table. Herbert shuffles the cards and begins dealing two more hands.

Their tankards pushed together on the corner is a sign, the landlord Ernie will notice them there. When he has a free moment, the stooges are never in a hurry, he'll come to the table, take them to the beer pump and refill them. Making absolutely sure to return them absolutely full to the brim, the slightest gap between the top of the tankard and the beer will cause unrest and Ernie will be subjected to repeated light-hearted banter about when is a pint not a pint, the common market and we fought a war for this country, we want a pint not some foreign metric half measure. When the stooges are ready to leave and shuffle the few hundred yards home they return their tankards to the bar where they have pride of place on their own shelf along with Jack's. Stan and Herbert insisted Jack's tankard remain as a mark of respectful memorial.

It's unusual to see the pub so full on a Thursday evening, mostly regulars. The moped gang in the far corner, five or six *mostly* well-behaved, leather jacketed, local lads. PC Baker does have to have words with them from time to time it is said, Comberley town centre is not Brands Hatch. One of them stands out very conspicuously, with dyed orange spiky hair, his black leather jacket has been highly...shall we say extremely personalised, teeming with shiny studs and pin badges...a wannabe Johnny Rotten in their midst. Ernie assures us that they are all now eighteen. Apparently their puny, tinny sounding mopeds have long since been replaced by altogether more potent machines. A couple of them have sulky looking perm haired girlfriends now too. To Kim and I though, they are still the moped gang...names stick despite the passage of time.

Then there's the ever-present mid-twenty-ish couple, I have no idea of their names. Him in his purple shirt and artificial leather jacket, sporting a noticeable beer belly overhanging his belt. His wispy gingery brushed back hair is thinning, If you catch it from the right angle, from the side you can see through it, receding quickly it will soon be at the point of being tragically so,...decisions, decisions. Be bold about being bald and cut it short, really short, it works well for Kojak and Yul Brynner. Or heaven forbid embrace that ridiculous comb-over look, confined to staying indoors on windy days for fear of looking like a bird of paradise when an errant gust catches it, before you know it eighteen inches of hair is blowing across your shoulder. Or simply do nothing, another year or two and his hairline will have receded far back leaving that curiously still hirsute tuft on the top of his forehead looking like a sparse gingery desert island at low tide.

His girlfriend interests me, no...not in that way. It's just that she seems to be...what am I trying to say...out of his league? She is really quite attractive, her glasses don't do her any favours at all...apart from allowing her to see but ignoring them she is pretty. Impossibly tall and slim, she often wears those shiny skin-tight black trousers, more suitable for a disco than the Fox...who am I to talk?...wearing a boob-tube for badminton. It would be easy to imagine her in the pages of the Gratton or Littlewood catalogues, minus the horrible glasses, modelling knitwear or maybe slacks on a seaside pier or perhaps in the garden of a country house or street café wearing a pretentious false smile, her hands positioned oddly as if shielding her eyes from the sun or waving to greet some imaginary friends.

They are sat happily, and they always seem to be just that, happy. I notice that about them, they always sit closely to one another and often smile and hold hands...good for them.

Kim is holding court with the three stooges, leaving me to my musings. Callum...the knoll...his wife, that was a revelation. The poor man, life can be so cruel just as it can be so wonderful.

And with that...he's...just walked in through the door. He isn't alone, turning he places his hand on her back and ushers her in while she shakes and collapses her umbrella in the entrance.

Of course he has a girlfriend, why wouldn't he? She doesn't have to be so damn beautiful though. I have an instant sinking feeling as they walk the few paces to the bar, my heart suddenly heavy, illogical, why should it feel heavy? I'm married, I love my husband, Callum is just a neighbour, a friend, but no more, so why do I feel like I have just been stabbed in the heart? I need to pull myself together, stop feeling like a silly schoolgirl with a crush.

Callum was bound to have a girlfriend, he is gorgeous, handsome, thoughtful, and fun. He has got it all...he had to have a girlfriend, she was bound to be stunning.

Perhaps he could have mentioned her though, not for any particular reason. With almost morbid fascination I am drawn, compelled to watch them from the far corner, trying to hide myself behind Herbert as he played his cards. This isn't their first date, their body language, they are at ease with each other, smiling, laughing, and talking comfortably as they wait for Ernie to serve them. Absorbed, they are only interested in each other, not looking around the bar. I don't mind that, I feel awkward, ill at ease with my reluctant, almost voyeuristic interest. I want to leave.

'Kim, I'll go home, I have a bit of a headache.' She is still discussing wills with the stooges.

"I bet you didn't say that earlier to the milkman." Giving me a cheeky wink, oblivious to the fact Callum is stood mere yards away, she hasn't met him, she doesn't know what he looks like. Swallowing the remainder of her cider.

"Give me two seconds, we'll go." She rises from between the two tweed jacketed stooges and slides past them.

"Right gentlemen, thank you for your company, Stan I'll see you next Wednesday afternoon at four. Good night." Looking to the bar, Callum and that woman have gone, I can just see a part of her back and her shiny long black hair in the snug. The pub is quieter now, but in there, the snug, they can't see the bar, I can leave without being seen. I feel torn, should I say hello or just leave? It doesn't take more than a milli-second for me to make my mind up.

The wipers rhythmically clunk back and forth, smearing the drizzle in a watery film across the windscreen of Kim's hay-littered Land-Rover on the one-minute drive home.

"Are you alright Teresa? you're quiet, you seem to be away with the fairies."

'Yes, just a bit tired, I'll take an Anadin and go to bed, I'll be all right in the morning...shit!'

The brakes squeal as Kim pulls up outside my cottage.

"What?"

'Tomorrow, Friday, it's my turn to host the dinner party...the Pitman's.'

# Chapter 11

## ***Triumphs and Tribulations***

*Primrose Cottage, Brookhayes.*

"T...T...T...wake up." Raymond is shaking me.

'What...what is it, what time is it?'

"It's early, I have to collect Paula this morning and take her with me to the office, her old rust bucket is on the blink."

'Raymond, it's really early, do you have to go *this* early?'

"Afraid so, we need to get cracking on last month's accounts. Don't forget tonight, we are hosti–."

'Mmmm, I know, the Pitman's.'

I receive special 'because it's early' dispensation this morning, Raymond amusingly walks gingerly on tiptoes trying to be quiet. I notice his expression, he is sort of wincing, how thoughtful, it's common knowledge that creeping around while wincing and moving one's arms in slow motion emits no sound whatsoever. No 'mwah' on my temple, but on the bright side, no Blue Stratos either, every silver cloud eh? And...he's...gone.

Trap, trap, trap down the stairs, jangle, clunk, whirr, whirr, roar...and he's really gone.

Thoughts of last night slowly enter stage left of my mind as the groggy blur of sleep gives way to a marginally less blurry semi-conscious state.

*That* woman in the pub with Callum, tall, slim, her confident pretty face packed full of bright white teeth, that lustrous long raven hair.

I feel envious of her, I imagine in her world she'll not be cooking dinner which will be subject to scrutiny under Yvonne's microscope.

Right Mr Wogan, play me a tune, I'll have ten minutes under the continental quilt before I seize the day. The radio alarm crackles into life. '*Love is in the air'*.

I love this song, it's one of my favourite dance around the kitchen songs at the moment. As to whether I'm being foolish or wise as the singer has just asked?

Mmmm... jury's out on that.

Right, time to get up, shower, I still smell of chlorine!

The new swimsuit is great, thanks for asking.

I'll just have my Weetabix and head to the butchers and greengrocers. Unusually for me, I'm quite organised. I have the menu planned mostly. Prawn cocktail, yes I know, how sophisticated am I? exotic, well it becomes exotic when you sprinkle a little paprika on it. It's something the guests can just peacefully eat, no need to be skilled in hand-to-hand combat like one has to be to tackle Yvonne's avocado pear.

At the last dinner party I...err...hosted I thought I'd do 'whitebait' as the starter. Well the instructions were somewhat vague in respect of how long I should cook them and how hot the oil should be, not that I have the slightest notion of the oil's temperature. In the far too hot oil for far too long; my embarrassment at serving dozens of tiny fish skeletons, sorry...tangent .

Kim's suggestion for the main course, bouef bourguignon, she's given me the recipe, apparently it's from a very loud, slightly eccentric American woman who lives in France and cooks like a boss. Kim has road tested it successfully on Mark's mum and dad. Approval from Mark's mum bodes well, a sterner test has yet to be devised. Kim has given it the thumbs up, she tells me it's a piece of cake to prepare too, so that's that sorted out. I have to say though Kim's idea of a piece of cake doesn't always coincide with my definition of it, the recipe looks quite complicated to me. Brown the meat the instructions say, well how brown is brown? It'll take quite a bit of time to prepare. Looking at all the ingredients I need and all those processes there is plenty of scope for disaster to strike, I mean the Titanic *only* had to sail across the sea and look how that ended up.

The only fly in the ointment is...is...dessert.

I'll just take a look in the pantry, what have we got in here.

A good start, I have a box of After Eights already, albeit opened, it seems light...it's...it's...fiddlesticks, the box is empty, no actual After Eights, just the wrappers. I must have 'just taken one' when I was in the pantry more often than I thought, I *thought too* it was getting harder to find a wrapper with an actual mint in. What else is in here? Something I can use for a quick easy dessert, Lord knows this fancy beef stew is going to take me an age to make. Angel Delight...a tin of gooseberries...no.

Dream Topping?...maybe...only kidding, I keep a packet of that for when Kim's kids come, there's a mousetrap, a candle, Ooops...twenty B&H, let's just push them to the very, very back.

No, there is nothing, nothing at all, except...except someone is knocking on the front door.

'Callum, good morning.'

"Good morning Teresa, are you free at ten?"

'Ten, ten, what ten, this ten, this morning ten?'

Calmly smiling, he is amused as I splutter and semi-panic, my mind is all over the place.

"I was wondering if you'd like to come ar–"

'I can't, I have to cook, it'll take ages, honestly Hercules had it easy, he didn't have to cook for Yvonne, it's the dinner party tonight, I have a million things to brown...burn...I mean cook, I'm sorry.' I'm still misfiring.

"Och, that's a pity, I was hopi–" I cut him off, his voice is starting to mesmerise me, intrigue getting the better of me.

'What were you wondering Callum?' Still on my mind, *that* woman in the pub with him last night.

"I was wondering if you were free to come around to mine at ten for a cup of coffee and meet my mum and dad?"

Well, that can't hurt can it?' not just for half an hour, after all I have all day to cook a simple beef stew and sling some prawns in a bowl, how hard can that be?

'I'd love to Callum, see you at ten.' Turning to leave he raises his hand close to his head with his finger pointing upwards.

“By the way, you’ll get to—” Callum stops speaking as the phone starts ringing in the alcove by the door. He silently mouths, “See you at ten” and walks away down the path towards the drive.

‘Comberley 419’.

‘Hi Yvonne, yes Yvonne, seven o’clock, no Yvonne just yourselves.’

~ooo~

*Ivy Cottage, Brookhayes.*

Ooh, that’s odd, a little purple car on Callum’s drive, I thought they came on the train. He definitely said his mum and dad were coming on the train.

How could they possibly have come all the way from Edinburgh to Gloucestershire in this tiny little car? I suppose it’s possible, it’s got two seats and a black fabric folding roof. Putting my face close to the windscreen peering inside, I’m being nosey. It must be *that* woman’s car, she must have stayed overnight. He only said come and meet his mum and dad, he didn’t say that the glamour goddess had stayed overnight.

“Hi, Teresa.” Callum suddenly appears by my side. I didn’t see him come out of his front door and approach, his voice makes me jump.

‘Did your mum and dad drive down in this?’ I ask, realising it’s probably a silly question but I’m startled.

He titters, “No, they came on the train, this is *my* car, Lionel brought it here this morning.” I’m not usually especially interested in cars, but this one is intriguing.

‘It’s...it’s very purple.’ Running my fingers gently over the smooth shiny boot. The car smells of polish.

"It's called magenta." He says correcting me...oh how very silly of me...it's magenta, well I say it's purple.

'Is it foreign?'

"No, it's a Triumph...a TR6," Callum looks at his car with pride and a modicum of glee.

'It's unusual, despite its purpl...sorry magenta colour it looks a little brutish, not obviously attractive but it has a certain something about it. It's a bit like Tom Jones in car form.' I proclaim with a grin.

"Why do you think my car is like Tom Jones?" his smile broadens accompanied by that Callum slight head twist, it's his subtle tell me more sign.

'Tom Jones, well he's not the most gorgeous looking thing in the world but he's blessed with a certain alluring brutish charm, such that you wouldn't kick him out of bed, well personally if I were not married I wouldn't, and have you seen him on stage? he's a bit of a mover, probably like this car, I would have thought this car is a bit of a goer isn't it?"

Laughing now, Callum nods enthusiastically,

"True enough, it does shift."

'There you are then, I'm right, Tom Jones in car form, just don't expect me to throw my knickers at your car Callum.'

While I'm talking I notice the direction of Callum's eyes had changed slightly and as the word knickers leaves my mouth I begin to get the overwhelming feeling we aren't alone. Taking my arm he ushers me to turn around.

"Teresa, let me introduce you, this is my mum and dad and this is Kellie, my sister, she's taken a few days off work to come down too."

‘Hi, it’s very nice to meet you Mr and Mrs Gilchrist, Kellie.’

Kellie...Kellie, so *that* woman with the legs and the teeth and the hair is Kellie, Callum’s sister. Not that *that* makes a jot of difference to anything you understand.

They look very friendly, warm smiles all round while introductory pleasantries pass between us.

“I’ve just put the water on to boil, Teresa would you like tea or coffee?” Mrs Gilchrist has the most lovely voice, sugary sweet, it has an adorable, squeaky mouse-like quality.

‘Coffee would be very nice thank you.’

Mr Gilchrist, his well-trimmed grey hair and neat pencil moustache give him a distinguished look, smartly dressed as his son always is. He is a little taller than Callum but a little shorter than Kellie. Lean and sprightly, his posture is very upright. He fixes his gaze on me, his blue eyes are intense, warm with a mischievous twinkle.

“Tell me, is it the custom here in Gloucestershire for the lasses to throw their underwear at cars Teresa?” quite high pitched and interrogative he finishes with a muted braying laugh.

‘Well...that rather depends on the car Mr Gilchrist, I don’t throw my underwear at just *any* old car.’

What...what? I know, I know what you are thinking. You’re thinking behave yourself, you’ve only just met them, show some dignity. But they snook up on me and caught me saying knickers fair and square, it’s too late for that, I might as well play along with it, it’s no use getting embarrassed now. We are all heading indoors now, I'll try to behave.

"Sorry it took so long for the water to boil, Callum you should really get a proper kettle, a saucepan takes so long to boil." Mrs Gilchrist mildly tutting carries a tray with cups, saucers, and a plate of biscuits into the lounge.

"Here we are, I've bought you some of those Jammie Dodgers Callum I know they are your favourite." I snigger to myself, thinking Callum normally so discerning and tasteful prefers children's biscuits.

"Teresa, Callum tells us you are having a dinner party tonight?" Mr Gilchrist, again that high pitched inquisitive tone.

'Yes every few months, just us and the neighbours the other side, the Pitman's.'

"What are you planning to cook Teresa?" Kellie asks.

'Prawn cocktail followed by Bouef bourguignon. But dessert, I haven't got a clue at the moment."

"How about a layered orange sponge cake, I'm making one for us for tonight, so I'll just make two and you'll nae have to worry about the dessert." Mrs Gilchrist smiles at me, I feel awkward, a kind offer, but a cake, I'm not sure if that would be suitable. I think seeing my hesitation Kellie reassuringly intervenes.

"Aye Teresa, don't worry, it's much more than a cake, it will be perfect for your dinner party. Mum's orange layer cake is spectacular, both the taste and visually, it's a fantastic dessert, you have to eat it with a spoon. It's covered in a sticky fruity syrup, topped with grated chocolate."

"So that's settled then, we'll hear no more about it, I'll take care of your dessert." Mrs Gilchrist rests her hands on her stomach with a satisfied look on her face.

'What job do you do Kellie, If you don't mind me asking?'

"I'm an air-stewardess." Well of course she is.

"British Airways, mostly long haul, Australia, Bahrain, Hong Kong, New York, occasionally I get to fly on Concorde." A dazzling smile, Kellie clearly is satisfied with her lot.

'How lovely and glamourous, that's every girl's dream.'

"You do get awkward passengers at times, some act like spoilt children, some a little over familiar but aye, on the whole it's quite an exciting and glamourous job."

"And Mr Gilchrist?"

"Och, call me Alistair, I'm retired now, have been for—"

'You don't look old enough to be retired...Alistair.' I butt in, genuinely surprised...no, really, I'm not attempting to deceive to flatter.

He smiles broadly, "I think you and I are going to get along nicely Teresa." Lifting a Jammie Dodger and narrowing his eyes he inspects it in careful detail.

"I was a superintendent in the Lothian and Borders Constabulary, I had the good fortune to be offered retirement at fifty-five years of age, hence my youthful good looks." His smooth braying giggle ends abruptly as he takes a sharp bite of the biscuit.

I make my excuses and rise from the chair, I really have to get a move on, the clock is ticking, the shopping, buy some wine, clean the house...Yvonne is coming...so really clean the house, iron the napkins, set the table, it doesn't set itself, the wine glasses don't polish themselves, the ice cubes won't freeze themselves...okay you got me, yes, technically they do freeze themselves as long as they are in the freezer, but they don't put themselves in the freezer do they? Anyway you get the picture.

"Kellie or Callum will bring the dessert around at about five Teresa, is that okay?" Callum's mum is so sweet I could just give her a huge cuddle...okay, I won't, not yet anyway.

'Thank you, that is so kind, you have no idea what a massive help it is." Callum shows me to the door.

As I make to leave he checks me with a hand on my shoulder and plants a brief peck on my cheek.

"Have a good day, thanks for coming around." I blush a little, his voice...or is it his little kiss I can still feel on the side of my cheek?

'Thank you...wish me luck!'

~ooo~

*Primrose Cottage, Brookhayes.*

'The Algarve?

"Yes T, it will be marvellous, The cool mornings out on the golf courses, the warm afternoons by the pool what could possibly be better?"

A lot of things, I think to myself clearing the starter plates. A Caribbean cruise, a romantic weekend in Paris, being stung to death by an angry gang of hornets.

The starter had been well received, peacefully passing muster with Yvonne after her gag about the presence of brick-dust...ha,ha, ha,ha, the paprika sprinkled on top of the prawn cocktail.

With the first bottle of Black Tower empty, Ralph, Yvonne, and Raymond were plotting. A week away in early October in Portugal, Yvonne informing us that Princess Amanda decrees that it's oh so far more cultured and sophisticated than mixing with the great unwashed hoi polloi, packed like sardines sizzling red raw in the sun on the beaches of Torremolinos or Benidorm.

The unfolding horror of it flashing through my mind, a week with Yvonne and Ralph. They are 'alright in short doses' type of people. How many times will Yvonne say 'Amanda', how many times will Ralph slap my behind? In a bikini or swimsuit it will be a sitting duck. With my oven gloves on, the casserole containing the Boeuf Bourguignonne is taken out of the oven, lifting the lid I smile, I am more than satisfied, the aroma, it smells wonderful. Thanks Kim, her advice...cook it slowly and don't be stingy with the wine and garlic...pure gold.

The dessert? Well that's a moral dilemma, do I say Callum's mum made it? Do I try and take credit for it if asked? hoping to God I'm not asked to say how I made it. Yvonne seems suspicious, I can't blame her, three courses in, and if I may be so bold...faultless so far and it's all going swimmingly. I can see her examining Callum's mum's beautifully layered dessert, alternating her gaze between the delicious looking precise layers with its glossy glazing and my eyes. Act innocent Teresa I tell myself, just as I think I'm about to get the third degree, she swoops down with her spoon and scoops into the cake.

With four empty dessert bowls on the table, the After Eights...new box, take to the stage. The brandy is waiting in the wings, Raymond and Ralph are still busy demolishing the four bottles of Black Tower I bought earlier at the Co-op. The conversation reverts back to the proposed 'Algarve' holiday.

"The thing is I've saved a wedge of cash on Yvonne's new car." Ralph looks pleased with himself. Raymond and I are confused, it's the first we'd heard about a new car.

"So, a week in the Algarve for us is easily affordable. We're going to Orlando for a week at the end of September, Amanda's birthday treat, she wants to go to Disneyland."

'Are you getting a new car Yvonne?' I ask, she hadn't mentioned it, I'd have thought the whole world would have known about that, but she'd kept it quiet. Disneyland for Amanda...well that isn't a big surprise, she'll be right at home there. Snow White will of course have to temporarily relinquish her title, she'll not be the fairest in the magical kingdom for the week Princess Amanda will be there on holiday.

"Mmm, yes." Yvonne doesn't seem thrilled.

'Are you getting it on August the first?' I want to know more, Ralph boisterously jumps in before Yvonne seemingly reticent can answer.

"No, the thing is I got a great deal by agreeing to get it registered in July, something boring about sales figures for the dealers so I saved several hundred quid on the price."

Yvonne glares acerbically at smug Ralph, it's rather obvious that she is not a happy bunny.

"That means it will be an 'S' registration." she hisses, making no attempt to hide her disappointment. "If he'd just waited a few weeks I could have had one of the new 'T' registrat–" Ralph somewhat exasperated, he exhales sighing then quickly butts in.

"Darling, If you rememb–"

Ralph moving on the defensive, it quickly becomes evident this is a bone of contention as an incensed Yvonne instantly cuts him off, attempting to launch a swift and decisive verbal counter attack, repeatedly jabbing an accusing finger at her husband.

"Don't you dare *darling* me...it was you...you could have registered it a few weeks later, I was happy to wait but...oh no, not *you*...*you* were the one that–"

Again Ralph wades in with unfamiliar, probably Black Tower fuelled courage, before Yvonne finishes, her face becoming increasingly annoyed.

"Yes, darling we've talked about this, it's just a number plate, it's still a brand-new car, remember what Amanda said, 'who cares about a silly little plastic letter on your car Mummy, the important thing is that I get to go to Disneyland.'"

The tension is rising, I can sense a full scale domestic around the corner. Do you think I should remove the knives from the table? I'm going to try and mediate...I know what you're thinking but don't worry, relax...I'm good with kids, even drunken squabbling adult kids.

'What type of car is it Yvonne ? it must be exciting getting a brand-new car.'

Raymond buys me cars that are two or three years old usually, better to buy them pre-wounded he says. He always takes great delight in explaining to all and sundry that it's much cheaper for him to buy my car with the dents already in it, he tells me that it'll save me the bother of having to dent it myself, generally telling me , 'not that that'll stop you from regularly adding to them, ha,ha,ha'. My plan seems to have worked, sidetracked, Yvonne looks calmer.

"It's a brand-new model...a Chrysler Sunbeam. It's a hatchback, it's going to be finished in metallic Montezuma Gold, the GL model with a push button radio and sunshine roof, top of the range, of course."

Of course it had to be the 'top of the range'...obviously.

Up to now Raymond has been quiet, contenting himself to watching the Pitman's cross swords, a bitter duel fought between Ralph's frugality and Yvonne's snobby pride, which is being as dented as my Mini. Finishing off the third bottle of Black Tower and opening the fourth bottle Raymond joins the active heated debate waging across the dining table.

"I saw an advert on the telly for that car...the Sunbeam, Petula Clark was singing a song about it."

Yvonne musters a weary smile, "Yes, that's it, it's been on several times."

Raymond reaches down under the table and takes my hand, worryingly he has that mischievous look in his eye.

“Have you seen it T?” grrrr, he announces loud enough for all to hear.

‘No, I don’t think so.’

“Well, Petula Clark is banging on, singing a cheery song about this new car...this Sunbeam, she says ‘put a Chrysler Sunbeam in your life, it’ll put a smile on your face.’” He grins before finishing his next glass of wine in one gulp.

I think Raymond is very observant, especially for someone who eschews commercial television, a BBC man to the core is my Raymond. Anyway he is not finished, and clearly the Black Tower is working its mischievous brand of magic. Raymond continues his appraisal of the television commercial.

“It’ll put a smile on your face she says, I suppose that’s easy for Ms Clark to say, she probably hasn’t got a penny-pinching husband who’s going to buy her an old S registration one...ooh, no, Petula will have the new T plate for sure.” This isn’t helping the already tense atmosphere between the Pitman's. Their smiles at Raymond’s jibes are insincere to say the least as he continues teasing.

“Poor old Yvonne, an S registration, it’s more than enough to *wipe* the smile clean off your face isn’t it darling?”

I’m going to switch Teresas now...going from a gentle diplomatic babysitter role to full blown United Nations blue helmeted peacekeeper.

‘Raymond why don’t you and Ralph go and listen to Mantovani or whoever while Yvonne and I make the coffee? I half usher, half shoo the men away to the lounge.

'Sorry about that, Yvonne?' I feel embarrassed. Raymond's stirring jibes were rude, and moreover they were deliberate at that.

"It's okay Teresa, we know they are like silly schoolboys when they have had a few too many, anyway I'd like to congratulate you on tonight's dinner, it was very nice, I mean it really, very nice, and yes I'm seething about not having a T registration," she mocks a horrified look with her palms flat against her cheeks.

"The shame, the shame I'll feel at the bowls club turning up in an old S registration banger."

I am honoured, it's usually enough for Yvonne to say nothing for me to consider the evening to be a success but open praise, that's a very rare honour. She seems different tonight, warm, strangely closer, and more friendly.

"Teresa, did you know Callum's parents and sister are visiting him from Scotland this weekend?"

'Yes, I'd heard that.' I try to sound glib filling the kettle.

"I took some dahlias from my garden around earlier to welcome them, brighten the place up a bit. Callum and his sister had gone out for a stroll. Callum's mother invited me into the kitchen for a cup of tea, we had a nice chat, she mentioned you'd popped in for coffee earlier." Yvonne gave me a theatrical wink before continuing.

"It seems these orange and chocolate sponge layer desserts are all the rage, do you know that Callum's mother was putting the finishing touches to not one, but two of them." As Mantovani bursts into life in the lounge, the men presumably marvelling at the stereo reproduction listening for crackles Yvonne moves very close to me and with almost motherly concern whispers to me,

"Talking with Callum's mum and reading between the lines I think Callum has taken quite a shine to you. Teresa, please tread carefully."

# Chapter 12

## ***Red Flags or Red Herrings?***

*Primrose Cottage, Brookhayes.*

'Comberley 419.'

"Teresa, Kim, how did it go last night?"

'It was a great success, the boeuf bourguignon was delicious, they wolfed it down like gannets. I got found out by Yvonne about the dessert though, Callum's mum made it for me, she's such a darling. Problem was Yvonne had seen her making it, but she kept mum bless her, in fact Yvonne was weird last night, out of character, in a nice way.'

"Listen, Mark can look after the kids for an hour or two, I'll come by and pick you up shortly, are you free?"

'Yes, Raymond is playing golf, but what are we going to do?'

"Something has been bugging me, something in Macsley, I want your opinion on it, see you shortly." And she's gone. Well that was very mysterious.

Look at all that washing up, it doesn't matter, I don't mind, I'm so pleased about last night. Raymond and his hangover have gone to play a round of golf with Ralph and his. I feel blessed, my life is happy. Right let's get these dirty dishes done.

Marigolds on...a big bowl of hot and soapy...

Abba cassette in tape player, volume at absolute max. Let's sing...come on, don't be shy, as loud as you can, louder ...can you dance?...can you jive?...

~ooo~

*Macsley, Gloucestershire.*

Kim has arrived in Mark's old Austin Maxi, and we are heading off towards Macsley. She is being quite tight lipped, 'A house', that's all she is saying.

She wants my opinion on a house? Looking out of the hazy car window I am still baffled. I know Kim sometimes behaves seemingly irrationally but it always makes sense in the end, maybe she is going to buy a house to sell on or rent out.

"So Callum's mum made your dessert ?"

'Yes, it was fantastic, most of the evening went well, Raymond made a bit of a silly arse of himself being rude about Yvonne's new car oh...oh.. and the three of them are planning a holiday for us all in the Algarve.'

"To play golf, when are they planning that?" Kim looks bemused.

'Golf, yes I think that is the general idea, October they mentioned, I wasn't paying much attention, I was busy with not burning the food.'

"That's so selfish of Raymond, and with the Pitman's too."

Kim gently reduces speed, looking at the houses lining the side of the road on the outskirts of Macsley. Large detached houses, they are beautiful, elevated on grassy banks they are nicely set back from the road. She slows down to a snail's pace and crawls past two or three before drawing to a halt. Following her through a rattly metal gate up a dozen gentle steps and down a path around the back of the house to a huge garden.

'Whose house is this Kim? it's beautiful.'

Still saying nothing we approach the back door, painted dark red with two frosted window panes set in towards the top.

Fully expecting Kim to rap on the black wrought iron knocker, she forcefully pushes her thumbnail into the door's shiny dark red paint. Inspecting closely where she'd pushed her nail she put her nose very close to the door and audibly sniffed.

'Kim, what on earth are you doing?' she looks at me expressionless.

"Is this the same colour dark red as the paint you asked me about on Raymond's shirt cuff?" She is speaking in quite a hushed tone, more than thrown by the question I think for a moment.

'Well, I suppose it might be, why did you sniff it?'

"Because it's quite freshly painted and soft, take a good look, think, do you think it could be the same colour, exactly the same colour?"

'I can't be completely sure, but it looks similar.' Kim grabs my hand and starts dragging me down the path.

"We need to go, we shouldn't really be here."

'Why not, what's the matter, whose house is it?'

"It's Paula's house, and I don't know if she is in."

'Paula, Raymond's secretary Paula?'

"Yes, that Paula, let's go to the Fox, it's a nice warm day. We can sit in the beer garden, I need to talk with you." I'm baffled, what on earth is Kim up to, it's all mysterious and melodramatic. There must be a very simple explanation.

~ooo~

*The Fox and Goose, Newell Cross.*

'What's this about Kim, what did we just do?'

Kim takes a long sip on her cider, looking at me possibly a touch vexed.

"Teresa, you know I have never meddled or opined in your private life, and I'm not meddling now, what you do with what I'm going to tell you is up to you, I'll still love you the same, crazy lady, but I don't like seeing you being lied to."

'I don't understand Kim.' I am actually quite worried, her tone, the look she wears, it sounds like she is going to deliver some bad news.

"I think Raymond is having an affair with Paula."

Well, that is quite an accusation and I automatically titter dismissively. Time for a B&H and listen to the evidence, and there will be some. This is Kim, and seemingly detective 'Columbo' Kim making the accusation, so I don't think it will be some fluffy fanciful notion; I still think it highly unlikely, Paula really?...highly unlikely...I mean, mechanical Paula. The whole notion at first thought seems ludicrous.

"Teresa, did you know that I do some contractual law work for the district council from time to time?"

'No, you quite rightly rarely discuss your work with me.'

"A week ago I had cause to go to the council offices near Stroud where Raymond's office is, and do you know what I noticed?"

'No.'

"You can walk through the entire building including inside Raymond's office and there isn't the slightest hint of dark red anywhere, nor a painty smell. Just to satisfy myself I asked the councillor I went to see there if there has been any repainting work carried out in the office buildings recently. He laughed in my face, thought I'd lost my mind, he told me with all the cutbacks, this building hasn't seen a lick of paint in at least five years, probably nearer ten."

'There must be an innocent explanation.'

"There is an explanation, but innocent...I don't know about that, I think Raymond is working on Paula's house when he tells you he is playing golf." She swills down some more cider.

"Cast your mind back a couple of weeks. I phoned you on a Saturday afternoon to ask if Raymond was playing golf or was he at home?"

'I remember, he was out playing golf, you wanted to ask him for a few of those plastic golf tees for William's school project model.'

"Correct, only I didn't want them for William, In fact I didn't want them at all, if you remember it was raining cats and dogs all day."

'Yes, I remember.'

"So when you said he was playing golf I asked you to give me a call immediately when he returned so I could come and get a couple of tees, under the pretence of having to urgently make William's fictional model in time for school on Monday. Well, when Raymond took me into the garage to get a couple of tees from his bag do you know what I noticed?"

'No.'

"His golf bag, clubs, shoes and umbrella were all bone dry, less than an hour after leaving the golf course in torrential rain, do you not think that to be a little odd?" Her gaze intensifies, seemingly gauging my reaction.

'Yes, it is odd, but there may be an explanation. He has a lot of golf equipment, perhaps he has another bag and shoes, maybe he put them in the airing cupboard when he got home to dry them.'

Kim nodded.

"Possibly, one more thing...last year at the silver jubilee do, Raymond didn't come with us to the castle meadows did he?"

"No, he was helping out at the Rotary Club event in Macsley."

Kim looks dismissive, "So *he* says, well I was having a working lunch with a client in Macsley the other day. A Rotary club member, well, my curiosity got the better of me, I thought I'd ask about the jubilee do. It turns out that on the day, only my client and one of the younger members were present for the Rotary Club grand charity event for the whole day, the Rotary Club stand was a 'hook a duck' paddling pool." Her eyebrows rise in that Kim smells a rat way.

'I imagine that he probably went off to play golf for the day, he probably used the Rotary Club do as an excuse to not come with us to the castle meadows jubilee day, slightly mischievous true but it's not compelling evidence that Paula and he are having an affair, you can't really blame him, the jubilee day celebrations weren't really his thing.'

"Fine, I'm just marking your card, I don't want you to get hurt Teresa."

'How do you know that house is Paula's.'

"My colleague is doing the change of ownership conveyancing work along with Paula's divorce, that house is Paula's mother's house. I might have just had a slightly unethical sneaky peak around the property last week, hence why I was suspicious about the red paint on the door, so don't mention it."

'I really don't think Raymond is having an affair, I don't think he has any interest in...you know, that sort of thing, I can't remember the last time he paid me any attention in bed, and I can't imagine Paula is going to inflame any man's wild primal urges but thanks detective Kim, thanks for watching out for me.' I feel confident that Kim is probably jumping to conclusions.

"Just keep an eye out for anything unusual in his behaviour."

'I will, but I'm not going to say anything, or accuse him of anything, I don't want him to think I don't trust him, because I do trust him, I love him, I really do.'

# Chapter 13

## *August Book Club Meeting*

*Mr Stamp's Garage, Comberley.*

"Eeeeuuuww, it's all covered in horrible slime, whatever happened to it blondie?"

'Well, it really wasn't my fault.'

The old, oil-stained mechanic eyes me suspiciously.

'It happened just five minutes ago, I had to stop and wait in the middle of the lane while the farmer's herd of Friesians walked by. One of them stopped right by my car, it looked at me through the window, it looked so cute with its big eye lashes, then it sort of slurped the mirror with its big slimy tongue, licked it clean off. Can you fix it back on?'

Holding my car mirror in one hand and with a horrified look at the slime on his other Mr Stamp inspects the little metal piece screwed to my Mini's door.

"Well, lucky for you the mirror's not broken."

'Lucky because it won't cost much to mend?'

"No, much more luckier than that, you have seven years bad luck if you break a mirror see, just think of that, seven more years before you can run away with me to Bognor. The mirror isn't broke so no bad luck, we can run away together tomorrow if you want?"

Mr Stamp laughs heartily, he always thinks himself terribly funny...sometimes he is.

"If you leave it with me while you're working at the library I'll put a new part on the door and refit the mirror, I have a little bag of they  somewhere, they'm only a few bob, it'll be ready when you finish work darling."

'Thank you very much Mr Stamp, I'll be finished at twelve.'  Right I have to go, it's a special morning at  the library. Mr Stamp shouts across the road to me.

"Mark you, I'm not going to clean all that cow slobber of it mind, you'll have to do that yourself."

~ooo~

*Public Library, Comberley.*

"Morning Teresa, are you ready, did you bring your tin helmet?"  Margaret greets me cheerily.

'Morning, yes, I'm ready, well as ready as one can be, they are so unpredictable.'

This morning is our monthly 'book club morning'.

Ahhh, that's nice I imagine you are thinking, the gentle folk of the town gather in the library...an inspired choice of location for such an event, where the old folk and not so old folk gather around the reading table and genteelly discuss 'The book of the month' selected by Margaret.

That's how Margaret started book club a few years ago, her own initiative and it was a peaceful enough event. However the county council's libraries coordinator implemented a few changes upon hearing about Margaret's club. I remember his visit well.

"Margaret, Teresa, let's expand things," he told us.

"Let's reach out further, widen the net."  Go on, tell us more we'd thought innocently at the time.

"Think of the bigger picture, let's have some blue sky thinking." At this point we had begun to switch off, this fresh faced just out of university er...ummm...boy had started spouting gobbledegook at us.

"Let's make book club more inclusive and attractive to different groups and organisations throughout the district." We were still a little confused.

"The WI, the Round Table, the Ladies Circle, the Lions, the Rambling Club, church groups, all of them." He was enthusiastic in his vigour.

"Let's fill this place, make it a hub for all, a focal point for all, a meeting place for all, let's spread our message...unity in the community." Those were his parting words to us as he breezed towards the revolving door which was being determinedly and speedily spun around in a game by a couple of teenagers, we laughed at the irony as he admonished them.

"Get out of here, we don't want your sort here."

Margaret rarely swears, very rarely, but she did say something about the library coordinator, something about shit for brains.

The 'New Model' book club got off to an inauspicious start, Margaret with her usual zeal had flyers printed and she distributed them. Once word spread that there were free tea and biscuits, it was warm in the winter, and it really didn't have much to do with books, numbers swiftly increased.

It quickly became a forum where the warring factions of the parish would air their gripes. The ramblers being savaged by the farmers wives about walking about willy-nilly and not closing the gates, the ramblers staunch in their own defence, claiming it's the likes of visiting week-end city folk leaving the gates open not *us* 'professional ramblers'. Recipe wars frequently break out between the WI and the Ladies Circle, trading punches with jibes about sticks in the mud and fuddy-duddies, the ramblers joining in with advice to the Ladies Circle about where to find the best blackberries, who are in turn countered by the farmers wives indignantly telling everyone *those* blackberries are on private land.

I think you get the picture. At times they do talk about a book, but that normally just polarises opinion and compounds the problem. Last month's selection, Wuthering Heights for example.

"That Cathy had no right to just wander across the moor willy-nilly, it's probably private land." The unanimous view of the farmers wives on Emily Bronte's classic novel.

"She definitely *does* have the right to roam the moors, it's common land. Anyway I saw that young Kate Bush singing the theme tune to 'Wuthering Heights' on Top of the Pops last week, she looked smashing in her skin-tight leotard." One of the ramblers was more embracing although not without adding a little lecherous devilment in his opinion of the book.

All the while the Ladies Circle complain, tutting about Heathcliff; he is either wasting food by throwing warm apple sauce in *that* Edgar's face or getting all unnecessary with Cathy, branding the classic novel nothing more than cover to cover filth.

Margaret has to be quite careful with the choice of book. Nothing that mentions Stalin, Hitler, or heaven forbid, the Common Market.

Book club does liven up the morning, it's never *actually* come to blows and it can be entertaining. Margaret and I are quite powerless to maintain law and order. We are but simple librarians, unlike policemen with their truncheons and soldiers with their guns, we are only armed with a slightly acerbic librarian strength SHUSH!

Talking of policemen, this morning in a change to the usual schedule, PC Baker from Comberley police station is giving a one-hour presentation with questions after. His white board with the title of today's talk is already set up close to the reading table.

Crime Prevention In The Rural
Community

At ten sharp, the first book club members begin filing in. Margaret and I busy ourselves with the tea and biscuits. We thought we'd do the refreshments at the beginning, we have no idea how the morning is going to end. How many arrests will be made; how many ambulances might be needed!

Marjorie Wilkins of the Comberley Ladies Circle gets things off to a good start by tutting her disapproval at the biscuit selection. I'd nipped to the Co-op and bought a tin of tea-time assortment. But Peek-Freen's finest offering was never going to cut it.

"Why didn't you bake some home-made shortbread, rather than giving us these...boughten biscuits?"
Margaret politely replying with a slightly sardonic edge as usual, "Sorry, we were a bit busy filling sandbags, next time eh?"

PC Baker made a good start, patiently explaining about window locks, leaving a light on when the house is empty, and reporting suspicious behaviour. Unfortunately for him the majority of the attendees hailed from either the Ramblers Club or the Comberley Vale Farmers Wives Union, interspersed by a smattering of WI and Ladies Circle Members. At best these groups when combined together are quite unruly...at worst they are a baying mob.

"We don't need to go messing around wasting our time and money on window locks Constable, we got dogs and shotguns." Betty Atkinson, the undisputed matriarchal mouthpiece of the Farmers Wives takes centre stage.

"What *we* want to know is when you are going to start arresting these...these...so called ramblers wandering about on our land as if they own the place, leaving gates open, why I even caught a couple of them in my barn last week, frolicking in the straw they were, naked as the day they were born."
One of her accomplices from the Farmers Wives can't resist a quick heckle.

"Let us know next time you see them Betty, we'll come and join them for a romp in the hay, it's been years."

"Ladies, please," PC Baker moves to prevent what he fears will become a bawdy escalation.

Betty glares impatiently at PC Baker, expectant of a reply, arms akimbo trying not to cast an accusing glance towards the assembled ramblers.

PC Baker in his response is a model of police professionalism.

"Well, Mrs Atkinson, If a rambler is on a public footpath and closes the gate as that individual passes through it then that individual has not committed any offence and will not face arrest."

He looks across the library and catches my eye with a weary grin, I return a smile of solidarity.

"Any individuals carrying out lewd activities on your private land or your outbuildings will of course be committing an offence." He takes a sip of his tea, turning his gaze towards the farmers wives.

"There have been reports from the ramblers that signs marking public footpaths have either mysteriously vanished or have been twisted on their posts to point in the wrong direction. Stiles have just disappeared into thin air to be replaced by barbed wire fences and on a few occasions there have been reports of bulls in fields through which public footpaths cross without any indication or warning signs that said field contains these potentially dangerous animals." PC Baker now returns the demonstrative arms akimbo stance to Betty Atkinson with a pleasant knowing smile.

"I suggest your two groups work together in harmony, as far as I'm concerned the Ramblers Club here in Comberley are responsible individuals."

"What about them blasted kids from the...the...those council houses, running around knocking on doors at all hours of an evening and scarpering."

Marjorie Wilkins from the Ladies Circle, looking aggrieved, "Five or so times a night they knock on my door."

"That's a fair complaint Mrs Wilkins, I *will* look into that, I *will* have a word with them, it's just youthful exuberance, hi-jinks if you like but it's not right."

"Get a dog and set it on the little buggers, that'll learn them." A voice from the Farmers Wives contingent pipes up accompanied by murmurs of agreement around the table. PC Baker raises his hands gesturing for calm.

"That won't be necessary, I think I know the names of the youngsters in question, I will have a word both with them and their parents now you have brought it to my attention."

"Are you going to at least give the little sods a good clip round the ear?" The farmers wives still baying for blood.

"No, we can't go around doing that anymore Mrs Atkinson...police brutality they call it nowadays."

"Bloody liberal softies, don't worry we won't say nothing Constable, you just go ahead and give them a clip round the ear, that'll teach the blighters a lesson."

The library is quiet now, the main belligerents' mouths chock full of bourbon and rich tea biscuits. The Peek Freen tin has been surreptitiously taken from our little kitchen area and placed in the middle of the reading table. There are a couple of soggy semi-circular pieces of rich tea biscuit lying on the table, maimed, each surrounded by a small pool of tea. Victims of reckless overly long dunking by the farmers wives, the tea sodden biscuits couldn't survive the short perilous journey twixt cup and lip, met with shrieks of laughter and 'oh bugger its'. Like locusts the ramblers dig in to the last few unpopular biscuits in the tin enthusiastically.

PC Baker casts his eyes around the reading table.

"Any other business, anyone?"

Miss Humble, from the church committee, diminutive, the most senior person present, well into her nineties, still smartly dressed and active, raises her hand.

"Yes, Miss Humble." PC Baker points a finger in her direction.

"I...I...don't want to be a nuisance or cause a fuss..."

"It's no problem, Miss Humble, what's the matter?"

Miss Humble is such a sweet old lady, PC Baker smiles affectionately at her.

"Constable, someone has been painting rude words on the back of the church wall, near the jester's grave."

This catches the room's attention.

"Oh, I'm sorry to hear that Miss Humble perhaps I can request that the council come and remove it, graffiti isn't nice, especially if it's offensive."

Miss Humble smiles, seeing the interest in her complaint, she addresses the room. "The grammar in common use today...it's shocking. Do you know they spelt 'fingers' with a z."

"Oh, I wasn't aware that fingers was a rude word Miss Humble," says PC Baker.

"Oh, yes, yes, I see what you mean, but when used as a verb it is, it's all in the context Constable, if you care to go and read what they have written you'll rather see what I mean, oh, by the way they also left the 'k' off of knob."
This gets the dry humoured spinster quite a laugh.

Mr Waldron, the Round Table bonfire night organiser thrusts his hand in the air determinedly.

"What are you going to do to guarantee the safety of the guy this year?"
Margaret and I titter at the comic irony of Mr Waldron's concern for the guy's safety.

"We discussed that at the last parish council meeting Mr Waldron. It is very simple, when the cubs have finished making him and doing 'penny for the guy' around the town we'll put him in the cell at the police station for safe keeping until his big night. Then he can travel in the passenger seat of your car to the castle meadows to be burnt."

I expect you might be wondering why it is that the Round Table's guy needs police protection. Well there was an incident last year. The town's bonfire night celebrations are always held on the first Saturday in November without fail. On the run up to the big day the guy had mysteriously disappeared from his lofty perch on top of the bonfire sometime during the Thursday night only to miraculously reappear again on top of the bonfire at some point during Friday night. The bonfire is a huge, really tall pile of scrap wood, old doors, tree branches and pallets. That very self-same week in a seemingly at the time unconnected incident there was a theft from the junk shop behind the café in Comberley town centre. A large cardboard box of mostly half empty aerosol car paint spray cans just vanished. The junk shop owner Mr Mayes thought there were probably about forty to fifty tins in the box.

Fast forward to Saturday night, the Round Table bonfire night event. Festivities had begun innocently enough with the grand lighting of the bonfire by the town clerk. Soon, the bright flames were dancing high in the air licking over Guy's old boiler suit and wellies. Guy hadn't been burning long when it became quite evident where Mr Mayes' stolen car spray paints had ended up.

The first couple of exploding cans causing several shocked gasps and screams from the large crowd circled around the now roaring fire; as the tremendous bangs and streaks of flame following the flying cans like fiery comets intensified, the panicking crowd stampeded towards the safety of the road. A mass exodus...leaving in its wake a trail of hastily abandoned still burning sparklers and dozens of discarded half eaten, tin foil wrapped jacket potatoes. The culprits remain at large to this day.

PC Baker winds things up. With a broad smile framed by his thick dark beard he says that statistically we live in a very safe, relatively crime-free area, accompanied by muted murmurs of dissent. He extends his thanks to Margaret and me for hosting the presentation. As he receives a brief round of applause I think PC Baker overall can chalk his morning up as a moderate success.

Margaret and I breathe a sigh of relief, PC Baker's white police Austin Mini van is leaving the car park as the last of the ramblers leave the library, the revolving door emitting a slight squeal as it turns... it always does that at this time of year.

It's a sign. We are now in high summer, the days are getting warmer.

# Chapter 14

## *A Saturday in August*

*Rosebank Cottage, Brookhayes.*

'Oooh, it looks lovely Yvonne, it's such a pretty colour.' Sitting in the driver's seat, breathing in that 'new car' smell I'm admiring her new car...her Chrysler Sunbeam.

"It's metallic Montezuma gold." Yvonne is beaming with delight as she demonstrates opening the sunshine roof.

Pid-pad, pid-pad noises slap on the drive, we are joined by Princess Amanda, still wearing her overly tight fitting pyjamas, and slippers. She's home from university for the month or so of the long summer break.

'Good morning Amanda, isn't your mum's new car lovely?'

"No, it isn't, it doesn't have rear doors, it's such an inconvenience, Mummy didn't think it through carefully, she's such a dummy." Amanda, sulky, her arms folded, looks at me with contempt. I think, quite fortunately Yvonne isn't listening, busily engrossed pushing the buttons on the car's radio.

'It isn't that inconvenient not having back doors, my Mini is the same, it only has two doors.' I reply, only to be met with a sarcastic false smile from Amanda, raising her eyebrows, pushing her lips forward. Oh, so clearly she thinks I'm a dummy too. No surprise there.

Next door the rolling metallic sound of Jack...I mean Callum's garage door lifts.

"Good morning, ladies." Callum, straddling his yellow motorbike rolls out of his garage, down the drive towards the road, squeezing between his boring Cortina and raunchy Tom Jones, his little purple Triumph sports car.

"Would you like a coffee Callum? perhaps you'd like to join Teresa and me, the merry 'golf widows'." Yvonne shoots a glance towards Amanda. "Go and get dressed darling, it *is* ten o clock."

Princess Amanda protests, "But it's Saturday I'm on holiday what's your problem?" Yvonne upscales her displeasure to a stern lingering scowl and her daughter pid-pads up the drive in the direction of the front door. Yvonne whispers to me,

"She's had those pyjamas since she was about fourteen, they are obscenely tight, they leave absolutely nothing to the imagination."

Callum joins us by Yvonne's car, "Golf widows?" he asks confused.

"Yes, Ralph has gone to play a round in Macsley and Raymond is in...is it Nuneaton for the weekend, Teresa?"

'Nuneaton, yes, that's right.'

A white van appears around the sharp bend by the derelict chapel at the end of our row of cottages and slows, the two men inside are looking at the cottages intently. Callum walks down to the road and waves his hand attracting their attention.

“Mr Gilchrist?” calls the driver, I smile as he pronounces Callum’s surname as Gil-Christ like Christ.

“Yes, good morning.”

The van is subtly sign written on its side, it’s from the motorbike shop in Stroud, the van’s two occupants open the rear doors, pull out a wooden plank and disappear inside.

Yvonne and I watch with growing interest. Yvonne’s early prophecies of our imminent doom had been wrong. When Callum first moved here Yvonne noticed he had a motorbike. She predicted that sleepy Brookhayes would quickly be overrun with gangs of leather clad Hell’s Angels; we’d be unable to sleep for the constant ear-splitting noise or worse still we’d be ravaged and murdered in our beds as we slept. In fact Callum hadn’t ridden his motorbike once as far as I know.

The Two men cautiously wheel a big motorbike from inside the van down the plank to the road. Kicking its stand down, they turn their attention to Callum’s yellow Honda motorbike, pushing it up the plank into the van.

Callum is grinning like a Cheshire cat as he gently runs his hand over the saddle of this...his new toy?

‘Have you bought a new motorbike Callum?’

“Aye, it’s a beauty isn’t it?

‘Ducati, is that a foreign brand?’

“Aye, it’s Italian, a new model, it’s called a Darmah.”

Well, I have to agree, I know nothing about motorbikes but it looks big and powerful. Gorgeous bright red with white striped paintwork, there is a stylish motif of a snarling tiger’s head on its red side panels. The engine is a huge mass of chrome and glinting metal, dazzling in the bright morning sunshine, even Yvonne is smiling approvingly. The men inside the van have finished making ratcheting noises and Callum leads them towards his cottage, calling across to us.

"If the offer for coffee still stands, I'll just pay the men and be round in five minutes."

Amanda reappears, hastily dressed in a T-shirt and jeans, immediately drawn to the new gleaming machine on the side of the road she uninvited slings her leg over it and begins making roaring sounds.

"Take me for a ride on the back" She calls to Callum as he emerges from the house with the two men.

"Och, I'm sorry, I dinnae have another helmet." He looks at her with a modicum of concern as she fiddles with the levers on the handlebars. Disappointed, she dismounts and flounces away pouting towards the house. Standing together watching the van pull away, Callum moves close to me.

"If you're on your own and have nae plans, do you fancy going for a drink this evening Teresa? We could go to that wee pub down by the river."

'The Comberley Hunt Inn, the one near the swing bridge?'

"Aye, it'll be a warm evening, it's nice sat outside there."

'Tom Jones?' I ask hopefully.

I have always wanted to ride in an open top car, I visualise myself looking glamourous like Audrey Hepburn wearing a silk headscarf, I imagine the reality would look far different...well, really, you don't have to agree with me quite so whole-heartedly.

"Why don't we go on my new bike?" Callum can't take his eyes off his new bike.

'But you told Princess Amanda you don't have another helmet, how can we both go on it?'

He whispers in my ear, lassoing me gently with his silky tone.

"I might just have fibbed; I dinnae want her sitting on my new bike, have you nae seen the size of her arse?"

I playfully poke him in his stomach whilst gasping in very insincere shock, replying in my best Victorian lady style voice.

"Why I declare, how very rudely of Miss Pitman doth thou speak Mr Gilchrist, though veritably, in truth she is possessed of a very broad beam." Giggling like children lowering his voice, again he whispers in my ear.

"I have a spare helmet, but she wouldn't like it, it does nae have a tiara," he chuckles as Yvonne calls to us from the front door saying that the coffee is ready.

"I'll pick you up at seven. Wear some jeans, a jacket, some gloves, and please dinnae wear your flip flops."

~ooo~

*Comberley Hunt Inn, Rupton, Gloucestershire.*

Well, that was *quite* an experience! I have never sat on the back of a motorbike before...not a moving one anyway.

Callum has gone inside the centuries old rustic inn to get the drinks.

My heart rate is slowly starting to return to safe levels; my legs aren't shaking quite so uncontrollably...I can just about stand unaided now.

His advice to me ten minutes ago as we were poised to set off from outside my cottage. 'hold on to the wee shiny handle behind you' he said, 'just relax and let yourself go wi'the movement of the bike' he said.

*Him*, looking over his shoulder at me, giving me his sage advice. *Me*, petrified, looking back at him feeling like a goldfish peering out of its bowl with the claustrophobic helmet and visor firmly strapped to my head while the motorbike's engine growls and throbs, sending tingling vibrations through my feet and fingers.

Now I know how Evel feels, motorbikes are terrifying, even just standing still. It took less than a hundred yards after setting off before I abandoned any notion about holding the 'wee shiny handle', wrapping my arms tightly around Callum's middle in a death grip, my eyes firmly closed. After a few minutes realising I was still alive and could breathe I opened them and begun to relax a little. That was until we reached the long sweeping bend in the road past the pig farm and Callum began to sharply bank the motorbike over to round the curve.

'Oh my God...oh my God...we're going to fall, I don't want to die, I don't want to die', petrified thoughts filled my head. The surroundings hazed into a blurry flash, the road was seemingly rising up to meet us, it appeared to be so close, almost as if I just had to put my hand out to the side to touch the dark grey tarmac speeding by. Shut your eyes Teresa I told myself, keep them closed until he turns the engine off. It's not far...the pub...it's not far.

The half dozen outside tables and chairs are all occupied, happily I head to 'the old pillbox' carrying the helmets and jackets while Callum gets the drinks. The concrete pillbox, a relic left from the war, well placed overlooking the river, well we didn't want the Germans getting their hands on our cider, did we? Nowadays it's mostly buried under a grassy bank, just a foot or so of it remains visible. The large flat concrete roof makes an excellent seat affording an unhindered view over the surrounding countryside and river. What makes the pillbox an especially lovely spot on warm days is the beautiful, mature walnut tree growing alongside it providing shade.

"Did you enjoy that?" Callum puts my cider on the pillbox roof.

'No, it was really scary, you are going to have to ring for a taxi to take me home." He smiles at me.

"I'm sorry, I thought I was going slowly, I didn't mean to scare you, don't worry we'll go even slower on the way home."

'Grease, the film, it's on at the pictures next weekend.'

I hastily change the subject, I've had quite enough of motorbikes thank you very much.

"Och, I know I cannae wait to see it." Grinning at me, it hurts a little. Callum has never been sarcastic to me before; I suppose I shouldn't be surprised, A 1950's American high school themed musical is never going to be of interest to him.

I really really want to go and see it, but Raymond laughed at me and refuses point-blank to take me. He only likes war films, 'I'm not going to see a bloody soppy musical like that with that John Revolting in it' he told me. Kim likes films and music, but she says, 'never the twain shall meet' and hates musicals with a passion. She says the instant people start singing in a film she has to leave the room, or she'll be compelled to uncontrollably put her foot through the telly screen in anger.

"I'll go with you, I want to see it although I don't want to go on my own, I love the songs from it." Callum is still grinning.

'Stop teasing me Callum, don't be mean.'

"I'm not being mean, I love musicals, I'm serious, I've been looking forward to going to the pictures to watch it, so let's go together."

I have to say, he looks like he means it, I'm still not entirely convinced. Shall we test him, to see if he is joking?

'Which musicals have you seen then, 'Mr I love musicals'?

"Och, pretty much every one that's ever been made, Singing in the Rain, Sound of Music, Thoroughly Modern Millie, West Side Story, Paint your wagon."

'Prove it, prove to me that you have seen these musicals, prove you aren't making fun of me.'

Callum looks deeply into my eyes, he looks a little hurt.

"Honestly, I'm not making fun of you; how can I prove it?"

'Sing me a few lines from songs from a few of the musicals you claim to have seen.'

Well, he amazes me; unsurprisingly he has a nice voice. What surprises me is that he doesn't seem to be held back by self-consciousness or taking himself too seriously. Moving very near to me he begins rattling through a medley of songs. We laugh as with a harsh gravelly tone he sings a few lines of 'Wandrin Star' then with animated arm movements and a good touch of sentiment I'm treated to a burst of 'Maria', leading into an energetic and enthusiastic 'Do-Re-Mi', at this point I join in, I love Julie Andrews. Finally, my heart begins to melt with his soulful heartfelt rendition of 'Summertime' from Porgi and Bess. Believe me, as long as you have a pulse and functioning ears the smooth Scottish acappella version of the song will move you.

Life is so full of surprises isn't it, he sings so beautifully. The two, sixty-something couples, the only remaining customers sitting outside the pub, obviously not hard of hearing applaud from their table. Callum responds, comically bowing with a smile and a sweep of his hand, blushing a little...I rather think he thought or hoped they were out of earshot.

“So, now do you believe me, my secret passion is musicals.”

‘Yes, I’m sorry, sorry for doubting you, it just seemed so unlikely.’

“So let’s go to the pictures next Saturday and watch Grease, as long as it won’t cause nae bother with Raymond, that is.”

‘I’d love to go with you Callum, I’m sure it will be okay with Raymond, would you like another drink?’

“No, thank you.” He has had one small glass of beer, I’m not going to encourage or try to persuade him to have another...I’m acutely aware that mixing driving and alcohol must be something painful for him...the tragedy of his pregnant wife.

‘Is it okay if I have a quick one?’

I think I better have a quadruple whisky to give me enough Dutch courage to face the three-mile trip home on that terrifying motorbike!

“Of course, take as long as you like, please don’t rush, it’s such a beautiful evening.”

Travelling back didn’t seem so bad, perhaps the whisky, or maybe because it was dark, maybe because I was getting used to being on a motorbike. Callum rode it considerately, not wanting to scare me witless again, he seems at ease on it, at one with it, naturally able to handle it confidently.

It has been a lovely evening and as I hand the crash helmet back to Callum on his drive, thoughts of ‘would you like a coffee?' or 'my place or yours?' are swimming around in my head, but it could possibly lead to somewhere I know it shouldn't.

'Thank you for a lovely evening Callum. The motorbike ride...interesting...terrifying but interesting. Would you like me to drive to the pictures next weekend?'

"I'll drive, if it's a nice evening would you like to go in Tom Jones?"

'I would like that very much, an open top car, that would be lovely.' With a fleeting peck on his cheek and a quick goodnight I turn and walk the fifty yards, smiling from ear to ear to my dark empty cottage. Thoughts running through my mind.

I have a week to find some stylish sunglasses and a silk headscarf...eat your heart out Audrey Hepburn, you only got to ride around with the likes of Cary Grant and Humphrey Bogart...I...I on the other hand...well I get to be fabulous in an open top car with Callum.

# Chapter 15

## *A Thursday in September*

*Nelson Park Leisure Centre, Stroud.*

It's crowded tonight, diving in and warming up with a few speedy lengths of crawl, I haven't ever seen the pool this busy before. Now for one of my stylish...stylish in my mind anyway racing turns and swim back, twenty-five metres to the wall. There is a man...a man...an older man, we're on collision course, he looks eerily focused, a gaunt, sallow face, eyes obscured behind virtually black goggles, his head covered with a glossy black rubber swimming cap with a white skull and crossbones motif on the front. Skimming the rope with its numerous red plastic floats dividing the lanes we pass, a near miss. Then ten yards away a large...very large woman is heading towards me preceded by a sizable bow-wave, large enough for me to quickly deduce squeezing by on the ropes again is not an option. Dive, dive, dive...what's wrong with these people tonight?

You're going to find this hard to believe, but no really it's true, I am quite graceful and agile in water, much more so than on dry land, a bit like a penguin. Diving down to the bottom of the pool under the oncoming behemoth holding my breath I twist through 180 degrees to look up to see when I can surface. The woman five feet above me slowly lumbering through the water like a giant turtle is wearing one of those pink Disney hippo swimsuits I told you about from the shop in Macsley. I have no control, I immediately blow my tanks, I'm sorry, I apologise, I feel so mean, but they look even worse 'on' than I had feared. Without air I have to surface immediately, the woman above me still not quite passed. I suppose it's karma, divine retribution from giggling at the lady that I get a hefty kick on my backside from her as I rise gasping to the surface.

When I reach the wall, the tall handsome lifeguard is there to meet me.

"Miss...Miss." He waves his hand to attract my attention, his whistle poised, inches from his lips he looks eager to blow it with venom, but I surrender without a fight.

'Oh, hi.' I just know I have done something wrong.

"Did you not read the signs on the cones?"

He is pointing to an orange traffic cone with a bit of cardboard stuck to it. Cones, signs, what is he talking about?

"Miss, the Painswick Pirates Swimming Club are having to use this pool tonight, the one they usually use has sprung a leak, we are using a swim up one lane down the next system tonight because it's so busy."

The Painswick Pirates, never heard of them but it goes some way to explaining the pirate zombie I'd nearly bumped into. You know I think I might need glasses soon, I can't make head nor tail what's written on the hastily scrawled note on the cone, don't worry I'm not totally blind...I can see the cone. I'll play it safe, I'll just tuck in behind Captain Morgan, the zombie pirate king and swim. I don't know where Kim ended up.

Anyway did you like the way the handsome lifeguard called me 'Miss' several times whilst admonishing me? Eat your heart out Vikki the hairdresser, what with your wrinkly forehead jibes. Talking of which I have booked an appointment with Tracey the hairdresser tomorrow ahead of my big night out to see 'Grease', I can't wait. I thought I might get a 'Grease' themed hair do as a bit of fun. I can't make up my mind whether to go for something like the innocent, shy, 'good' Sandy or the raunchy leather clad, 'bad' Sandy. No doubt Vikki and her sister will have opinions, probably quite robust ones they'll happily discuss with Tracey.

Heading home, as we near the pub Kim begins tittering.

'What's so funny Kim?' Her laughter increases.

"At the pool, you know the lane system, I'd been practising butterfly, you know how I struggle with it."

'Yes, butterfly, something I can actually do better than you...probably the only thing.'

"Well, I collided with that gloomy looking old man with the black cap, he wasn't happy."

'Ah the zombie pirate king.' Sniggering together, we pull up outside the pub.

"I heard him complaining to the lifeguard, you'll never believe what he said."

Kim giggles briefly, "He said, 'oy, lifeguard, have a word with Madam Butterfly and that blond bimbo in the Special K swimsuit will you, swimming the wrong way they are.'"

~ooo~

*The Fox and Goose Inn, Newell Cross.*

"How was Raymond's golfing weekend in Nuneaton?" Kim, inquisitive, she is keen to find out the result of a somewhat devious plan we'd hatched as we sit down in the beer garden, deserted apart from two men I'd not seen at the pub before.

'Yes, he saw it and read it, he thought it was nice. He is at the Rotary Club meeting this evening.'

What had I done? Well, I had put a little note in the ball pocket of his golf bag saying, 'have a nice time' and 'I love you'. It was Kim's suggestion, she reasoned if he'd been 'playing around' instead of 'playing a round' then he wouldn't have seen the note. A weekend playing golf without...excuse me, taking your balls out of their bag would indeed be suspicious.

"Are you getting excited about Grease on Saturday night Teresa?" I think she can see my face light up before I answer.

'I can't wait, I have a silk headscarf, some trendy retro sunglasses, and I'll wear my cute little sheepskin jacket, I'm getting my hair done on Friday.

"And *those* Levis?" smiling, she knows the answer.

'I think they would complete the look.'

"I can't stay long, I have to give Mark a helping hand." Kim knocks back her cider with determination.

'That's fine, you go, I'll just have a quick ciggie while I finish my drink then wander home, it's a nice evening.'

"Okay darling, I'll just give you your swimming bag and head off." I laugh, relieved, thankful Kim remembers everything; I would have got home and discovered I didn't have my bag and be locked out.

Kim places my bag on the table, "You have a lovely time at the pictures, tell me all about it on Sunday, take care." A quick kiss on my cheek and she walks away to her Land Rover.

'Bye darling.' Lighting my illicit B&H, the man from the table nearby approaches with an unlit cigarette in his hand.

"Excuse me, can I borrow  lighter please?"

A foreign accent, not unusual, seamen often walk the mile from the docks for a drink here, this accent is unusual though, not French or Spanish.

'Of course,' I hand him my lighter and with a broad smile he takes it.

"On your own?"  His English although broken is good.

"You want drink, what is it?"  He looks at my virtually finished glass on the table.

'No thank you, it was cider but I'm just about to go home.'

Without asking he lifts the glass and hands it to his companion who'd now walked across to my table, saying something in his own language; the other man takes the glass and heads towards the door of the pub.

'Oh, I really don't want another, I am about to go home, I have to cook dinner for my husband.' A little fib, but I don't want another drink.

"Nonsense, stay, your husband can cook his own dinner, have drink with us." His dark eyes burn intently into mine. Fiddling with the strap on my bag I feel nervous.

"A pretty woman like you shouldn't be all alone, what is your name?" Normally I wouldn't mind a light-hearted complimentary remark like this...but something isn't sitting well with me, the butterflies nervously rising in the pit of my stomach increase greatly as the other man returns with a pint of cider, placing it on the table in front of me. He sits down beside me, uncomfortably close, our thighs touching, too close, I shuffle along the bench seat. Not wishing to appear ungrateful or rude but another whole pint of cider on an empty stomach will definitely get me tipsy. Is that what they are intending?

They could be brothers, somewhere between thirty and forty, tall and muscularly lithe with swarthy olive skin. Both wearing black leather jackets. Their heads seem quite long and narrow, topped with slicked back dark hair.

'My name is Teresa, where are you from?' I am feeling very uneasy, something visceral, my instincts tell me to get my bag and head to the bar.

"Teresa...a pretty name for a pretty lady, we are from Albania, do you know where that is?"

The man in front of me smiles, I notice one of his front teeth is entirely made of gold.

'No, I'm not sure.' I answer. Reaching across the table he takes my hand shaking it as one would; he doesn't let it go, retaining his light grip on it. I notice he has several small tattoos on his fingers and hand, strange symbols.

"My name is Nikolai, this is Pavel." He gestures with his free hand towards his companion.

"Relax little lady, there is nothing to be afraid of, let's get to know each other." I'm sure he can sense my discomfort; this is just making me more afraid. Feeling vulnerable, there is no one else in the beer garden, the car park unusually is eerily empty. They say something I don't understand between themselves, laughing lewdly, running their eyes over me. You don't need to understand Albanian to know they aren't discussing the weather.

"Have you eaten this evening?" Nikolai asks, raising his eyebrows questioningly. Foolishly but truthfully I say I haven't eaten yet.

"It's settled, we get a taxi, we are staying in hotel by docks, you come with us, we have dinner. We have a room there, is not luxurious, but it's clean and private. After we eat you come to our room, we...relax, have good time, we have plenty of vodka."

Foreboding waves of apprehension flood over me, my heart is pounding in my chest, what does he mean 'relax'? I can guess. With a queasy smile he tells Pavel something, before turning his intense gaze back towards me, taking my hand once more.

"I tell him to go and ring for a taxi."

My stomach is churning making me nauseous, I get the impression these men are used to getting what they want, not used to taking no for an answer.

My mind is made up, the fight or flight instinct kicking in. I have to head for safety inside the pub.

'Excuse me, I must nip to the toilet.' Just as I stand, picking up my bag I hear my name.

"Teresa...Teresa." Ernie, the pub landlord shouts from the pub door and starts half-jogging across the beer garden towards me.

"Excuse me Teresa, you have a telephone message, come with me to the bar." Huge waves of relief flow over me as Ernie moves very close to me, protectively close. The two Albanians talking to themselves stand, Nikolai takes my hand, in an elaborate, almost chivalrous gesture he kisses the back of it.

"A pity, we could have had enjoyable evening together, maybe another time, good night Teresa."

'Good night Pavel, Nikolai, thank you for the drink.' They'd already turned and were hurriedly walking away towards the road. I feel hugely alleviated by their abrupt leaving, I was never going to go, not willingly at least to their hotel room, drink vodka and 'relax' with them but all the same there was something I didn't feel comfortable with about them, an aura, something quite menacing.

'Ernie, what is this message?'

"A policeman phoned the pub, asking for you, thought you might be here, from a call box by the sound of it, he said there had been a break-in at the library and you need to go there straight away with your key, he said Margaret didn't answer her phone when the police rang her."

'PC Baker?' My mind is awash, I have no idea how the police would know I was here.

"No, it wasn't PC Baker, the caller wasn't local, he sounded like he was from London judging by his accent."

Ernie ushers me through the bar to the rear of the pub, picking up his car keys, he shouts towards the half-ajar kitchen door.

"Lisa, look after the bar for ten minutes please, there's only Stan and Herbert in."

'I can walk home Ernie, get my car and the keys and drive to the library, it won't take long at all.'

"No Teresa, I insist, I'm going to drive you home, I really didn't like the look of those two men, I'll feel happier driving you home rather than you walking alone down your lane."

He is so kind, and what's more I'm not going to argue, Ernie is right I don't want to walk down the lane alone as I would usually, feeling safe, confident, and care-free. This is Newell Cross, where if you forget to lock the house door or leave the key in your car what will happen? Absolutely nothing...but this evening I don't feel so self-assured, there was something quite threatening about those two Albanian seaman.

~ooo~

*Comberley Public Library.*

Well this is very mysterious, there are no policemen here, I've done two laps, walking around the outside of the library; looking as carefully as I can in the darkness for any signs of a break-in, but everything looks as it should. Still shaking a little from the Albanian seaman episode; I'm certainly not going inside the library alone at this time of the evening, it's pitch black inside. I'll go and ask at the police station, it's only a minute's walk.

"Good evening Teresa." PC Baker is sitting behind the desk in the small functional reception area of the police station. A copy of 'Horse and Hound' magazine opened in his hands, a recently made mug of tea steaming lazily by his side.

"What can I do for you?" He smiles warmly, peering over the top of his magazine.

'I was given a message that there has been a break-in at the library.'

Putting the magazine down he stands and walks to the counter. "It's the first I've heard of that, a break-in you say?"

This is becoming more baffling, 'Yes, a policeman, apparently with a London accent phoned the Fox and Goose and left a message with the landlord that there has been a break-in at the library, and could I go there with the key, a policeman would meet me there.'

"And did you and was there?

'Yes I've had a look, there was no sign of a break-in, but I didn't go inside, I was too frightened to; there wasn't a policeman there.'

"And do you have the key?' I nod to him as he takes a mouthful of his tea before picking up his helmet and large rubber torch.

"Right, let's go and have a look." On the short walk past the chip shop, hardware shop, the Dragon public house, and the bank, PC Baker is curious to know, as am I how the police knew I'd be at the Fox. There is no answer to that.

The inside of the library is just as Margaret and I had left it earlier this afternoon. Apologising to PC Baker, he is equable.

"Don't you worry about troubling me, better to be safe than sorry, it must be someone playing silly beggars. Anyway you get on home now Teresa, I'll keep an eye out during the night. Good night."

# Chapter 16

## ***All dressed up…but***

*Vikki's Hair Salon, Comberley.*

"Morning Teresa, what are we doing today?"

Sitting in my usual chair next to the door, Tracy smothers me with the huge white nylon cape.

'I'm going to see Grease tonight at the pictures, I thought it'd be fun to have something 'Grease' themed, but I'm going to the cinema in Gloucester in an open top car, although the weather looks iffy.'

"Hmmmph…give me a moment, I'll go and see what Vikki and Sharon think." Don't worry, I'm not going to follow her and inadvertently eavesdrop like last time!

It's nice this chair, comfortable; you can see all the comings and goings in Comberley High Street.

Well, it seems I have sparked a little interest as Tracey returns accompanied by Vikki and Sharon both cradling mugs. Vikki pushes her lips forward in contemplation.

"So, you're going to see Grease are you?"

'Yes, this evening.'

"And you want a hairdo like Olivia Neutron-Bomb's?"

'I thought it might be fun.'

"Tracey says you're going to the cinema in an open top car."

'Yes, that's right.'

I can see Vikki and Sharon in the mirror behind me, narrowing their eyes looking at me objectively, their hands slowly rubbing their chins side to side.

Vikki lifts my hair, twisting it gently.

“You’re not driving it are you, this...this open top car?”

‘No, my friend is.’ I reply, Vikki with a slight snigger turns to Sharon.

“Well thank God for that.” The pair of them titter.

“A fella is he...this friend of yours?”

‘Yes, he is...just a friend, my next door neighbour.’

Vikki turns her attention to the weather, it’s been heavily raining all morning and shows no sign of stopping.

“It’s piddling down all day and tonight according to the forecast mind.”

‘They may be wrong; it might be nice by this evening.’ Always sanguine, nothing is going to spoil my day.

“Glass half full, that’s the spirit, don’t worry, even if your ‘friend’ has to put the hood up you’re still going to look fabulous.” Sharon, cackling, shares my optimism.

“Are you planning on wearing a hat or something?”

‘Silk headscarf and retro cat-eyes sunglasses.’

“Let me see, silk headscarf and retro sunglasses, open top car and a...err...’friend’...mmm.”

Rubbing her chin Vikki turns to look at her sister they nod at each other, their smiles broadening.

“Are you thinking what I’m thinking Shar?”

“I’ll get my Kirby pins Vik,” Sharon excitedly skips away.

“Tracey, leave this to us...watch and learn!”

I’m happy, they clearly have come up with an idea; it might be nice if they shared it.

"The trouble with open cars is they play havoc with our artistry." Vikki catches my eye in the large mirror on the wall. "If you had a 'Bad Sandy' teased out curls hairdo by the time you get to Gloucester you'll look like the Dulux dog...no offence. The 'Good Sandy' ponytail, Alice band and fringe? Nah...too goody goody plain Jane, you'll look like a librarian." Sharon returns with a basket, tittering about me looking like a librarian.

They are unusually quiet by their standards as they work, beavering away, focused they look as if they are really enjoying themselves. I can see the concentration as they backcomb, twist, and pin my hair. Sharon has taken command, tutting she prods Vikki with the sharp end of her rat-tail comb on seeing something not meeting her exacting approval.

"Ouch, you mare, what was that for?" the two of them giggle as Sharon pushes Vikki's hands away.

"Leave *that* bit alone, just twist *that* bit in the chignon you narna, we need that bit there left loose for the bangs when we'm finished with the bun. Put the kettle on Trace we're nearly done."

Watching in the mirror I had seen their work gradually taking shape and as it nears completion I feel very happy, Sharon makes a few finishing touches before pronouncing with an excited ta-da, "It's done."

Wow, it's as if they read my mind, these two hairdressers are worth their considerable 'robust' weight in gold, my hair looks fabulous.

Sharon is rightly proud of her creation. Shaking a can of hairspray.

"The Audrey Hepburn up-do, it's ages since I've done one, it suits you well, close your eyes Teresa."

The cloud of hairspray clears, looking in the mirror turning my head from side to side I can't help but beam with delight, a low-slung bun, skilfully twisted and pinned with two broken sections of short fringe. Just gagging for a tiara, eat your heart out Princess Amanda.

More Dusty than Audrey in shade; I absolutely love it.

At the salon door I prepare to pop up my brolly for the short walk to the library. The three hairdressers are looking outside at the rain teeming down.

"Do you think your 'friend' will like it?" Vikki pushes her tongue into her cheek, nudging and winking at her sister.

'I'm sure he will, but he is just a friend.'

~ooo~

*Comberley Public Library.*

'Margaret, did you get a strange phone call last night so say from the police?'

"No, I didn't get any phone calls last night, I was indoors watching the telly with mother all night, we'd have heard the phone if it had rung."

The library was quiet, just Group Captain Jelf, sat at the reading table intently deciding if he wanted to borrow our copy of 'The Thorn birds'.

"What's this novel all about ladies, is it any good?" calling across to us standing by fiction and romance.

Ex RAF Group Captain Jelf is an elegant gentleman, always smartly dressed, courteous with a refined accent. He walks with a slight but pronounced limp, a legacy from the Battle of Britain. Unlike many of the exaggerated or fictional 'old soldier' tales one hears, he was indeed wounded during the war. We looked him up in the detailed reference book we have for that particular battle. It mentions him as a Squadron Leader Leonard Jelf back in those days. Badly injured after being forced to land his damaged Spitfire in a field near Rye in East Sussex. He never talks about his exploits during the war, a modest man, he'll just tell you, 'we had a job to do, we just got on with it'. We respect that and never pry, we just quietly admire him, a proper gentleman.

Margaret flounces across to him, they are quite good friends, they have met for lunch on a few occasions at the Dragon public house in the town centre. The Group Captain now a widower is a regular to the library. In his early sixties he still cuts a dashing figure. I sometimes imagine, hopeless romantic that I am, him getting together with never married Margaret, she's only seven or eight years younger than him, I think they would make a nice couple but any mention of it and Margaret scornfully dismisses my fanciful matchmaking notions. I suppose she could be right, he is always precise and exacting, stylishly formal in dress and manner. Margaret is flouncy and ethereal. At times her life is chaotic, often she is 'away with the fairies' with a very bohemian sense of dress. One of the gentlest sweetest souls I've ever met. Opposites attract I tell her, but she is content that they remain friends over a tomato juice in the Dragon.

Time passes slowly, but eventually it's three o'clock, coffee-time, as I'm waiting for the kettle to boil PC Baker pulls up outside in his police Mini van and heads for the library, entering after a swift tussle in the revolving door with Group Captain Jelf exiting at the same time.

"That was a complete mystery last night Teresa, baffling, I've spoken with Macsley police station, no one knew anything about a break-in here, so as I said, probably a silly beggar messing about, but it's someone who must know you or knows you work here."

'I don't know anyone with a London accent though, just my uncle from Bromley, but he is seventy and lives in a care home I can't imagine it was him in a million years.'

~ooo~

*Primrose Cottage, Brookhayes.*

5:15PM, 'Grease' minus two hours...an hour to get ready, a quick bath...mindful of Sharon's masterpiece of course and get dressed. I am so excited...'Grease', being driven there in an open top car, ruefully I look outside, stair rods, it's raining cats and dogs, oh well. We'll still have a nice evening even if we have to travel in his Cortina.

Speaking of which, Raymond's revolting beige Cortina is backing up on the drive.

"Hello, T," 'grrrr', "I have the golf club AGM this evening, I'll have a quick shower, change, and go." As he trap, trap, traps up the stairs.

Oh, so no your hair looks nice Teresa, enjoy the film Teresa, I like your new top Teresa. He doesn't say anything, I still feel fabulous if somewhat invisible as he hurriedly breezes out half an hour later.

6:15PM...I'm hovering in the kitchen, ready, looking, listening expectedly, straining to hear Tom Jones or the Cortina roar into life to whisk me away. The seconds...the minutes...tick by.

Knocking on the door of Ivy Cottage; I have tottered next door in my red stilettos under my umbrella. It's six thirty, the house seems empty. No lights are on, suspicious, although it's daylight the weather is very murky and overcast. I notice Callum's red Cortina isn't parked on the drive.

My heart is sinking, back at home sitting in my kitchen, the film starts in less than half an hour and there is no sign of Callum.

It's an indescribable feeling, desolate, I want to cry, surely he could have at least phoned, I feel foolish, I have looked forward to this evening for so long. A glance at the clock.

7:15PM, the exact time the film is starting, I can't help it, the first tear tracks down my cheek...All dressed up and no place to go.

It's nearly eleven when Raymond returns home. Trap, trap trap up the stairs entering our bedroom with a very large tumbler of whisky. He looks across to me, sitting at the dressing table in my nightie, brushing my hair, the table top littered with Kirby pins.

"How was the film?" he asks, unbuttoning his shirt.

'I didn't go, Callum didn't come.'

Slipping off his shirt, Raymond picks up his whisky and knocks it back in one gulp, I look at his reflection in the mirror, he smirks to himself as he sits on the bed to remove his socks.

"So, Prince Charming stood you up, he must have had a better offer."

'Don't be unkind Raymond, we are just friends, there must be a very good reason that he couldn't make it.'

"I'll tell you the reason, he has had a better offer, an offer from something a bit younger, something that doesn't need to wear skin tight jeans, something with big enough tits she doesn't need to wear a push-up bra to flaunt herself, maybe something in her twenties with not so many miles on the clock." Sliding into bed huffing he switches off his bedside lamp.

My light sobs, now torrents of tears, freely tracking down my cheeks, why is he saying these things? He has never been so hurtful, so unkind before. In the bathroom, brushing my teeth I hear Raymond's cruel words still echoing in my head. Feeling thoroughly miserable as I turn out the bathroom light, pausing for the briefest of moments with my hand resting on the bedroom door then opening it...not *our* bedroom door, for the first time ever...the spare bedroom door.

# Chapter 17

## ***An Enchanted Evening***

*Primrose Cottage, Brookhayes.*

I can hear Raymond moving around, opening my eyes getting my bearings, a little disorientated, oh yes...the spare bedroom. I don't know what time it is, no idea at all. This room has no clock. Thoughts of last night...Callum not turning up, Raymond's wounding words, I feel small and very foolish. Lethargic, I just want to wallow in self-pity and sadness in the warm bed. Only yesterday I was feeling so happy and blessed and twenty-four hours later well...my world seems a cold and empty place. Raymond moves about quietly...almost as if he is creeping down the stairs, moments later the clunk of the back door, followed by the whirring of his car's starter...and he's gone, not a word, golf?

A knock on the front door, Saturday morning, perhaps it's the postman or maybe Kim or Yvonne wanting to know all last night's goss? I am going to feel so embarrassed when I explain what happened. Wandering downstairs in my nightie; an unkempt bird's nest on my head in place of last night's beautifully styled hair. Opening the top half of the front door, still sleepy, my mind is confused...mixed feelings.

'Callum.' I'm at a loss for words, still bitterly disappointed but...well maybe there is an explanation.

"Teresa, I'm so, so very sorry, last night something came up at work, I can't go into it but I really couldn't get away, I have only just this minute got home." The apologetic look on his face suggests sincerity. He looks tired and pallid. A number of red puffy semi-circles under his eyes, unusually he has a dark shadow of stubble on his face. His shirt is creased and his hair hasn't seen a comb in a while.

"Look, can we go tonight? if it's okay with Raymond. Perhaps you'll allow me to take you to dinner afterwards, a small gesture to at least try to go a small way to make amends for last night."

Can I go tonight? What do you think, should I?
As for Raymond...well after last night's vitriolic diatribe he's the last person I am going to ask for permission to go to the pictures. Looking skyward the weather is much improved today, there isn't a cloud in the sky, the warm sun shining on my face is swiftly drying up the remnants of yesterday's puddles on my path. I'm picturing Tom Jones looking attractively brutish with the roof down, but what of my fabulous hairdo? I wonder if Sharon and Vikki the narna have time this morning to fit me in without an appointment for an 'up-do re-do' alongside their usual Saturday morning throng, 'the charge of the blue rinse brigade'. I try to look stern and probably fail.

'You are not in the clear yet Callum, just where are you thinking of taking me to dinner?' This better be good, if he is thinking of the Wimpy by the cinema...well.

"There is this little French restaurant I know, between here and Stroud, I took mum and dad there; it's in a tiny village, Hillerton, it's called the 'Chat Rouge'. The food is very good there." He said the 'Chat Rouge', I've long wanted to go there. That restaurant has a tremendous reputation, he has such good taste.

I've suggested to a certain someone for us to go there on several occasions, but my requests have always been met with contempt, 'have you seen the prices T?' or 'I'm not eating that foreign muck T.'

Oh, that's settled then...Callum is now definitely in the clear.

'Okay, you've twisted my arm, but don't you need to book that place well in advance?'

"Already have, we were going to go there last night, I was going to surprise you after the pictures, I've rung them this morning and explained, they were very good about it, very understanding. We have a table this evening if we want it. Shall I pick you up at four?"

Good taste and quietly confident without any trace of arrogance, he really is quite something. I had no idea we were going there last night.

'Yes, four o'clock, that's great, now if you'll excuse me, I have to go and grovel to the hairdresser.'

~ooo~

*Vikki's Hair Salon, Comberley.*

Vikki and Sharon both stare at me with incredulity, first at my hair, then lowering their gazes to the numerous Kirby pins in my outstretched palm whilst they listen to my pleading request. I lay it on thick, one can almost hear the violins. They look horrified, after a sharp intake of breath Vikki shouts to Tracy several times towards the back of the salon over the hum of the driers, all occupied by Women's Realm reading pensioners, with three more lined up, being processed like cars on a factory assembly line.

Enter stage right, Tracey, my saviour...quickly weighing up the scene she springs into action.

"I'll take care of the rinse, set and dry ladies." As she pushes me down onto the chair, I'm cloaked ready for emergency repair work as Vikki and Sharon get busy with their brushes and combs.

"Here, Teresa did you hear all about that commotion down the docks last night?" Vikki's voice sounds a little strange, the combination I suppose of excitement from some juicy local gossip and half a dozen Kirby pins gripped loosely between her lips.

'No, what happened?' I had heard no commotion.

All *I* knew about last night was rain, humiliation, bitter disappointment, a few huge Cinzanos to drown my sorrows and my husband berating my in his view, inadequate tits.

"Errr, Shar, Teresa don't know about last night down the docks." Vikki blurts to Sharon, accidently spitting a few hair pins on me; her mounting excitement reaching fever pitch.

"She must have been too busy with her 'friend', the one with the open top car, that explains how her hair got this wrecked so quick. That's why she never heard all the commotion."

They cackle, a dirty laugh accompanied by cheeky winks at me in the mirror.

"Oh my God, it's all over town this morning. My Dave was working at the docks last night when it all kicked off, he saw it all." Sharon is close to hyperventilating.

"Last night right, The police, proper serious police like on the Sweeney not like ploddy PC Baker, well they stormed this ship in Leighbury docks, apparently it had loads and loads of drugs on it, tons. And at exactly the same time, some soldiers, hard looking bastards with big machine guns, some with balaclavas, Dave reckons it was, what was it he said?...the SAS or something, whatever that is, well they stormed the Pier Hotel, they come in three black Range Rovers. You know the Pier Hotel right, the one by the docks, the soldiers rounded up this gang of foreigners that was staying there. Dave's mate Stuart was having a pint in the hotel bar with his mate when the soldiers burst in all of a sudden. Stuart shit himself and legged it outside, Stuart reckons the foreigners was some Albanians, nasty bastards, he was sure they had guns. Stuart said the soldiers gave them a right good kicking before the police came and took them away in handcuffs in vans." Their increasingly animated excitement was obvious as they worked restoring 'Audrey's up-do' to its former glory.

For me, nestling under the huge cape, my ears ringing from the excitable high-speed verbal assault they'd just received, my brain's cogs began ticking and whirring, albeit slowly; as once again Sharon pronounces with a flourish her artistry finished with a proud, 'Ta-da'.

Turning my head from side to side in the mirror I beam delighted at her beautifully recoiffured masterpiece.

Just one word needed...Fabulous.

~ooo~

*The Regal Cinema, Gloucester.*

Well, finally here we are, at last. The cinema is full, you can feel the buzz of anticipation and excitement in the air. All summer long the country has been subjected to if not bombarded by many of the songs from the soundtrack from 'Grease' virtually non-stop on the radio and 'Top of the Pops'. Now, released barely a week ago the film is in the cinema.

The journey from Brookhayes to the cinema in Gloucester was like being in a movie itself, not a cloud in the late afternoon sky, feeling like a movie star my silky headscarf feeling glamorous while keeping Audrey's up-do under control while I watch the world go by through my dark cat-eyes sunglasses. If you could keep your comments to yourself please.

The film was incredible, everything I'd hoped it to be, and more. Callum had bought me a tube of smarties, even the letter on the underside of the red plastic lid was a 'T', he said with a wry grin it was just coincidence.

He produced a hankie for me when Danny made Sandy cry, so naturally I cried. We laughed together when the three boys 'mooned' at the dance, we sung 'Summer Nights' together, and he held my hand at the scary part when Danny was racing against the nasty man with the cratered face at Thunder Road.

~ooo~

*'Le Chat Rouge' Hillerton, Gloucestershire.*

"Your hair looks beautiful tonight Teresa, it's very elegant, classic, it has more than a touch of Dusty Springfield about it...my favourite singer of all time."

'Thank you, I had it done at Vikki's, she decided what I was going to have when I mentioned open top car, I had no say in the matter.'

Picking up the crisply starched white napkin and placing it on my lap you can feel the quality. The waitress arrives at the table, looking immaculate in common with everything else here, the silverware, linen tablecloth, crockery. Everything is immaculate, tasteful and of a certain quality, rather like the diners!

We order aperitifs and enthuse about the film, the soundtrack is still coursing through my veins, I find it hard to stop myself fidgeting...I just want to dance, control yourself woman. We eat pate with melba toast, followed by a filet mignon, I drink Côtes du Rhône and Chablis, a glass of Sauternes with dessert, the most delicious apple tart with Crème Anglaise.

Over coffee we are still talking about anything and everything, but I'm conscious that we have spent the whole evening carefully tiptoeing around the elephant in the room.

'Callum, when I was at the hairdressers, Vikki and her sister were telling me all about some drama at the docks last night.' I lock eyes with him, hoping to capitalise on the element of surprise.

"Oh, is that right?" straight faced, he stirs his coffee.

'You work at the docks, you were working there last night, I thought you might have noticed something.' Remaining quite expressionless, he glances at me, most matter of fact.

"There was a drug seizure, some traffickers were arrested, that's what I'd heard."

'Don't you think it odd, that you have taken lots of photographs from the knoll, but you've never shown me any?' Switching tack, maybe I can wrong foot him.

"Och, no, not really, I have nae got around to sending them away to be developed yet." Maybe that's true, I'll try another angle.

'Do you know that two Albanian men from the docks approached me at the Fox the other evening after Kim left, they were quite pushy, they sat at my table, bought me a drink. They were going to get a taxi, they wanted me to go back to their hotel room with them. I have no idea what they're intentions were.' His expression changes in an instant, surprised disbelief I'd call it.

"Teresa...what goes on in that pretty little head of yours? Their intentions probably weren't to go back to their hotel room and play scrabble, it could very easily have ended up badly for you." Well, that got a reaction.

'What makes you think that? they may just have wanted to have a chat and a drink.'

"Oh, good God, wake up Teresa, you always see the good in everything and everybody...and I love that about you, but those men at the pub, those Albanians, they are ruthless, extremely violent criminals, they wouldn't be interested in a cozy little chat over a Babycham, discussing the library, dinner parties, swimming or any of the other lovely things going on in your lovely world." Resolute and assertive, he pauses briefly to finish his coffee.

"They live in a far different world, a hard, nasty, violent world; inhabited by hard, nasty, violent people." He exhales, taking hold of my hand, with his other hand he traces light soothing circles around my upturned palm with his fingertips.

'The strange thing was that when the Albanian men were talking to me at the pub Ernie came across and told me a policeman with a London accent had rung the pub saying there was a break-in at the library.' He calmly looks at me, half smiling, patiently listening to me as only Callum does.

"That does sound strange."

'There was no break-in, the local police knew nothing about a break in.'

"The plot thickens."

'So just who do you think it was, this mysterious London policeman?'

"Who do you think? it was me, I phoned the pub from the call box opposite the school."

'*You*, you did it, but how did you know I was at the pub and potentially in danger?'

"Because I was watching, I was with a colleague in a car parked on the crest at the end of our lane overlooking the pub, two hundred yards away. Ernie and you drove past us when he was taking you home. We'd followed those Albanians from Leighbury to Newell Cross. We've been watching them for several weeks. By the way, smoking isn't good for you."

Well, that confirms that, he saw me having my sneaky weekly ciggy, he *must* have been watching.

'But Ernie said the man had a distinct London accent.'

Callum with a smile on his face comically clears his throat and theatrically begins talking.

"This is Detective Sergeant Gilchrist of the Met, can you tell Mrs Sheen there has been a break in at the library."

Wow, he can really throw his voice. He sounds just like a cockney barrow boy.

'That was incredible, you're like Mike Yarwood, who else can you do? Do Larry Grayson, go on, say 'shut that door' the way he does.'

Callum smiles at me, I have to say his finger tips tracing very light circles around my palm is rather delightful.

'Why didn't you just come to the pub and rescue me if you were concerned for my safety, what if the pub phone was engaged or Ernie was too busy to answer it?'

"It could have ruined months of work, ruined our operation, I was worried sick watching you through my binoculars, you looked scared. But what worried me the most was that if they'd have tried to bundle you in a car then I would have had no choice, I would have had to help you, I couldn't have risked anything happening to you."

I feel flattered.

'Wouldn't they have guns though, these dangerous criminals?'

"Probably, but so do my colleagues and I. One thing I ask of you is that you promise, solemnly promise to keep everything I have told you to yourself. The work my department does, its success and the safety of its personnel is reliant on keeping things very much covert. I should nae have told you any of this, but I know I can trust you, but everything I have said is strictly off the record."

'Yes, of course, I promise.' I can't believe it, Detective Sergeant Gilchrist of the Metropolitan Police, Callum is an undercover police detective, a good one too, I had no idea, no idea at all.

My head is swimming, Callum letting go of my hand raises his arm and requests the bill. I make a move towards my clutch bag thinking we can split the bill, he shakes his head.

"No, I'll get this, my treat, I stood you up after all."

'Yes, you did, you rat bag, but did you not potentially save me from something awful?'

"Thankfully we will never know."

'Thank you, thank you for everything Callum. This has been such a lovely evening, the film, the meal...the company...everything.'

Walking across the car park towards Tom Jones I take hold of Callum's hand, I so like this man. He opens the car door for me, gentleman that he is.

"Teresa, I have to say, *those* jeans...they are...you look...they–" I cut him off before he says too much.

'You aren't the first to say that.'

The journey back home from the restaurant is magical, under a majestic blanket of stars, a beautiful balmy clear cloudless evening, one of those rare evenings we get like this in England just a few times every year. It was as if one were on the French Riviera, with the nearly full moon lying low on the horizon in front of us. I felt like I had been transported to a mystical utopian world where everything seemed to be just a little too perfect...just a little too romantic. The tensions, disappointment and drama of the past few days had melted to a distant place far away in the back of my mind.

I have enjoyed this evening very much, more than I have enjoyed myself in a long time, a very long time...dare I say ever?

Looking across to Callum as he drives, his attention fixed on the road, I can just watch him, half smiling as always, his face bathed in just a little greenish light shining from Tom Jones' array of ghoulishly lit gauges and dials.

He said I live In a lovely world earlier, a lovely world doing lovely things, well I agree, I think that tonight at least my world is rather lovely and what's more, with my Audrey's updo under my billowing headscarf I feel rather fabulous.

# Chapter 18

## *All good things...*

*Primrose Cottage, Brookhayes.*

"Good morning darling...I've made you a cup of coffee." A chinking clunk from the bedside table near my head. Raymond sits on the side of the bed his hand on my shoulder.

"So, you went to the pictures last night instead, did you?"

'Yes.'

"Did you have a nice time? I know how much you wanted to see it, was it good?"

'Yes.'

"Don't let your coffee go cold." He has made me a cup of coffee...so the motive is?

"By the way T, I've been invited by a pal to play a round with him today at Chepstow...yes Chepstow, that's a rare opportunity, you wouldn't mind, would you?"

There it is...the motive, the reason behind him pouring some nearly hot water on some horrible Mellow Birds instant coffee powder, the motive is that despite me spending two nights in the spare bedroom he wants to play golf both days of the weekend.

'That's fine Raymond, you go and play golf, have a good game.'

I get a 'mwah' on my forehead, well that's something but no 'I love you', and he's gone, but the smell hasn't...Blue Stratos...for golf? That's not going to improve his handicap, is it? perhaps it'll put off his opponent.

Sunday morning, on my own, shall I have a lie-in or breakfast in bed? Over the last few years these formally special fun things have lost their magic, not for me but for someone...someone trap, trap, trapping down the stairs to pack their golf bag in his car. Sunday mornings we'd sometimes stay in bed until noon, we'd have breakfast in bed, read the papers but just lying snug and cozy being cuddled by Raymond was my favourite part.

Nowadays it's a whining chorus of 'there are toast crumbs in the bed T', or 'you have got marmalade in your hair T', or 'don't do that T, your hands are sticky.'

Perhaps I'll just go for a stroll, it's a fine morning, maybe I'll go to the knoll. Should I ask Callum if he'd like to come? No, we spent time together yesterday, I don't want to be overpowering, be too much, come on too strong, we all know about too much of a good thing don't we? ...well really, that was quite uncalled for, surely I'm not 'too much' am I?

No, better to take a nice solitary stroll, I'm sure Callum will have plans, let him have the day to himself or maybe I may just...

~ooo~

*Ivy Cottage, Brookhayes.*

'Hi, Callum, I am going for a walk, would you like to join me?'

What...what? I know what I said but he is rather moreish.

"Sure, give me ten minutes to hang my washing out and I'll join you." His voice, I still swoon as his words caress my ears.

The first subtle inklings of autumn are showing themselves as we stroll through the fields. Oak leaves hued more jaundiced yellow than their rich deep green of spring, the hedgerows rich bounty of blackberries withering unpicked on the brambles. Groups of swallows and swifts chirruping excitedly, line up along the telegraph wires readying themselves to soon take flight to warmer climes for the winter. A country girl albeit city born doesn't need these clues to know autumn is around the corner, she can feel it, smell it, taste it in the air. Summer, the lovely high summer I have enjoyed so very much this year is on borrowed time.

'No camera today, Callum?' We are sitting by the conker trees, Callum seems intrigued with one of the fallen horse chestnuts, pushing his thumbnail into a split running along the length of its brown leathery casing, extracting and fastidiously examining the brown glossy conker from inside its pithy casing. He has a faraway look in his eye.

'Are you okay Callum, you seem quiet, preoccupied?'

"Teresa, I have to leave."

'Leave?'

“Aye, my job here, here in Gloucestershire is done, the Albanian gang have all been arrested, nailing them was my job, Lionel is relocating me.”

‘When,’ taking in what he’d just said my heart slowly starts to sink.

“I fly out next Saturday.” Sinking lower and lower.

‘*Fly out*, so soon, wherever are you going?’

“Canada.” It feels like there is now a huge cold heavy stone resting where my heart normally is. The enormity crashing down, he is going to the other side of the world in less than a week. I am welling up.

‘How long will you be there...in Canada?’ I can feel an uncomfortable lump forming in my dry throat.

“There is no way of knowing, a couple of months, maybe more, maybe a year, maybe more.” I have to look away, he mustn’t see the tears now slowly beginning to trickle down my cheeks.

Crying in front of him about my son, crying with him over the death of his wife, crying while we watch a soppy film in the afternoon, these things are okay, I don’t mind him seeing me cry about these things. Him seeing me cry because he is leaving, perhaps we’ll never see each other again. Him seeing me cry because my heart is shattering and he has no idea why, I can’t allow that. Him seeing me cry because he’s leaving and I have totally and hopelessly fallen in love with him, that I can’t allow.

“It would be nice to stay in touch Teresa, we can talk on the phone every now and again if you’d like, I want to hear all the Brookhayes gossip.” He tries to chuckle. Stop sniffling Teresa, I command myself.

'Um, yes, erm, yes I'd like that.' Trying to pull myself together. How could I possibly like that? I'd hate that, a brief phone call now and then? Irrational but nonetheless excruciatingly painful thoughts tear through my soul as I imagine future conversations, listening to him over the coming months as he excitedly tells me, 'I'm having a great time in Canada Teresa', or 'I have met someone Teresa', or worse, 'We are going to get married Teresa, would you like to come to our wedding'? All the while I'm being slowly, agonisingly torn apart. I have to change the subject.

'What about Jack's house, who'll live there now?'

"I don't know, Lionel took out a six-month let, which is just about up, I imagine the letting agent will find new tenants."

I have lost my appetite for conversation, I just want to be alone.

'Callum, I have to go, I need to get Raymond's shirts ironed and his sandwiches made for tomorrow.'

The stroll back home felt awkward. Starched, dry throated conversations and meaningless stilted niceties. I knew it, I'm sure he knew it, this wasn't us. Not the usual zany 'Callum and Teresa show', missing the silly songs and silly rhymes and daft games that provide the lovely background to our strolls through the woods and fields.

It wasn't until I got home in the privacy of my empty cottage, my bedroom, the spare bedroom I'm sleeping alone in at the moment whilst Raymond and I negotiate a deep bump in the road that I took the brake off and gave my emotions free rein and boy did I let them go.

~ooo~

Three days have passed since Callum gave me his news. From my upstairs window I have glimpsed him wash and polish Tom Jones only for Lionel and another man to arrive later and drive it away. I glanced briefly as he cut the grass in the back garden...for the last time.

When I'd caught sight of him from my window before, my heart would skip a beat, now it feels like I've been stabbed in the heart. It's painful, I ask myself, trying to be rational, why should it hurt so much, what was I expecting? I'm married, he's single, he's gorgeous, I'm the wrong side of forty, he is...probably not, I still don't know his age. Why was I deceiving myself, thinking he'd see me as more than a friend; what right do I have to think he'd stay here, living next door to me forever?

In a state of melancholy limbo, I have to accept he is going but until he is actually gone...this coming Saturday, only then can I get on with moving on. Moving on? That is going to take some doing.

The phone is ringing in the alcove.

'Comberley 419.'

"Teresa, Yvonne, I imagine you have heard about Callum leaving?"

'Yes, I know.'

"Well, I've just popped around and invited him for an impromptu dinner party on Friday evening to see him off. Just the usual four of us...oh and Callum of course. Amanda says she would like to cook the food, so don't make plans see you at seven."

# Chapter 19

## ***Accusations and Proclamations***

*Rosebank Cottage, Brookhayes.*

"Come in, come in you two." Ralph greets Raymond and me with a broad smile, looking dapper with a paisley cravat instead of his customary tie. I give him a brief peck on his cheek, he returns the compliment by giving my behind a light playful slap...my own fault, tight blue jeans.

Ralph buzzes around the drinks trolley, soliloquising in a comical Italian accent as he pours our drinks.

"A wh-his-ky for the a-gentleman and a Cin-a-zano for the 'bee-ut-ti-ful la-hay-dee'." He does make me laugh, I like Ralph, I regard him as the sort of 'Swiss Army knife' of husbands, a journeyman, he doesn't appear to do any one thing perfectly but does everything to a reasonably acceptable standard. And in common with the Swiss knife he's rugged, he has emerged with his spirit and sense of humour and fair play intact, more or less unscathed from many years of marriage to Yvonne and twenty years as the father of Princess Amanda.

A light knocking on the door, Ralph scurries towards it.

"This must be our guest of honour...or it's the TV detector van." Pulling a mock horrified face he shoots a glance to me, "You know I really should buy a licence for the old gogglebox eh?" Opening the door he animatedly invites Callum inside.

"Come in, welcome, welcome, how was the journey, traffic wasn't too bad was it?" Callum looks amused by Ralph's enthusiastic greeting.

"Come in, come in, sit yourself down, what can I get you to drink?"

Amanda appears in the lounge , she wears that stressed because she's trying to be perfect expression, a tray of little china bowls with some peanuts, cheese balls and twiglets in her hand.

"Good evening everyone, dinner will be ready in fifteen minutes, meanwhile here are some 'amuse-bouche' for you." She says placing them on the table.

As she returns to the kitchen Ralph scoffs and titters.

"I think she means nibbles." He doesn't say it quite quickly or quietly enough as a somewhat elaborately dressed Yvonne appears into the lounge from the bottom of the stairs looking glamorous. Wearing a full length emerald-green pleated evening dress, its deeply plunging neckline showcasing Yvonne's more than ample cleavage.

"Amanda possesses a far more sophisticated lexicon than you Ralph, you are such a Philistine."

The starter was, Princess Amanda tells us with glowing pride in honour of our soon to be departed neighbour Callum. 'Cock-a-leekie soup', a traditional Scottish favourite. Very nice it was too, not unexpectedly Ralph and Raymond resorting to a few childish jibes about its name, something about incontinence whilst they rapidly demolish the first bottle of Black Tower. Across the table Callum's eyes and mine meet a few times, lingering a little longer and more warmly than maybe they ought, although the glances are for me tainted bittersweet. This evening holds very conflicting emotions for me.

The main course arrives and with it the first hints of the unruliness that often enliven our get-togethers.

Amanda lifts the lid from the large casserole on the table and announces in exaggerated French the fruits of her labour, "Bouef bourguignon."

Quiet descends around the table with everyone tucking in, the second bottle of Black Tower came and went.

"Boeuf bourguignon, isn't that what you cooked for us at the last dinner party Teresa? I recall it was absolutely divine."

Fiddlesticks, I was rather hoping that little detail would pass unnoticed, but Ralph, clearly wine-emboldened raises it.

'That's right.' If I just say it quickly and quietly enough, perhaps no-one will hear.

Princess Amanda, up until now has been quite subdued, but the suggestion, the very suggestion of her culinary endeavours being just mentioned in let alone compared *to* in the same sentence as something an ordinary everyday housewife had cobbled together was beyond the pale, her claws until now retracted are out.

"Hardly the same thing Daddy, I implicitly followed the Cordon Bleu recipe, as they serve in Maxims in Paris, Teresa probably threw hers together using the Ladybird book of cooking."

She affords herself a smug grin. With the third bottle of Black Tower entering its death throes and Ralph's sense of self-preservation critically impaired he proffers further comment.

"Well, I'm sorry, I think Teresa's was tastier, it had a richer, fuller flavo–"

"Don't be absurd Ralph," he is instantly hacked down by a bemused Yvonne with a scything glare. She quickly moves to shore up Amanda's easily bruised ego.

"Take no notice of him darling, it's not as if he's Egon Ronay, just who on earth would be interested in the opinion of someone who is so fond of those frightful Findus crispy pancakes, and don't get me started on his penchant for Heinz sandwich spread, I mean...what on earth could possibly possess one to consume that revolting vomit willingly...not at gunpoint."

Perhaps I should have warned Callum how these dinner parties often turn out, he looks uneasy, he shoots me a quick glance with a raised eyebrow as we are treated to an elegantly high peaked lemon meringue pie, nicely tart, Amanda has done well. As I'm telling her how much I like it, she stands and takes her leave. Curtly addressing us all gathered around the table.

"I'm meeting some friends shortly at the Fox, good night."

Callum is very appreciative of the pains she has gone to on his behalf, warmly thanking her as she puts her coat on and leaves.

Raymond as usual has been quiet, with all the Black Tower now finished, Ralph has produced a bottle of Blue Nun.

"So, Callum, Canada?" Oh God I think, please don't start Raymond.

"That's right." Callum hasn't really ever spoken at length with Raymond before, just polite inconsequential good mornings from across the garden or drive.

"Which province, it's a big country?" I see that certain look in Raymond's eyes, half focused, half glazed over.

"I don't know yet, I'll be told that nearer the time."

"Oh, will you? will you indeed, well one thing is for sure, it'll be cold and there'll be fuck all to do."

Yvonne simultaneously raises both her eyebrows and voice.

"Raymond, please curb your language, there is no need for that." She is right, our dinner parties no matter how contentious a subject we may stray upon, how vehemently we sometimes disagree we always maintain our propriety when it comes to language, I like that. Raymond offers a not entirely sincere apology. Callum responds to Raymond's terse outburst.

"I imagine it will be cold but I'm sure I'll find something to entertain myself."

Pouring yet another glass of wine Raymond scoffs derisorily.

"No doubt you will, no doubt you'll soon find someone else's wife to sniff around while her husband is out working his fingers to the bone."

I chide my rude drunken husband with a sharp venomous 'Raymond' whilst Callum remains reticent, unmoved he just wears that half smile.

Bullish now, Callum's lack of reaction seems to further irk Raymond, he enjoys contention around the dinner table when he has become inebriated sufficiently. He's done it time and time again in the past, he just lurks quietly and unnoticed on the sidelines, drinking more than is prudent but not enough to incapacitate him, more's the pity. Then, when least expected he hurls a controversial or cutting personal remark onto the table like a grenade waiting for the fireworks to begin.

"Did I say something funny Callum, why are you smirking?" The until now relaxed ambience is fast becoming streaked with Raymond's hostile overtones, intolerably so. I want us to leave right now, before it escalates further. I feel awful, embarrassed, it's been a nice evening, now sadly being spoilt by Raymond as he pours another glass of wine.

'Come on Raymond, let's go home.' Standing up, hovering by my chair feeling uncomfortable.

"Not yet T, sit back down, what's the big rush, or are you hiding some guilty secrets eh you two? Going off on your so say walks in the woods together. There is still some wine to drink, and our friend Jock here hasn't told me why he's smirking, I'd like to know why." Raymond is beginning to slur his words.

Callum stands, he looks embarrassed as do I, uneasy in the tense atmosphere. He shakes Ralph's hand and plants the briefest of pecks on Yvonne's cheek.

"Goodnight Yvonne, Ralph, good bye, thank you for your hospitality and for being good neighbours, it's been a pleasant evening." His eyes briefly look wearily towards

Raymond, his voice and look suggesting the evening has been pleasant but now Raymond...well.

"Where are you going Jock?...come on...spill the beans, we're dying to know, did you manage to get your leg over Teresa?"

Mortified, I don't know what to say, where to look, this is horrible. Callum remaining placid but compelled to try and mollify Raymond.

"Raymond, you are embarrassing your wife and our congenial hosts, why don't you go home and sleep it off. I suggest you apologise to Teresa in the morning, she is a good woman, a faithful woman, you dinnae realise just how lucky you are to have her as your wife."

"So you did, how else would you know she's good and that I'm lucky?" With a queasy smile and a short burst of laughter,

"Who'd have thought it?...Jock and T shagging in the woods." Yvonne's dining room fell into a momentary excruciatingly awkward silence, before sounding increasingly foolish Raymond continued.

"Let's go outside; sort this out like men, I used to box in the army you know."

"Good God man, that's enough." Ralph raises his voice, this is getting out of hand.

Callum remains unshaken, cool self-confidence etched on his face in defiance of Raymond's outrageous accusations and his quite frankly, ridiculous threats. Unsteadily staggering, Raymond picks up his wine glass, swallowing the contents in one gulp. Pointing towards the back door he manages two uncoordinated steps before his balance deserts him, falling backwards with a crash between two chairs, overcome by his drunken stupor he becomes motionless and silent...passed out.

With a sigh and a shake of his head Callum bids goodnight to us once again and heads for the door.

I panic, he is going, I won't see him again, I don't want it to end like this, not like this. Yvonne tutting, righting her overturned chairs turns to me, taking hold of my lower arm, she can see my tears, compassionately she tells me to follow him.

"We'll take care of *him*." She casts a disgusted look at Raymond sprawled lifeless on the floor, "Go and say goodbye to Callum properly."

Dashing to the front door, it's still raining incessantly outside, perhaps more so than earlier.

'Callum, Callum wait.' I shout above the noise of the wind and rain lashing down. He stops at the bottom of his drive.

'I want to say goodbye properly, with dignity. I'm sorry about Raymond.'

"It's okay, it does nae matter what he thinks, we know the truth, we've done nothing improper."

We quickly become saturated. I take hold of his hands in mine, feeling lost, lost for words, lost inside my heart as I nervously raise and lower our arms in fidgety little movements, trying to find the words.

'Well, is this *it* then, is *this* goodbye?' Crying now doesn't matter, it's raining so heavily who will ever notice.

"This is goodbye, don't think for a single moment that I'll ever forget you Teresa." There is a melancholy edge to his voice I'd not heard previously.

'I feel the same, I've so enjoyed your company.' My heart is churning, this pain, the pain of parting is unbearable, restricting myself to just saying what I think to be appropriate, merely lip service, not daring to tell him how I truly feel.

'Will we ever see each other again? it all seems so very...final.'

"Who knows?  it's possible but in all honesty is it not better, less painful if  we don't ever see each other again?"

'Why not, how can you say that? I thought we meant something to each other.'

"Aye, we do and for me that's the trouble, it's not going to be enough."

'I don't understand, what's not going to be enough?'

Callum looking up with angst at the impenetrably dark, rain laden sky, pitifully cursing in exasperation as we are pounded by the downpour. Forcibly pulling me by my hand up his short drive to shelter from the rain, shivering under his porch.

"It'll nae be enough, a phone call or letter every now and then, it'll just open up the scars again, remind me of *you*, how much I *miss* you, how much I *love* you."

Shocked, struggling to find words, appropriate words.

'I had no idea you felt that way.'

"Och, don't be coy Teresa, you must've felt it, I have fallen for you, something happened to me that very first day I saw you." Laughing and shaking his head.

"With the hosepipe and the bucket washing your car, I have had to try so very hard to stop myself kissing you...I mean kissing you like a lover not a friend." Encouraged, now I know we feel the same way about one another.

'I have those same feelings for you, when I see you, when I hear you, when we are close. I want to hug you, kiss you...and more...but–'

"But you are married, and it's the way you loyally hold on to that despite everything that makes me admire and respect you all the more, I'd never want to get in the way of your marriage, jeopardise it...damage it, only to run the risk of you hating and blaming me later so this *has* to be goodbye."

Before I can respond, dragging me by my hand down the drive we run together to my cottage, dark and empty. Reaching the back door he seizes me, spinning me around to face him, firmly pushing my soaking wet back against the cold hard wall, our faces mere inches apart. His hands clutching the back of my head we kiss, not on the cheek, not fleetingly, but with emotionally charged fervour, our lips pressing together passionately. Just as I begin to feel *that* fire rising within me, knowing with every sinew this is wrong, but powerless to stop he breaks off, opening the door, he pushes me inside .

"Goodbye Teresa." The sound of his footsteps in the puddles on the rain-soaked path fade as he walks away.

# Chapter 20

## ***Rat trap***

*Primrose Cottage, Brookhayes.*

Housework...something I do that Raymond is totally oblivious to...that is unless I haven't done it, this morning's parting comment as he left for work, choking me with *that* aftershave...by the way I'm still in the spare bedroom, it's been three weeks now.

"Have you seen the cobwebs on the kitchen ceiling T?" grrr. Meaning *you* need to get busy with the pink feather duster and get them down. Housework is something I find much more fun done to music.

My Earth, Wind and Fire cassette in the tape player, volume knob on max, and I'm off, singing, dancing, dusting. Fee-fi, fo-fum, look out spider here I come.

Despite the fairly considerable...very considerable raucous din I'm making I become aware of a knock on the door. Fiddlesticks, it's Lionel, stifling his amusement. Impeccably dressed as usual, he's looking at me through my huge kitchen window. Well, that's rather embarrassing, as you'd imagine, I wasn't holding back, dancing and singing with hearty aplomb as the dangling webs and one of those spiders with pin head size bodies and ridiculously long legs are swept up in the feather duster, I'll pop him outside in a moment, he can enjoy freedom in the garden.

'Lionel, what a nice surprise.'

"Good morning Teresa, how are you?"

'Very well, thank you.' Embarrassed, simultaneously I laugh and snort a little, 'Just doing a spot of dusting.'

"Yes, I can see that, very energetically, you are doing a sterling job."

'How is Callum?'

"He is fine, settling in well, actually Callum is the reason behind my visit here this morning. You see, he'd wanted to give you a little something...a gift, but for one reason and another he couldn't get hold of it in time before he left, his relocation was quite sudden. It's next door, I'm just picking up his last few bits and pieces, if you'd care to follow me."

A gift? I wasn't expecting that, two weeks had passed since Callum had left. Not a day goes by where I don't think of him in some way or another, I just tell myself to remember the fun times we shared, the good times, there were a lot of them crammed into six short months, I tell myself to just be thankful I met him.

Outside Ivy Cottage my he rt melts, propped up against Jack's...Callum's...whoever's garage door a shiny new bicycle.

"It's very much bespoke." Lionel tells me.

"Callum went to great lengths, he is a stickler is our Callum, he was most insistent that every detail be correct, even down to having it repainted this particular colour."

'Do I like it? I absolutely love it Lionel, thank him for me will you?'

"Yes, of course, I'm sure he'll be pleased you like it."

'Would you like a cup of tea, coffee maybe?'

"No thank you Teresa, that's very kind of you but I have to head back to London now, too much tea and I'm afraid the journey would be plagued by frequent stops for a gentleman of a certain age." He titters as he reaches into his pocket removing a small manila envelope.

"He gave me this letter to give to you before he left, now if you'll excuse me, I best get cracking, cheerio Teresa."
Wheeling my new bicycle around to my cottage and putting it in the garage I can't believe it, I am incredibly touched.

Every little detail, he has thought about every little detail. I had told Callum about my old bicycle one sunny afternoon at the knoll. Seemingly dozing contentedly, he was sat propped up against a chestnut tree, eyes closed, his chin on his knees, his arms wrapped around his legs, a trace of a smile. I thought he was miles away, maybe asleep even. I prattled on about it endlessly, telling him about how my mother had bought me a bicycle for my sixteenth birthday, we had little money then and she'd saved up for it. It was a beautiful deep purple colour with white mudguards, a wicker basket on the handlebars along with a shiny silver bell which I rang at every opportunity. How I loved it. Callum must've listened very attentively and remembered everything I'd said as I told him how I'd looked after it carefully. My bicycle and I, especially my knees had been through some scrapes over the years as you'd imagine, and although it was over twenty years old it worked perfectly well.

Except two years ago it started making a funny noise and the back tyre was flat. Jack had a look at it and said it needed a new back wheel. Raymond took it to the bicycle shop near his office to get it mended; I never saw my bike again. He told me the bike shop said it was so old rather than mend it it would be wiser to throw it away and put the money towards a new one. I suppose the sentimental value it held for me was of no consequence to them, I suppose that they just wanted to sell a new bicycle. That's just what Raymond did, he threw my beloved bicycle on the tip in Stroud. He didn't ask me first, he didn't care it was a permanent reminder of my mother, something she'd saved so very hard to buy me, something that I loved, something I used often, he didn't buy me a new one.

The note in the manila envelope. The note Callum had written, short and to the point.

*Teresa.*
*I very much hope you like it.*
*Love always, Callum. x*

That's settled then, this afternoon when I go to work at the library I'm going to ride my new bicycle. It's more than a bicycle, more than two wheels, a basket, and a bell. It's a tangible reminder of that man who came to Brookhayes for six fabulous months, unintentionally stole my heart and left abruptly taking it with him.

~ooo~

Returning from work in the evening Raymond backs up on the drive...I think we need to talk. It's been a little over two weeks since Princess Amanda's dinner party showdown, I have gravitated to sleeping in the spare bedroom permanently, I feel that now, now that there are more of my clothes in the spare bedroom than *our* bedroom it is high time to grasp the nettle and have a heart to heart.

'Raymond, how was your day?'

"Same old same old, but I can't complain." Pouring himself a large glass of scotch before he has even taken his jacket off.

'I'll go and get fish and chips for supper, would you like that?'

"Yes, if you like."

'Afterwards, I think perhaps we should talk.'

"Oh, and why is that? we're just having a bit of a rough patch, every couple have them from time to time, it'll soon blow over especially now Prince Charming has been banished to the colonies, that'll help you to stop filling your head with fluffy romantic nonsense."

I am slightly...no, deeply incensed but tell myself, deep breaths Teresa, keep calm and rise above it as Raymond just smirks thinking himself amusing.

"Look T, I have to go to Nuneaton again in a fortnight's time, I'll stay over again for the weekend and play a couple of rounds after the Friday conference, when I get back we'll book a weekend at that little guest house you liked in Torquay. Things will sort themselves out, you'll see."

And for the next two weeks 'things' just carried on the way that they had been carrying on. I slept alone, we barely spoke, I pined for Callum's company, the sun came up, the sun went down. Raymond left for Nuneaton on the first Thursday in November.

~ooo~

*Primrose Cottage, Brookhayes.*

The phone is ringing in the alcove by the door. Sitting, reading the Comberley and District Gazette I jump out of my skin in the quiet...too quiet kitchen.

"Teresa, love it's Vi." Vi is Raymond's mother, seventy-two years old, her sharp mind and reasonably agile body more akin to those of a younger woman.

'Hi, Vi, this is such a nice surprise, how are you both, how is Arthur?' She hesitates, remaining silent for a moment.

"That's why I'm ringing, it's Arthur, he's...he's." I can hear her lightly sobbing.

'Oh, no, I'm so sorry Vi, I had no idea that–'

"No idea that what Teresa?" she interrupts abruptly.

'Something's happened, is he ill, don't say he's passed away?'

"Oh, no, he's not dead love, it's much worse than that, he's run away with a go-go dancer from Bromsgrove."

And there it is...too silly to be true, not one of her more believable ruses. She tries to maintain her veil of desolation, lightly sniffling but I've rumbled her. My mother-in-law is an incessant trickster and she frequently attempts to exploit my gullibility. Not on every occasion we speak, but she relishes the opportunity from time to time. She starts cackling,

"No, I was only joking, he hasn't, I don't think he has the energy for that sort of thing these days, he's fine, just lying on the couch looking at the horse racing on the telly, the useless lazy oaf."

'You are such a joker Vi, I'm glad you are both well.'

"Yes darling we are both fine, still breathing, that's the main thing isn't it? Is our Raymond about?"

With her strong West Midland dialect I love the way she enunciates the word 'Raymond'.

'No Vi, he is in Nuneaton playing golf all weekend.'

"Can you ring him at his hotel? Ask him which weekend in December he wants us to come and visit you two in the wilderness. Only I want to book a winter break see, I fancy Majorca, the travel agent says there aren't many places left so I need to book it as quickly as possible."

'Yes Vi, I think I can ring him or leave a message at the hotel.'

"Good, only I don't want to get my weekends muddled up, you know how our Raymond can get." I like Vi, we've always got along well, she was quite supportive to me when Anthony died and I admire her strength, she doesn't take too much nonsense from either Arthur, her husband or Raymond, her son.

"I'll wait to hear from you then Teresa love, bye."

Now...just where did I put that scrap of paper with the hotel number on or shall I just call directory enquiries?

~ooo~

"Good afternoon, Nuneaton Edge Golf Resort Hotel, how may I help you?" The phone at the hotel is answered by a chirpy, probably quite young man with a twang of Birmingham in his voice, I think maybe trying to tone it down to better fit the more up market requirements of the golf club and I must say making rather a good job of it.

'Good afternoon, I need to speak with Mr Raymond Sheen, it's quite urgent.'

"Okay, I'll give his room a buzz, Sheen, Sheen, Sheen, ah here we are, room 41...no wait." Listening, I can hear the receptionist rapidly tapping something lightly and repeatedly, a pen on the register maybe?

"One moment, I just need to talk with my colleague." The phone becomes muffled, the receptionist stops tapping the pen on the register and the irritating piped music playing nearby becomes indistinct although not inaudible.

"Adam, what room is Mr Sheen in?"

"The cleaning cupboard."

"Eh?"

"The cleaning cupboard, there are a few tins of Mr Sheen in there or maybe it's Pledge?" I hear muted childish tittering.

The receptionist's attempt to mute the phone while he talks with Adam, his colleague is ineffectual to say the least. Quite the comedian is Adam, how many times have I heard furniture polish gags over the years?

"No," the receptionist's colleague continues, "seriously he *was* originally in 41, but when his missus turned up this morning, he requested an upgrade, a de-luxe double, we've put them in 32."

"Hello, Madam, sorry to keep you," the receptionist's voice becomes louder, "I'm buzzing their room now, are you alright to hold."

'Yes, it's okay, I'll hold.' I'm baffled, 'missus turned up' I wonder if they have more than one Mr Sheen staying. The receptionist, his accent slipping, is back on the line.

"No, there is no answer, I think I may have seen them going out together a little earlier." Confused and more than a little alarmed, the receptionist definitely said '*them*'.

'Do you have more than one Mr Sheen staying?'

"Let me see," a pause punctuated by more pen tapping.

"No Madam, there is just the one Mr Sheen, a Mr Raymond Sheen." Miraculously, I haven't turned to jelly, thinking quickly and clearly. Calmy assuming the role of Raymond's secretary I further probe the receptionist.

'I'm Mr Sheen's secretary, can you give me his address to confirm I have the right hotel?'

"No, I'm sorry, I can't give that information out." Understandable, I pause briefly collecting my thoughts.

'What about if I give you an address can you confirm it.'

"I shouldn't...I'm not supposed to but go ahead."

'Raymond's address is Primrose Cottage, Brookhayes, Comberley, Gloucestershire.'

"I didn't tell you but yes, that's the address he's registered under, now do you want to leave a message?"

'Actually no, on second thoughts it's okay, I can ask one of his colleagues in the office, I don't want to disturb Raymond with boring work matters, let him have a nice weekend, thank you, bye." Putting down the receiver my heart is pounding, *now...now* I'm turning to jelly.

Slowly crashing down on me, Kim's suspicions and dire warnings could be coming home to roost, all the little pieces making sense. Picking up the receiver again.

"Comberley 363."

'Kim, I've just had the strangest conversation with the receptionist of the golf club where Raymond is staying this weekend.'

"Mmm, go on."

'Raymond changed his room to a double room this morning, apparently his 'missus' turned up unexpectedly for the weekend, I am very much here in my cottage...not in Nuneaton.'

I know I can rely on Kim to give me nothing other than solid support and good advice. There won't be the slightest hint of gloating because it looks horribly like she was right, no trace of a 'told you so'.

"The receptionist was talkative, he shouldn't give out information like that."

'He didn't, he just didn't mute the conversation he had with his colleague effectively...I heard them talking between themselves.' Kim on the other end of the phone remains quiet.

'Kim, what am I going to do, you must have been right, Paula, it all makes sense now, when you told me you thoug–.'

"Calm down Teresa, we don't know it's Paula, we don't know anything...yet." She knows me so well, picks up so easily my foibles, frailties, and idiosyncrasies, she knows I'm on the verge of panicking.

"Calm down and put the kettle on."

'Calm down and put the kettle on? I've just found out my husband is having a dirty weekend probably with his secretary, my life is just about to fall completely apart, and you want me to put the kettle on...I don't want a fucking cup of tea Kim.'

"No darling, put the kettle on and make a flask of coffee, *your* coffee, not Raymond's god-awful Mellow Birds shit. I'll just have a word with Mark, I'll be with you in ten minutes or so. We're going to pay Raymond a visit in person, let's find out what's going on."

Mark's tatty, dull maroon Austin Maxi pulls into my drive more or less ten minutes later. Kim bursts into the kitchen, hurriedly heading for the downstairs bathroom.

"I'll just nip to the loo, I forgot to go when I was at home."

'Do you want sugar in the coffee Kim?'

"Better not, the dentist told me off about too much sugar last week." The toilet flushes and Kim appears by my side in the kitchen, placing a supportive hand on my shoulder.

"Look, I know you probably don't want to do this, I'd feel the same, but it's important we do; you don't have to face this alone.

'You're right, better to know one way or another.'

The first half hour of the journey we remain unusually tight lipped, I watch the bridges, junctions and scenery go by as we head north on the M5. Listening to 'Kid Jensen' on the radio regularly drifting in and out of tune while I fiddle with it trying to find a stronger signal, the radio accompanied by the whining 5th gear on Mark's decrepit Maxi.

"If we catch him red-handed, what do you want to do about it?" Kim asks, her eyes fixed ahead on the road.

What indeed? I am not in any state to make any potentially life-changing decisions, but if we did...catch him red-handed, it will shake my confidence and faith in Raymond fatally.

Nearing Nuneaton, Kim with her road atlas and hastily scribbled down list of towns and road numbers has got us here with unerring precision...it's Kim, don't be surprised about that.

"You need to prepare yourself, what we are stumbling into may be very distressing."

'Sure, but it's better for us to find out, it might not be what we think.'

"Maybe, now should we find him in a compromising situation we don't want to make a big scene, we just make sure they know we have seen them then quietly leave. Maintain your dignity, don't slap her or Raymond no matter how tempting. We can plan what you want to do later, for now just think it through in your mind, prepare yourself."

Kim is trying her best to embolden me, I think mixing roles, those of being a caring friend but with one eye on soon potentially becoming my solicitor. With each passing mile, every mile we get nearer my anxiety level is rising, The turmoil in the pit of my stomach is about to boil over.

'Kim, Kim, pull over, I think I'm going to be sick.' A few moments later I find myself strenuously heaving on the side of the road. Kim soothing me, her hands rubbing lightly over my back whilst undignified I convulse with next to nothing to show for my efforts. Trying in vain to spit the stringy clear drool tenaciously hanging down from my mouth, Kim, motherly, produces a tissue from her pocket and wipes my lips.

"Close your mouth as I wipe, the tissue might have a bit of William's dried snot on it; it's all I have."

I don't really care, I just appreciate having a friend like Kim. Whilst rummaging in my bag for my ciggies she hands me a little coffee in the plastic cup from the top of the flask.

'I never thought I'd get a divorce Kim. What am I going to do?'

"It might not be necessary, maybe there's an explanation, let's not jump the gun, one step at a time, are you feeling better?"

I am, a mouthful of coffee, a ciggie and a hug from Kim, I'm ready, or at least as ready as I'll ever be.

'Yes, let's get it over with.'

Five minutes later we are parking in the hotel car park, it looks very posh...Nuneaton Edge Golf Resort Hotel.

"Did his last visit here...last month, wasn't it, did it show up on your bank statement Teresa?"

'I don't know, I never look at that sort of thing, Raymond handles all the banking things, why?'

"Oh, I was just wondering if he is fiddling expenses, if he is I can use that as a powerful lever if you want to divorce him; it'll focus his mind into not being anything less than generous in any settlement."

Confidently striding through the hotel's front door Kim is on a mission, I am in pieces! she tows me along by the hand. Sweeping briskly through the reception area unnoticed, heading for the stairs, up to the third floor. The corridors smell of new carpet, the little gold signs on the walls with arrows, rooms 30 to 39. It's around quarter past nine. Kim takes a deep breath standing outside room 32, she looks at me with steely determination and gives a nod. With a couple of sharp raps with her knuckles she shouts at the polished teak coloured door.

"Room service". With an exaggerated shrug, raising her upturned palms she whispers to me with a nervous smile. "Sorry, it's all I could think of, how corny."

Long, anxious moments pass, the hotel is eerily quiet, my heart skips several beats at the sound of the door latch being turned from inside the room.

Though considerably shorter and lighter than Raymond, underneath Kim's usually smartly dressed nine to five solicitor façade there is a rough, tough, rugged country girl. As the door begins to open... Raymond's voice.

"I didn't ask for room serv–"

He was unable to finish his sentence. Immediately upon the door opening enough for Kim to see beyond doubt it was Raymond, she forcefully charges into the door like a rhino. With the element of surprise she pushes a grunting Raymond hard against the wall, bursting into the room with me following a few steps behind.

Any questions are answered instantly, Raymond wincing in pain, his nose bleeding profusely from the harsh panning it has just received from the door, his dressing gown dishevelled enough to make it obvious it's all he's wearing.

"I should report you to the police for assault...I think my nose is broken." Raymond incandescent brandishes his finger towards a blithe Kim. Both knowing that Raymond can do nothing but wag his finger.

"Good luck with that." Kim is coolly self-assured and dismissive.

Paula, Raymond's secretary is sitting up in bed covering her modesty with the thin white bedsheet, pulling it up to her chin, her face a picture of abject shock. Kim turns her attention to Paula. With incredible speed and force she grabs the edge of the sheet at the bottom of the bed sharply pulling it free from Paula's grasp, it falls to the floor crumpled in a ball leaving a terrified stark-naked Paula frantically sliding from the bed, fleeing towards the bathroom shrieking, her chubby behind wobbling. With a harsh slam she closes and bolts the door. Kim looking disgusted moves close to my side; speechless I can only glare at Raymond with venom. Nauseous I just want to leave, but Kim is intent on entreating my perfidious husband with a few preliminaries...she means business.

"Raymond I respectfully ask you not to go back to Primrose Cottage for the foreseeable future, make alternative living arrangements until such time Teresa has considered her options."

Raymond looking incredulous at what he'd just heard.

"Where am I supposed to live, do you seriously think I'm going to just walk away, walk away from my house, I bought the bloody thing, I paid the mortgage, just who do you think you are?"

"Paula's house," Kim scoffs dismissively, "The house with the red door. Listen Raymond, I have a pretty good idea what you and Paula are up to, her divorce is still a fair way from being finalised, wouldn't it be a pity, a very costly pity should Paula's husband find out about Paula's mother's house and the considerable assets she has? So let's just all be reasonable." Kim fixes him with that lingering, stern look she has.

"But what about my clothes and personal things I'll need in the short term?" Raymond blubbing holding his blooded nose as Kim's patience wears thin.

"Oh for God's sake, stop crying, it's always all about you isn't it, what about Teresa, how do you think she feels? Your personal effects will be in bags in the garage of Primrose Cottage by tomorrow afternoon, you may collect them at a mutually convenient time but please do not attempt to go in the house."

Lawyer Kim striking the first decisive blow.

She takes my hand, leading me through the door and along the landing to descend the stairs. I'm speechless, stunned into silence. It's one thing imagining it, thinking about it but when confronted with it, before your eyes your husband in bed with another woman, facing the brutal reality...it violently slaps you across the face sucking the breath out of you.

'If I wind the window down can I smoke in Mark's car, he won't mind?'

"No darling he won't mind, just don't go dropping it on the floor, all that tinder dry hay on the floor, the car will go up in flames like a barn."

Kim is busy, negotiating the unfamiliar dark roads leading back towards the motorway. I let her concentrate, I have nothing much to say anyway, I just feel hurt, betrayed, and humiliated. Hurt, Raymond didn't appear to show the slightest shred of remorse, bereft of any contrition for his infidelity. I feel that is possibly the worst part; it's as if he has totally given up on us...places no value on our long marriage.

At last we descend the slip road of the M5 junction heading southbound. I begin to wail, as soon as she has persuaded Mark's car's stubborn gearbox into 5th gear, she holds my hand.

"We'll stop at the services at Strensham, we'll get a coffee if that's what you can call it. I'm sorry darling but we are going to have to make a few decisions, nothing long term or definite but we need to put some short-term measures in place until such time as you know what you want to do."

'Such as?'

"Such as, well tomorrow we'll get your locks changed, put Raymond's clothes and his other nik-naks he needs for the short term in your garage."

'Locks changed! that's drastic and who is going to do that on a Sunday.'

"I have a locksmith I use for such cases, you'll be surprised how often I need to call on his services for my clients. It's imperative that Raymond be denied access to the house, he'll have to arrange access through his solicitor." Kim, calm and matter of fact is in full flight now, to her this rotten mess is an almost daily event, to me it seems like the end of the world.

"On Monday, meet me at my office at ten to nine, we'll go to the bank immediately and clear out the bulk of your joint account, do you have your own personal account?"

'I do, but it's only a deposit account.'

"That'll do, as long as he can't get at it, we can put the money in there for the time being."

~ooo~

*Strensham Services, M5, Worcestershire.*

Slowing down, we pull off the carriageway onto the slip road then into the motorway services. Cradling a thin weak coffee in a crinkly cellophane cup, I watch Kim hungrily tucking into a plate of chips and beans.

Between mouthfuls she looks at me with Kim's focused 'under the microscope' stare.

"Do you have any idea what you want to do?"

'I don't, I'll need time to think, right now, I don't ever want to see Raymond again, how *could* he?'

Agitated, I fiddle with the red plastic tomato on the table as Kim demolishes her chips. I can't get the scene out of my mind...back there at the hotel, I subconsciously squeeze the round plastic tomato a little...much too hard, a line of ketchup bursts flatulently, from the container's green plastic stalk top landing in a deep-red broken trail across the table.

Putting her knife and fork together on the now cleared plate, Kim wipes her mouth, relaxing she leans back in her seat.

"Tell me, what did you feel when you spent time with Callum, just the two of you?" Unexpected, not sure it's relevant to what has happened today, but I'll answer.

'It wasn't like that Kim, Callum and I, well what we had was delicate...subtle...nothing sordid. Sure I had feelings for him, strong feelings, one doesn't stop being human just because one is married, but honestly we didn't cross any boundaries.' She lightly shakes her head.

"I didn't ask *that*, although I like your answer. What I want to know is how *you* felt, you, inside you, what emotions did *you* feel?" Her gaze is intense.

'Happy, very happy, contented, respected, alive...yes very much alive but mostly scared.'

"Interesting...scared, I wasn't expecting you to say that, why is that?"

'Because at times I felt *it*...whatever *it* was to be running out of control, it was only a matter of time before I felt I wouldn't be able to contain my feelings, do or say something I'd regret; ruin everything, that's why I say scared. He helped me to rediscover how enjoyable life can be, with someone like him, how I'd love a life...with him, but knowing it was just a fantasy, a temporary fantasy.'

Kim nods, her lips pushed together, absorbing my words while I pause, collecting my thoughts to continue.

'I loved him Kim, I loved him so much, but I knew it could never be, turns out he felt the same, he told me so that evening we said goodbye.'

"Scared is okay, it's better than feeling nothing at all." Kim picks up her flimsy beige plastic cup with a disapproving scowl gulping the coffee. Scrunching the cup into a ball she tosses it on the plate where it miraculously springs back with a crackle very nearly into its former shape.

"And Raymond, what about when you are alone with him, what do you feel?" Now I can see what she is driving at. Considering a reply I feel more than a twinge of guilt, Raymond and I have had so many good times over the years. I have loved him all those years with all my heart, for me it was always only ever Raymond but now...

'Nothing, numb, at a push on a positive note I'd say secure, but the past few years I'd say controlled, ignored, taken for granted, unloved, is it awful to say that?' I feel terrible thinking it, it feels even worse saying it, speaking about my husband like this.

"No, not if it's the truth, I could see it in your eyes, they lit up when you told me about things you'd done with Callum. Those big blue eyes are windows to your soul, limpid, without curtains or blinds, there's no hiding place." She beams fondly at me.

"When Callum lived next door you were radiant, floating; it took me back to the Teresa from the old days. Your dizzy energy, your zest for life—crash, bang, boom, Teresa's in the room." She's right of course, I felt like a teenager again.

'You know Kim, he's gone, I accept that, but there are very powerful emotions that haunt me since he left. There are songs I no longer dare listen to, no longer sing. Places I fear to go; the streets and fields we walked are in my mind still littered with his footprints. The trees almost seem to echo to his laughter as if he were still here. I'm sure it will pass and lessen in time, this pain and sadness I feel, but for now the memories won't leave me alone.'

A brown and beige gingham clad waitress approaches our table, lifting Kim's plate, she wipes over the surface with a damp looking cloth, tutting with thinly veiled contempt as her cloth now comprehensively stained with ketchup struggles to clean the formerly cream melamine table top to anything more than a streaky rosy pink. She huffs in annoyance, Kim and I feeling like delinquent schoolgirls lock eyes and stifle our giggles until she saunters away with the plate and scrunched up beakers muttering something incoherently. Kim continues,

"You asked me what I'd do if I were in your shoes, well I would get the divorce ball rolling. Then either follow my heart and set off in pursuit of a certain Scottish policeman in Canada or use my head, give myself time to think things through, perhaps a month, somewhere, far, far away. You've long wanted to go, but you've told me Raymond has always whinged and blocked the idea. Why don't you go and spend a month with your mum in Australia?"

Food for thought, but Callum? I don't want him to become embroiled in the worsening tangled wreckage that passes for my life. He's such a kind, special man. It hurts me, selfishly and not without assuming a great deal I'd love to have him all to myself, forever. But such is the depth of feeling I have for him, my love for him, wanting only what's best for him, I know I'm not what he needs. I'd like him to find someone as special as he is, settle down and live the life he deserves.  Australia though? Now that's an idea!

Heading back to the car to go home it's after midnight. Taking the last ciggie from the pack, standing by Mark's car Kim puts her comforting, supportive arm around my shoulder, what would I do without her?

'Kim, it's asking a lot, can you stay with me tonight?'

"Of course darling, let's have a sleepover, a mug of hot chocolate and a midnight feast." Kim is so sweet. Tearful I give her a hug. 'Should I get a divorce Kim?'

"You decide in your own good time what you want to do. I have everything I need to nail Raymond well and truly to the floor." With a gently comforting shake of my shoulder then producing her little tattered paper hankie she wipes the tear from my cheek.

"Teresa, I can unlock your cage...but only you can fly out of it."

# Chapter 21

## *Fly...fly away*

*The Fox and Goose, Newell Cross.*

Well, it's been a lonely, reflective, busy few weeks since Nuneaton, that evening. Divorce...such an ugly word, Kim has started the ball rolling on the whole sordid affair, she's in the bar getting the cider while I have a ciggie. It took me no more than a few days, sad really, just a few short days to decide that I wanted our sixteen-year long marriage to end. I had a wobble last week, thought I was making a huge mistake. Reminiscing on all the good times Raymond and I had shared throughout the years while I was putting some of Jack's dahlias on Anthony's grave. I talked to him about it, my son, telling him my news, I always do. I wonder what a ten-year-old Anthony would think, would tell me to do?

Ironically, it was Raymond himself that firmly made up my mind, he thinks us divorcing to be for the best. We met at the Walnut Inn pub near Macsley last week, neutral territory! Much as he loves me, so he claims, he says our differences have become insurmountable. Talking without any emotion, like a programmed automaton he reeled off a list as long as your arm about why he feels we are no longer compatible. Gems such as I just haven't grown up, I have too much energy, he doesn't find me attractive, I dress too young, I flirt, I'm just too darn noisy and so it goes on. He is happy that we divorce so he can be with Paula, that's where he is living now, Paula's house, the beautiful big house with the red painted door...anyway he tells me he will be fair in the divorce settlement...well that's most magnanimous of him.

I'm leaving all that to Kim to sort out. The important thing, to me the most important thing is I'll get to keep my gorgeous cottage although I may have to get a full-time job when I get back from...Australia!

Yes, I did it, I took my solicitor's...my best friend's advice. take yourself somewhere far, far away and clear your head she told me, so I am.

My mum is delighted, I'm flying in ten days' time, Heathrow to Sydney, then an internal flight to Brisbane. My visa is being hurriedly sorted out. While I'm away, Kim and Yvonne said they will look after my cottage with its shiny new locks. It's strange now...my cottage, nearly all material traces of Raymond have disappeared, he cleared his things out so quickly. I found a few little odds and ends here and there, I found the gold Parker fountain pen I bought him for his fortieth birthday in the sideboard...that brought a little tear of sadness to my eyes. I found he'd left a jar of his Mellow Birds coffee in the pantry...that brought a smile to my face as I hurled it in the bin with venom.

Yvonne has been so supportive of me, she's been like a mother, so things are on the up for me...do you know I actually feel empowered, I feel stronger, more independent.

Here she comes with the cider...my rock, Kim.

"How about we go on a bit of a girly shopping spree to Bristol on Saturday, you'll need some light cool clothes for Australia, it will be hot." She is right, I will need a few things and our shopping sprees for a few hours in the big sophisticated city are always such fun.

'Yes, I'd like that.'

"And the following Saturday it's the Newford Towers disco, let's go for old times' sake, a few drinks and a boogie to send you on your way, I'm so going to miss you."

'It's only a month Kim, before you know it I'll be back, but yes, the disco, I'd love to, when was the last time?'

"Got to be ten years ago."

'Got to be.'

~ooo~

*Newford Towers Motel, Newford, Gloucestershire.*

"It hasn't changed at all," Kim, grinning she takes in the familiar surroundings of the once thriving motel on the main road heading south through Gloucestershire towards Bristol. Since the M5 motorway opened trade has gradually dwindled as the formerly very busy A road it stands alongside has become quieter. It was a regular haunt for us, in our twenties and early thirties, dancing for hours at the monthly dances which gradually evolved into discos.

'Only us, it's only us that has changed Kim, I feel like an antique!' Shouting above the music as the pulsing multicolour lights seemingly at random mysteriously roam around the room. Kim taps my arm, shouting in my ear.

"Remember back in the day, we needed a couple of Southern Comforts before we'd let our feet off the lead." Turning, she heads purposefully towards the bar, so it's the nostalgic, slightly mischievous Kim that's come out to play tonight. While Kim is at the bar, I notice an alternately green, blue, red, and yellow Princess Amanda has put in an appearance, accompanied with a couple of her friends, they are propping up the bar. Repeatedly changing colour as the flashing disco lights play across them. Kim scuttles back towards me from the bar, holding two glasses, wearing a rascally grin on her face.

Wow, that unique taste, that takes me back, pure nostalgia in a glass, Southern Comfort.
The times we got hammered on it, only for later in the evening it to hammer us back with interest, we would vow never again...that was of course only until the next time we found ourselves here again...The Towers. It takes three glasses of it and Blondie's 'Heart of Glass' before we're up and on the dance floor.

It feels so good, so exciting, today Comberley, tomorrow Australia, the Southern Comfort doing its heady work. It's been so long since I've danced, once I'm up and dancing I don't want to stop, just a quick refuelling stop between songs to top up on Southern Comfort and I'm back dancing again. Kim has spotted an old acquaintance, sitting herself down with them for a chat.

A young man...a boy really, moves in quite close to me as I happily dance in my own world. We sort of bond in that weird, hedonistic on the dance floor kind of way, temporarily detached from reality, circling, exchanging a little smile, he's in front of me, he's behind me. He looks a little familiar, something looks a little familiar about him; after mainlining on Southern Comfort all evening and the pulsing multi-coloured disco lights everything and everybody looks different...all cats look grey in the night!

As the evening begins to draw to a close Kim approaches me while I'm dancing, taking my arm.

"I'd better be off, I've rung for a taxi, are you coming with me? She shouts in my ear as the DJ excitedly announces he's going to liven it up...let's have everybody on the floor he orders as he fades in 'Y.M.C.A.'

'No, darling I'll stay for a while longer, I just want to dance, I'll cadge a lift home with Princess Amanda later.'

"Right, don't *you* be too late getting to bed, I'll pick you up tomorrow at around noon okay. Now, are you all packed, passport, visa, tickets etcetera?"

'Yes, Mum, I'm all packed, see you at noon.' I kiss her as she leaves. I love that woman, she is literally a life saver.

Disappointingly, after a few lively disco numbers, the DJ with his cheesy practised patter announces he's going to slow things down, things are going to get a little smoochy...smoocharoony even according to him. Smoochy on your own? I'll perhaps just get another drink.

Crossing that threshold where the dance floor gives way to tables and chairs, those few yards where people heading for the dance floor transition from walking to dancing, the young man...boy from earlier approaches me, looking nervous, shyly asking me if I'd like to dance with him. The DJ has started his smoochy segue...The

Commodores, 'Three Times a Lady'. The young man looks quite cute, he asked me politely, where's the harm?

Okay, so he isn't John Travolta, but he's respectful, placing his hands with care on my waist and my shoulder before moving his body close to mine. Stepping awkwardly on my feet a couple of times, sheepishly apologising , he feels very tense. I whisper in his ear, just relax, let the music flow over you. By the time the song has finished he's smiling, holding me with more confidence, feeling far less rigid. The DJ keeping it smoochy with the Bee Gees, 'How Deep is Your Love?' one of my favourites, so we stay loosely clinched together for another smooch, my arms just resting on his shoulders close to his neck, slowly circling around the floor with young man...boy.

"Can I buy you a drink?" He asks me at song's end as the DJ announces last orders at the bar.

'Thank you, just a quick one, I better go home shortly.' At the bar I look for Princess Amanda and her ladies in waiting, nowhere to be seen, blast, she must have gone when I was dancing. I'll just have to get a taxi myself, there are, well there always used to be plenty outside. Young man...boy, hands me a Cinzano and lemonade.

"Thank you for dancing with me." He looks happy, he has a nice smile.

'My pleasure, you dance nicely, once you relax.'

"Will you be coming to the next disco here?"

'No, I'm going to Australia tomorrow for a month, the following month maybe I'll come again.' Well I can please myself now can't I? One of the upsides; a soon to be divorcee.

I really should go home, saying goodbye to young man...boy, I head to the motel's car park in pursuit of a taxi, it's gone eleven-thirty now. I have thoroughly enjoyed my evening but tomorrow...well tomorrow I fly to the other side of the world.

~ooo~

*Primrose Cottage, Brookhayes.*

My head...oh my poor head, I'm paying the price for last night...the legacy of the Southern Comfort, I wonder what the time is? It must be early, but I don't have to worry, everything is packed...my head though, it'll take a couple of Alka Seltzers and a strong coffee; I'll soon be right as rain. Can I face opening my eyes? Not just yet, give it ten minutes, I'll just lie here and run through in my mind the checklist Kim wrote for me. Turn off the water, unplug the telly, unplug the milk, cancel the TV aerial, something like that.

Ouch! something sharp in the bed is digging into the back of my thigh. Reaching under my leg there is a square piece of what feels like...tinfoil? It probably got there when I was packing my suitcase. I must have been a bit worse for wear last night, I didn't even put my nightie on. With one eye slightly open I take a look, a roughly torn silver packet, some blue writing, no idea what it says. My eyes! definitely in need of some reading glasses these days.

A gentle yawn...now just hang on, that wasn't me! sensing movement by my side, an unidentified arm...definitely not one of mine brushes over my chest, its hand lightly grips my waist, gently hugging me. Still not entirely compos mentis, miraculously I resist the urge to scream. Lifting the continental quilt a little, I peep underneath, endeavouring to discover just who is sleeping in my bed, as am I, perfectly naked. I'm more than a little shocked to discover it's 'Young man...boy'.

Oh my goodness, it's slowly beginning to come back to me, last night.

'Ahem.' With a gentle shake I try to rouse him, it works after several increasingly firm shakes.

"Good morning," he says with a soft yawn. "Last night was fantastic."

'The dancing?' He must mean the dancing.

"Yeah, I suppose, the dancing *was* nice too, but I was meaning the sex really."

He slides his hand from my waist, rolling on to his stomach with his chin propped on his palm, gazing at me contentedly.

Last night's events, slowly it *is* all coming back to me now. As soon as I'd gone outside in search of a taxi, the cool fresh air and Southern Comfort overdose combined. I became woozy. Young man...boy, concerned for me, wanting me to get home safely, found a taxi and accompanied me. By the time we got to my cottage, I'd more or less recovered from the 'wooze'. I invited him inside for a coffee.

As it was very late, I thought he could sleep in my spare bedroom, I could run him home in the morning.

As we waited for the kettle to boil, we started dancing together in the kitchen. We forgot about the coffee as one thing led to another. It began on the landing at the top of the stairs, things got steamy in the shower and it finished in the bedroom.

'You look familiar, have we met before?' I'm sure even with my fuzzy head we've met before somewhere.

"The library, a few years ago when I was in sixth form, you'd help me to find books for my A level biology classes. I had a massive crush on you, still do as it goes." He playfully titters, he has a nice friendly smile, warm.

"I'd go to the library far more often than I really needed to, not always to get books, mostly I just wanted to see if you...well you had some tight blue jeans, they left—"

'When you say a few years ago?' Interrupting him, I'm struggling; the combination of my lightly pounding head coupled with my ineptitude with all things numerical.

"I left school four years ago."

Relief, even *I* can add four and eighteen without a calculator, he must be at least twenty-two years old, close to half my age, not ideal, but not the crime of the century.

I can picture Yvonne's horrified face should she discover what she'd regard as my wanton, age inappropriate alcohol-fuelled crime of passion. In fact, rather devilishly I feel a little flattered...a much needed ego boost...it has been quite a while since I...er...you know, yes, moving on. Happily, everything is still in good working order, but as far as young man…boy is concerned it certainly ought not to happen again…the age gap.

'Do you have a name?' That sounds awful doesn't it?

"It's Vincent, and you're Teresa." Oh so he knows mine.

"You used to wear a little name badge at the library, 'Mrs Teresa Sheen, Librarian', although I was always more interested in trying to peep down your blouse than what was written on the badge."

'*You*…are a very naughty boy Vincent.' Looking at my watch on the bedside table…it's nearly half past ten!

'I have to get up, I have to go to the airport soon.'

He reaches across me, stretching to the bedside table, picking up his condom packet, rattling it with a shake.

"There's one left, poor little thing all alone in there."

I smile at his hopeful opportunism, but now, stone cold sober I know we *really* shouldn't be doing this. Although I have to say last night, even through my fairly blurred recollection he surprised me, he was a considerate and accomplished lover for someone so young. Clearly he'd paid *very* close attention to those biology text books I'd found for him at the library. Last night he certainly knew his way around!

'Why don't you save it for someone your own age? I'm old enough to be your mother.' Well, it's true I am. Laughing heartily he drops his condom box back onto the bedside table.

"For your information I have slept with a number of girls of my age and based on my experience of sleeping with you last night, I have to say the old proverb is right."

'Oh, and what old proverb might that be?'

"The one about good tunes and old fiddles." Kissing my forehead playfully accompanied by a saucy wink he leaps energetically out of bed. Self-confident, he isn't abashed in the slightest about his nudity, relaxed he casually wanders around the room collecting his strewn-about clothing. I giggle to myself about his quip; the cheek of it, calling me an 'old fiddle' indeed. Right, time to get out of bed.

'I'll make you a coffee and afterwards I'm sorry Vincent, you'll need to go, I need to get ready.' Thoughtfully he passes my dressing gown to me.

"Certainly, no problem, I really enjoyed last night, If when you get back from your travels you want to meet up, I'd like that."

I don't think that would be wise, I quite like him, his easy manner, witty and caring. Responsible, he didn't need to be asked to use condoms, quite good looking too but the age gap is just too yawning...talking of which I need to get cracking.

# Chapter 22

## ***A land down under***

*Terminal 3. Heathrow Airport.*

"Just sign these papers for me darling, when you get back your divorce will be just a couple of months from being finalised. At last you'll be free." Kim, lawyer mode engaged, noisily clicks the top of her silver pen.

'Am I doing the right thing Kim?' Although sure I am, her constant reassurance is welcome.

"Absolutely, yes you are, I can see the difference in you already, a stronger, more independent Teresa. Now you have your tickets, passport? phone me when you get there."

'Yes. Mum.' Kim is so caring and thoughtful, she must have asked that a hundred times, but I don't mind.

"I'll check on your cottage every day, so you don't need to worry."

'Thank you, darling, thanks for the lift, now if you'll excuse me, I have a flight to catch.'

I'm so excited, the airport is a confusing busy place, but I take my time and systematically negotiate all the bewildering hurdles for the very first time ever. It always fell to Raymond to circumnavigate passport control, check-in, and boarding gates. My only job was just to people-watch and sniff the perfume in the duty-free shop, but well...he isn't here now is he?

Anyway I manage everything with for me surprising ease; in less than two hours I'm amazed walking along a funny tunnel and without really noticing I find myself inside the cabin of a massive Qantas jumbo jet. Sat reasonably comfy next to a sixties-something I'd guess couple about to see their son in Melbourne for the first time in twenty years, the Ramsbottom's from St Albans. Mrs Ramsbottom giving me chapter and verse accompanied by countless photos and amusing, amusing to her anyway anecdotes of every member of her...excruciatingly large family, including an exhaustive, frankly unwelcome insight into the copious and various illnesses and conditions they suffer from. You could say it's a lengthy flight, I try feigning sleep at repeated intervals to get some respite but by half way I feel I have accumulated enough in-depth knowledge about the Ramsbottom's huge extended family spread across all the furthest flung corners of the globe to appear on BBC tv's Mastermind. Supremely confident to face Mr Magnuson and his notoriously difficult questions.

"Your name"...'Teresa Shee...Taylor'.

"Your occupation"...'Librarian'.

"And your chosen specialised subject"...'The concise life, times, and ailments of the Ramsbottom's of St Albans.'

Arriving in Sydney via Hong Kong around twenty hours later, transferring to an Ansett airlines internal flight north to Brisbane. I'm excitedly met in a tearful happy reunion with my mum and for the first time I meet my six-year-old niece, Cindy. The heat is stifling in the taxi, and I'm subject to sensory overload looking out of the window taking in the strange surroundings whilst excitedly chatting non-stop with Mum and Cindy.

~ooo~

*Toowong, Brisbane, Queensland, Australia.*

I laugh with my mum as we arrive in her suburb...Toowong. 'Too wongs don't make a white eh mum?'

It's a fairly nice neighbourhood in the suburbs, far different from my sleepy Brookhayes. Her house, the house she lives in with my brother Robert and his daughter Cindy is single storey, its overlapping wooden planks painted a rather calming shade of bottle green. Blending in amongst the lush verdant surroundings, the houses lining the street are generously spaced apart from one another.

My brother Robert is an engineer in the mining plant industry. His work, located far away from Brisbane means he's away for weeks at a time, coming home once or twice a month for a week or so before returning to the mining areas. His ex-wife just upped and left five years ago leaving a one-year-old Cindy to be raised by Robert and my mother. Cindy is a pretty little creature, long blond hair in a ponytail and a mischievous carefree look in her eye.

Full of beans, I hope to be able to have fun with her and give my mum a bit of a rest.

My mum looks well, sounds the same, as if she still lives in Deptford. Now in her mid-seventies, clearly life here suits her, I hope the years will be just as kind to me in the future.

"Are you tired love? what with the long flight an all."

As the kettle boils she puts some tea in the pot, the Typhoo she specifically requested I bring her.

'No, maybe later it'll catch up with me.'

The house has a lovely semi-covered wooden 'deck' area attached to the back, the open section covered with trailing creeper plants growing over a timber lattice frame providing shade from the scorching sun. A chilly early December at home, here it's approaching the middle of the Queensland summer, it's like a furnace. The house is raised on wooden stilts, a few wooden steps lead down from the deck into the garden, full of very exotic looking plants that unsurprisingly I don't recognise, they are sort of palmy.

"So, how have things been? I was shocked to hear about you and Raymond."

'It was hard Mum, emotionally very hard, but I'm getting there. Our relationship sadly had deteriorated over the past few years, I was naïve, I didn't see it happening until it was too late, I suppose I didn't want to see it happening.'

"Are you financially okay, *he* ain't left you short has he?"

I can detect more than a hint of venom as she says *he*.

'No, Mum, I have a very good solicitor, she's made sure I'm okay, I'm keeping my cottage and I have money in the bank.'

"A woman solicitor?"

'Kim.'

"Ah, say no more, she's a good 'un' that one."

Mum knew Kim very well, almost like a surrogate mum to her, a teenage Kim spent half of her life at our house.

"Have you ever considered emigrating out here with all us convicts?" she laughs picking up her tea.

'No, I haven't, I love Gloucestershire, it's my home Mum, I belong there.'

A girl of a similar age to Cindy runs through the house. A shock of frizzy bright ginger hair, pink dungarees and little bumper boots dashing across the deck screeching, 'G'day, Mrs Taylor' as she passes us in an excited blur to join Cindy playing in the sandpit on the dry scrubby grass in the garden.

"It's Lydia from across the street, she's good friends with Cindy, thick as thieves them two, always in and out of each other's houses."

"And *you* must be Teresa, welcome to Straya." A booming, very thick accent, leaving the 'Au' from the word Australia. A huge man appears by the door, wearing a vest and knee length khaki shorts, his calves are absolutely enormous. Mum calls to him.

"Whatcha Jim, come out here love, sit down and take the weight off. Teresa, this is Jim, he lives opposite, he's Lydia's dad."

I shake hands with him, his hand is like a bear's, my dainty little hand is engulfed as he shakes it firmly but without squashing it beyond repair.

"Robert never said his sister was so pretty, Rose."

Mum giggles, "He kept it quiet, he don't want the likes of you sniffing around his little sister, do you want a cuppa love? or there are stubbies in the fridge if you'd prefer."

'A stubby, and a stubby is?' I have things to learn here clearly.

"A beer, a beer in a stubby bottle, we keep it simple here Teresa, we Australians tend to just call things what they are." Jim chuckles as he rises from the chair and heads for the kitchen.

Relaxing in the shade is pleasant, still hot but bearable wearing a pair of shorts and a light top. The three of us spend a pleasant couple of hours talking, laughing, and drinking chilled Castlemaine 'Stubbies' while I suffer a huge defeat at the hands of my mum and Jim playing 'Aussie rules scrabble', I'm sure they just make up words willy nilly.

"Maybe you'd like to come out to dinner one evening with me Teresa, once you've settled in." Well Jim wastes no time does he? I feel a little awkward, he seems like a nice man, with a friendly, genial if not somewhat loud and boisterous disposition. Mum certainly is at ease with him, but the last thing I want at the moment is any kind of relationship or even the merest hint of one. I push my head back looking up at the leafy creepers growing across the roof trusses.

‘Ahhh, Jesus Christ.’ Instantly, sooner in fact, I’m on my feet and hightailing it screaming inside. Jim laughs heartily as I peer at him terrified from the doorway.

“Strewth! that’s quite a reaction, it’s just dinner, I didn’t ask you to marry me.”

‘There’s a spider, in the roof, there, there above my chair.’ I point animatedly up towards the massive creature.

Mum and Jim look up with calm nonchalance, bordering on disinterest they remain seated.

“It’s just a Golden Orb spider, he ain’t going to hurt you love.” My mum just titters while she rummages in the biscuit tin all the time the behemoth monster wanders about in the foliage above her head.

The thing is huge, it looks bigger than my hand, I’m amazed they remain so calm.

‘Wouldn’t hurt you?...It would if it fell on you, the size of the bloody thing, it’d cause permanent brain damage if it fell on your head.’ Feeling in equal measure nausea and admiration I watch Jim stand up, pluck the huge spider with its long legs wiggling out of the creeping plants and carry it off, smiling at me as he places it gently in a shrub to the side of the garden.

Sitting back down, my palpitations decreasing I inspect the roof carefully.

“Rose, have you told her about redbacks? better she know about them.” Jim removes the cap from another brown glass bottle of beer, hooking it on the table edge and smacking the bottle with a sharp tap of his hand, gulping from the bottle.

"No, I haven't yet." My mum pours me another glass of beer, well you don't seriously expect me to drink beer directly from the bottle do you? You can take the girl out of England but...

"Maybe you could show her one Jim, I think there is one of the little buggers in the ball-hitch of Robert's trailer." Jim beckons me to follow him across the deck.

"Come with me young lady, I'll show you a redback, so you know what they look like, they are tiny, but they can give you a painful bite. Make sure you always take a look under the seat of the dunny, you don't want to get bitten on your backside." My mum thinks this highly amusing as I follow Jim down the few wooden steps to the garden, around the side of the house to a carport with a dust covered, gold hatchback car and a small two wheeled trailer.

Poking around the tow hitch with a twig Jim forces a small black spider to drop to the floor, its tiny round glossy body streaked with a vivid red flash.

"This little fella is a redback, they don't *generally* come inside the house but it's possible, their bite is very painful but not usually too serious; just don't touch them." With his huge leather booted foot he stamps hard on it while twisting his ankle with grim determination...just to make sure!

"I'd like to go to dinner one evening with you, no funny business, no ulterior motive, just for some grown up conversation. I'm a widower see, a single dad, outside of work I only get to talk with Lydia, and well, she's six.

Colouring books, Lego and Barbie dolls are okay in small doses, if you know what I mean."

'Okay, that will be alright, I'm happy with that as long as we are clear, I'm in the middle of a divorce at the moment and I'm not ready for any kind of relationship.'

"No worries, just let me know when, maybe next week or something, no pressure, I'll look forward to it."

Mum joins us in the car port and wipes a finger over the layer of fine dust pitched on the car.

"Can you charge up the battery and pump up the tyres on Robert's old banger Jim? He's gone and put Teresa on the insurance, I thought we'd take a trip out to Bribie next weekend, maybe Lydia would like to come along."

"Sure, I'll do that, it'll do it good to have a run, I'll ask Lydia, I bet she'd love a day at the beach." Jim has found another spider not to his approval under a window sill, flicking the poor creature out onto the floor with his trusty twig he summarily squishes it into a small round damp spot on the concrete floor.

Wait a moment, did you hear that? my brother 'put' me on the car insurance, is that wise, me driving? I know my mum doesn't know how to, but me, here?

Jim can obviously see my concern, my furrowed brow.

"No worries, I've driven in Britain, I know what it's like there. It's much easier here. We drive on the same side as you poms, but we have thousands more miles of much wider, straighter roads and there are less drongos haring around the place, relax you'll be right."

Ah well, that's okay then, Jim thinks I'll be 'right'.

Over the next few weeks I ease myself into the laidback semi-outdoors lifestyle of the mostly quiet suburbs of Brisbane. Panicking one night, running to my mum's room at an ungodly hour, terrified.

'Mum, Mum, there are rats in the ceiling above my bed, I can hear them scratching about.'

"There's no rats here Teresa, it's only a possum."

Then one morning just before breakfast, all hell seemed to be breaking loose in the garden, I couldn't see anything, but the noise...

'Mum, Mum, there's a troop of raucous monkeys in the back garden somewhere, going crazy.'

"Those aren't monkeys Teresa, it's just a flock of kookaburras."

Mum and I had great fun one evening, we spent a few very enjoyable hours at the 'RSL' club, the 'Returned Services League', it's a bit like the Royal British Legion back home. In true 'Aussie' style a bit more laid back and laconic. We played the 'Pokies'...one armed bandits to you and me, and a few games of bingo...I won five dollars...I know, I couldn't believe it, maybe, just maybe my luck is turning around.

# Chapter 23

## *Just another day in paradise*

*Bribie Island, Queensland, Australia.*

Jim thankfully was correct, with his seemingly flippant prediction that 'I'd be right', driving here was indeed rather straightforward. With Mum giving directions and the two girls, Cindy and Lydia, happy in the rear seat, singing and looking at their books interspersed with trying to imitate Aunty Teresa's English accent. I am flattered and amused; I think they may be pitching me a little too posh, their attempts sounding more 'Her majesty the Queen' than 'Mrs Scatterbrain Sheen...I mean Taylor.' An hour's drive in my brother's battered Datsun car from Toowong and we arrive at Bribie Island.

Beautiful warm turquoise water, golden sand and an unbroken azure sky, to me it's a tropical paradise. The presence of a netted-off section of the sea as you'd imagine causes me to ask a few questions. I'd been afraid to even get in the bath since Raymond took me to see 'Jaws' a few summers ago. He didn't mind going to watch that particular film...with a 'body count' of just five half-eaten corpses which is a bit on the low side for his somewhat morbid tastes; he found it just about acceptable to satisfy his blood lust. To me it was the scariest film I have ever seen. Never mind mythical scary entities like ghosts, vampires and werewolves, the thing with great white sharks is that they are very much real and what's more they live in the sea here, here in Queensland...and surely they must get hungry!

Mum laughed at my concerns, "It's just a net to stop box jellyfish stinging you, as for sharks...there aren't any, they have all been eaten by the salties."

'Salties, and salties are?'

"Saltwater crocodiles, they love a shark as a tasty little snack between meals." She chuckles as she looks at the horror on my face.

Mother!...that really isn't helping. Despite everything I put my little red swimsuit on...my Special K bimbo one and I swim, the water so warm and clear. The kids are real water babies, once they are in, collecting seashells, swimming, and splashing about shrieking with laughter they just want to stay in, they just want to have fun. They are a little grumpy because Mum wouldn't let them go back in the water for half an hour after eating our picnic lunch. With the sun blazing down on the beach I admire the way she diligently plasters them with sun screen and produces hats for them from her bag, not optional she insists they wear them, and they don't complain about it.

'It's beautiful here Mum, I can see why you stayed.'

"It is, you've been here a fortnight now, you like what you see, would you consider a permanent move here?"

That question again, this place, Queensland, it has such a lot to offer, the weather, the wide open spaces, the cost of living is cheaper, it's beautiful; although it seems like all the creatures here are out to kill you. English creatures seem so gentle and polite in comparison don't they? I suppose I *could* sell up and move here permanently, true, but I wonder would I want to live here? here in this seemingly too good to be true idyllic land.

'I don't think so Mum, I love it here...but it's not home, not for me.'

"Robert will be back home on Wednesday, he's so looking forward to seeing you."

'Me too, it's been so long, just over sixteen years.'

"Has it really? time goes by so quick, you were always very good at remembering dates, anniversaries, birthdays, surprising really."

'Surprising, why is that?' I wonder what she means?

"Because, and I say this with all the love for you in the world, you are so dizzy, as a child you were, and you haven't really changed, you're still loveably ditzy."

'It's one of the chief reasons Raymond told me he wanted to divorce me. Mum, am I supposed to change because I'm getting older, try to be someone I'm not, is it so wrong to just be me?'

"No, no it isn't, you just stay being you, you'll find someone, someone who'll appreciate and love *you* for who *you* are, exactly as you are, you'll see, you are a lovely, wonderful woman, full of fun, full of life, you just need to be patient. Mr Right is out there somewhere. You'll find him, or he'll find you, God help him!" with a loud shriek of laughter Mum stands up.

"Let's get an ice cream then we'll think about wandering back, eh?"

Enticing Lydia and Cindy out of the water is easy with the tempting bribe of an ice cream. On our way home, the hours spent in the sea playing quickly catch up with them, in the back of the car the little cherubs are fast asleep inside five minutes. Mum, sitting in the passenger seat wants to know about things back home… my home.

"Do you ever go over to Lydney anymore Teresa?"

'No, not since Uncle Victor died, I have no real need to anymore.'

"Ah…Lydney, I didn't mind it there." A quick glance across I can see Mother has put her head back and is smiling…I think nostalgia mode has been selected and I'm about to be told for the umpteenth time one of her 'Lydney tales'. I don't mind a bit, she so enjoys recounting her memories and we are having such a lovely time.

"Did I tell you about that time in Lydney when there was a bank robbery?" She pitches it as a question but…well I'm going to hear the one about the soldiers and the robbers again.

"It happened when I was walking your brother to school in Lydney. It was when we was staying at Uncle Vic's and Aunty Daphne's, you'd have been what?…probably about seven, anyhow Aunty Daphne was taking you to the girl's school the other side of town. We were walking along the High Street, Robert and me when all of a sudden this massive soldier comes bounding up and bundles me and Robert behind a car, next thing I know all hell breaks loose, there's shooting and screaming, robbers lying on the floor covered in blood where the soldiers shot the thieving buggars. Then the big soldier, South African I think he was, he came back and told me to go home. He was such a nice friendly bloke, proper gentleman, I often wonder about him, what became of him, did he survive the war? Me and him made up some cock and ball story about a horse being loose in the street so Robert didn't get scared."

'It all happens in Lydney eh Mum?'

~ooo~

*Toowong, Brisbane, Queensland.*

Well, that was a great success, we have safely arrived home without mishap. Four, still round wheels; four occupants gloriously free of bruises. The girls are awake and have their second wind as they get out of the car. Lydia thanks my mum for having her as she disappears down the drive to go home.

"Nanny, Nanny, Nanny, can I play Lego with Aunty Teresa?" Cindy is bounding with enthusiastic energy.

"Yes, but it's shower time first, then you can play for half an hour before supper." Cindy is a little poppet, with a smile she dashes off to the bathroom in a blur without a hint of complaint. I think perhaps she is a little hasty, she's back in a few minutes, her hair dripping wet. It's nice for me as I towel dry her hair, it's sometimes just the little everyday things that are so nice, the simple little things. I only have three living close relatives left now and I feel a warm bond has developed with little Cindy, almost a maternal feeling.

"Teresa." Mum yells to me, she is taking the beach towels and picnic things from the car.

'Yes, Mum, do you want a hand?'

"No love, there is another envelope with your name on it pushed into the letterbox, hand delivered it is, must be from Jim."

'Oh, thanks Mum, put it on the side.' I was far too busy with Cindy, she'd brought her huge box of Lego onto the deck and upturned it with a huge crash. A quick check at the plants on the roof...that spider...no sign of it, right let's play.

Still impatient Mum shakes the envelope near my face. Taking it from her, the front of the otherwise plain envelope just says 'Teresa'. I push my lips forward contemplating.

"Go on, just open it, tell him you'll go out to dinner with him and Robert next week if you want a chaperone."

'Put it in the bin Mum, let's pretend we didn't see it.'

I feel guilty, Jim is sweet but I feel he is pressurising me. Mum looks aghast, sighing she flips up the kitchen bin lid with a push on the pedal and drops the envelope inside.

"He's asked you three times to go to dinner with him, put a couple of notes through the door, brought you lovely flowers twice, invited you to the pictures to see Grease, he's really keen on you."

Jim is being a little persistent, mmm...very persistent. I like him as a friend, listening to his tales over a cold beer but I don't feel any attraction to him. I told him I *would* go out one evening in a while as friends, but he has asked me a number of times. And now it seems he has resorted to putting it in writing...again!

'Mum, I told him I've already seen Grease, it's sweet him buying me flowers but it makes me feel awkward. I don't want to go to dinner with him yet. To keep you happy I'll go out with him next week, next week when Robert is home, okay?'

"Look, look Aunty Teresa, I've made a Lego flying car." Cindy excitedly thrusts a hastily snapped together collection of multi-coloured blocks, wheels on each of the corners under my nose. She's clipped on some flat grey strips, probably originally intended to be used for a Lego house or garage roof but Cindy has creatively recruited them to act as wings.

'That's fantastic Cindy, you have such imagination, I love it...just one thing.' A quick noisy rummage through the pile of Lego blocks on the floor, picking up a small square translucent block I clip it on the top to complete Cindy's engineering masterpiece.

"Ah, that's where the man sits to fly it right Aunty."

'Well, actually Cindy, it's a lady, get a lady to fly your car...plane...creation, they are altogether far more dependable than men.' Cindy, I think nearly understands and laughs.

"You're funny Aunty, what are you going to make?" So cute how she runkles her nose as the smile spreads across her lightly freckled face.

My mum laughs too, she's been so supportive to me, I think she finds my women's lib take on Cindy's pilot dilemma amusing.

Cindy and I continue playing with the Lego while Mum prepares dinner, our imaginations running wild as we construct a tall, far too tall and skinny wobbling tower; with for no real reason a Lego fireman and a one-armed pirate clipped to the top. In excess of my 5ft 6inches the result was inevitable. A crescendo of noise and widespread fall-out of scattered various coloured blocks strewn all over the deck accompanied by our screams turning into giggles of delight. It's funny, despite my being forty-one years old, Mum arriving on the scene immediately post skyscraper collapse to see what the commotion is I still feel like a naughty little girl expecting to be told off.

I suppose it was inevitable...Mum is many things...many lovely things, however one of her at times perplexing characteristics is being a bit of an interfering busy body. Handing me the note from inside the envelope she'd retrieved from the bin, speckled brown with some soggy spots of tea and a little worse for wear from having damp potato peelings land on it. Her curiosity had got the better of her, wanting a sneaky peek she'd opened the envelope languishing in the bin. Without words, just a puzzled look, she hands it to me.

*Ms Teresa Sheen.*
*According to my records, you owe the sum of £11.99 incurred for the replacement of Evel's motorbike.*
*May I request you make payment over dinner this evening.*
*8:30 pm. The Atrium, Stamford Plaza Hotel. Brisbane.*
*Dress code while optional...Fabulous, is of course preferred.*

I can only smile, it occurs to me now, as I'd looked at the envelope, the writing, it had something familiar about it...the handwriting, that note Callum gave to Lionel for me with the bicycle. What can I say? I say nothing. Both nervous and elated, I just feel butterflies rising inside me, tears of joy perhaps prematurely forming in my eyes.

The note will make absolutely no sense at all to Mum, how could it?

'It's from Callum, has he travelled half way around the world just to take me out to dinner?' I can't contain my joy, I'm bursting with excitement.

She giggled, "Well, if that's the only reason, if *you* are the only reason he's come to Australia then I'd say that it tells you he's rather sweet on you."

'Mum, where is the Stamford Plaza, how far, how long will it take to get there?...it's already a quarter to eight...shit.'

"Don't worry, it's only ten minutes by taxi, go and have a shower and wash your hair, you got time. We can do something with your barnet between us, it's all matted and salty, it looks a right state. You'll need to put your best glad rags on, it's posh that hotel, got money has he...this Callum?"

'Do you know, I have no idea, he's never talked to me about money, I know he has very good taste though.'

I'm trying to remain calm, Mum says it isn't too far, I have a little over half an hour to get ready...I've got this under control. Except...what to wear, my red dress or...*those* Levis? I know he likes those.

The ten-minute taxi ride mostly alongside the Brisbane river gives me time to get my breath back. Showered, hair washed and dried and dressed inside twenty minutes. Fanning my face with my hand, it's stifling inside the taxi, I will myself not to perspire. I wonder what is he doing here, has he really come all this way to see me or is it just a work thing? Maybe he just happens to be in the area. How does he know I'm even here and where my mum lives? I suppose I shouldn't be surprised...he is a detective after all. I'm also very nervous, this is so out of the blue, I was playing Lego one minute...the next...well I don't know.

~ooo~

*Stamford Plaza Hotel, Brisbane, Queensland.*

Mum was right, this is a very posh hotel. Relieved that I'm only five minutes late. A doorman in a grey suit and top hat is standing outside on a green carpet.

"Good evening, Madam." Opening the door I'm ushered inside to a refreshingly cool, tastefully opulent entrance foyer. A tranquil haven of polished marble, mirrors, and teak.

At the reception desk I hurriedly ask where the bar is, that sounds rather desperate, doesn't it? Anyway I'm escorted by a concierge to a huge, leafy, mostly glass room, an atrium...orangery...conservatory?

Seated close, but not too close to the pianist who is gently tickling some jazz from a grand piano...Callum.

I can't help but beam with joy as we move towards each other, hugging each other tightly. I want to hug him forever, never letting him go; I have so many questions.

It's only been around eleven maybe twelve weeks but it seems a lifetime ago, so much has happened since we said goodbye.

'Callum, what on earth are you doing here, why aren't you in Canada?'

Sitting down on two of the cane chairs dotted around a glass table, they creak adorably as our weight settles into them.

"The assignment in Canada has finished, it was quite straightforward. Some Panamanians were trying to sneak their wares into Canada, complete amateurs, unlike those Albanians, they were altogether far more professional." Callum titters whilst gazing intently at me, his tawny eyes glinting from the sun streaming in through the glass panels of the roof.

"That's a beautiful dress, I love the colour and style."

'Oh, this old thing, I've had it ages.' Brushing his remark aside flippantly, I *may* have just fibbed a little. The dress is brand new and cost a small fortune. Kim and I saw it when we went on our shopping expedition to Bristol just before I left for Australia. Displayed on a mannequin, the centrepiece in the window of Debenhams in Broadmead. Go and try it on Kim demanded, believe me she did demand it, so I tried it on. When I came out of the fitting room to give Kim a twirl she said 'wow'. I looked in the mirror, it looked fabulous but...for some reason I was hesitant, Kim wasn't.

There ensued one of our high speed, active debates of few words. We often do it...verbal tennis.

Buy it she said, just *look* at the price I said, just *look* in the mirror she said, can I afford it I said, you *can* afford it she said,
Are you sure I said, don't argue she said...so I bought it.

The colour, style and fit...that old adage, you only get what you pay for. Quite frankly after the past two, please cover your ears, 'shitty' months I'd had I was really in the mood to treat myself. Glad I did, Callum seems to like it.

'Thank you, and I'd like to thank you for the bicycle, it's beautiful, I love riding it.'

"My pleasure...anyway where were we? Ah yes, Canada and coming home. When I came home no matter how hard I tried I couldn't get you out of my mind, I wanted to see you, even if it was just for a cuppa. I know what we said when I left...I remember that night only too well, but I couldn't fight it, I had to see you." He smiles with that endearing slight sideways twist of his head.

"The second night after I returned from Canada I couldn't sleep. Tossing and turning there was no way I could sleep, I got in Tom Jones and drove all night from Edinburgh."
Well, that really didn't take very long, I'm swooning, him and that voice of his.

"When I got to Brookhayes you weren't there, so naturally I asked Yvonne. I must have looked a fright. She made me a cuppa and cooked me a massive breakfast...she filled me in on all the recent news and where I might find you. She told me you and Raymond are getting divorced?"

'Yes, we are.'

"I don't want to pry or appear–" interrupting him, I think I can anticipate his train of thought.

'It was going to happen sooner or later. Raymond had been having an affair with his secretary, he was going to leave me for her, he was just biding his time. *You* aren't to blame, *you* aren't the reason Callum.'

Entwining his fingers together, as if praying, lightly tapping his hands against his chin, deep in thought.

"Did you not think to let me know, your divorcing, doesn't it change everything?" He is putting me on the spot; I am only going to be honest with him.

'Of course, it more than crossed my mind, but the truth was I was too scared, what if you had found someone, what if you didn't want me, how could I face more heartbreak, more rejection? My self-confidence had hit rock-bottom. My husband had just left me for another woman; a woman nearly ten years older than me and not a particularly attractive one at that. I couldn't take the risk of being torn apart any further.' This is harrowing, but I steel myself to be candid.

'What's more, am I really what you need? Yes, I fell in love with you, imagined to myself how I'd love to be with you; honestly though, in the long-term can I give you what you need, what you want? Maybe the novelty will wear off, the thrill, the allure of an older woman? Perhaps you'll want children. I'm forty-one, who knows if I can give you a child? how old are you anyway Callum? you've never told me, I've never asked you...early maybe mid-thirties?'

All the time he remains motionless, gently rocking his hands back and forth against his chin. Exhaling with a sigh, he moves his hands away from his face, his expression earnest. Indignantly he thrusts an outstretched wagging finger towards me, his tone agitated.

"What gives you the right...the right to think you know what I want, that you can decide what I need? It's you that I want, that I love. Why do you think I am here; do you seriously think I travelled all this way just for a glass of chardonnay? As for your remark...the novelty wearing off, the short-lived allure of the older woman, you know me Teresa, you know me better than that." He scoffs dismissively; I just feel a little indignant and foolish at his telling me off!

"I'm forty-one years of age, the same as you lassie, like a good wine we've aged well haven't we...you and I?"

His tone softens as he sees the surprised look on my face, I had no idea we were exactly the same age. He looks a little remorseful, apologising for the finger wagging and the acerbic tone in his voice; he plants a light kiss on my cheek.

"So where does that leave us?" He asks, uncertainty in his voice, "I remember that somewhat eventful rainy night before I left for Canada, we said some things to each other."

'We did, we said some things, the question is...did *you* mean them? I know that I meant the things I said.' My thoughts flash back to that night.

That torrid night, the torrential rain, drunken Raymond, that passionate stolen kiss, my agonising heartache.

"Aye, I solemnly meant every word I said. Do you think we could make a life together Teresa?"

'When you say together?'

"I mean together as a couple, live together, maybe get married one day, if that's what you'd like. I could transfer from the Met to Gloucestershire." Right now, the swooning is twice as bad...good. It's not just how he's speaking, it's what he's saying.

'Are you telling me that you'd be prepared to give up your exciting job travelling around the world apprehending baddies to settle down with me in sleepy Comberley, where the most job excitement you'll ever get is ticking off kids cherry knocking or misspelling knob on the church wall?'

"That is exactly what I'm saying, you belong there, there in Comberley. I loved living there." I have to say he looks sincere. Needing time to absorb what he has said I change the subject.

'How long are you planning to stay in Australia Callum?'

"Until *you* go home, I don't want to impose or assume anything, I thought maybe we could fly home together, how does first class sound?"

'Expensive!'

"Kellie, she gets very favourable discounts on tickets for family members."

'In that case, it sounds delightful.' Wow, flying home first class, how fabulous.

'The thing is I'm here for another fortnight, do you not have to work?'

"Lionel has given me extended leave, things didn't go entirely as we planned in Canada, one of my Interpol colleagues got hurt, badly hurt. I was long overdue some leave, Lionel told me to have as long as I needed, I'll probably take a month."

'Oh my God, *you* weren't hurt were you?'

"Och no, it has shaken me up, it's time I think about settling down; I'd like to put down some roots and live a quieter life."

'And are you going to stay here in this...this palace for the next fortnight?'

I pick up my wine, a refreshingly chilled Hunter Valley chardonnay. Callum putting a hand to his chin looks pensive.

"The reservation for my room is for a week, I suppose I can always extend my booking."

As if I'm going to leave him here...no, definitely not. He is coming to stay with me at Mum's.

'Come home with me in the morning; come and meet my mum. You don't need to stay here, you can stay with us at the house until we go home, there's plenty of room.'

I consider the sleeping arrangements, I know what I'd like!... but one step at a time.

'I think for propriety's sake we probably ought to have separate rooms, except for one particular night.'

"I don't want to be a burde–"

'You won't be, I won't take no for an answer, Mum and Cindy will love you, and you can protect me from all the creepy crawlies, it's settled, don't argue.'

"Then it will be a pleasure, I'll check out of the hotel in the morning. A moment ago you mentioned one particular night, what particular night would that be?"

'Christmas Eve of course, three days before I...we fly home. Once Cindy has gone to sleep, I'll sneak into your room and give you your Christmas present.'

"I feel guilty, I haven't got anything for you."

'Oh, I think you might have, Mr Gilchrist.' Giggling mischievously, taking one of his hands in mine, the lightest of touches with my fingertips, it's Callum's turn to enjoy those delightful soothing palm circles.

The impeccably dressed pianist finishes playing 'On The Street Where You Live' to modest applause from the assembled hotel guests. Turning the page on the music book in front of him. Taking a brief break, he lifts his glass of water from the top of the piano for a much needed, well-earned drink; the atrium is rather warm, as you'd imagine.

"Excuse me one moment Teresa." Walking the dozen paces across to the pianist, a few words quietly spoken in the musician's ear, a couple of banknotes exchange hands; Callum returns to our table with a broad smile, looking pleased with himself.

It had to be I suppose, minus the haunting lyrics, the melody and the memory of that moment flood back. How we laughed at the time, how we were tempted at the time.

I gently squeeze Callum's hand whilst the pianist softly plays Dusty's 'The Look of Love'.

'Are you hungry Callum? I'm not, not for food anyway.' I attempt to give him a cheeky wink, I've never mastered winking, it probably actually looks more as if I have a piece of grit lodged in my eye.

"Hungry, no, not really. When you said a while ago, 'come home *with* me in the morning', are you suggesti–"

'You have a room here in the hotel, right?' I butt in again, the newly resurgent, newly empowered Teresa strikes again!

"Aye, but it's only a small room, wi' just a single bed. It was the only room available at such short notice."

'I'd better give my mum a quick call, let her know I won't be home tonight; then we can sneak up to your room. As for your single bed, I really don't think that's going to be a problem, do you?'

# Chapter 24

## ***Goodbye 78***

*British Airways, Flight: BA5705*

I can't believe it, the space, the opulence...first class, no wonder it's so expensive. Relaxing comfortably on the first leg of the journey home, my head pleasantly spinning, the champagne, reflecting on the past month. How my life has changed, it seems like a dream, sitting here in my huge first-class seat, next to *that* man, *that* man with *that* voice.

Just a few days ago we were swimming on the Great Barrier Reef, the two of us and Cindy. I worry that I'm going to wake up, alone in Brookhayes, worrying that this is all just a pleasant dream. I prod a snoozing Callum, just to make sure...nope it all seems pretty real.

He had organised a three day trip for us last week, flying to Cairns, staying in a log cabin, swimming on the Great Barrier Reef and exploring the nearby rain forest. The experience although wonderful, far beyond wonderful, stirred something inside me. It gave me a brief albeit rose tinted snapshot of how the future might be, how it might feel. Callum and me along with our 'borrowed daughter' Cindy forming a temporary little family. Relaxing, having fun and very much enjoying simply spending time together. I have thought long and hard on Callum's proposal for us to be together, and haven't once had the merest doubt, not the faintest hint of cold feet, quite the contrary.

So, tomorrow I will be home, my beautiful cottage in Gloucestershire.

In a few short months Callum...my boyfriend, I like the sound of that, he'll be moving in with me. In a few short months my divorce will be finalised...goodbye Teresa Sheen...hello again Teresa Taylor.

No doubt those few short months will drag seemingly eternal, but they will pass.

And it's nearly time to say goodbye to 1978, hello 1979, just three days left. 1978, quite a year for me...a memorable year, although not always for the right reasons; it's ending with a huge smile. Just another year? I rather think not.

Right, I think that's about it, all's well that ends well right? But before we say goodbye for now though let's just fast forward in time a while, there is one tiny little thing I should perhaps just mention...relax...we don't need yet *another* new pope and at long last the dustmen have gone back to work. If you'd like to flick over to the next page.

# Chapter 25

## ***A lovely evening in May...1980***

*Comberley, Gloucestershire.*

'Callum, *this* is all your fault, *all* of it.'

Soothing my forehead with one hand; he traces those enchanting fingertip circles on my palm with the other, whispering sweet nothings in my ear, the way he does.

'That's not going to get you off the hook; it's all your fault, I hate you.' I pretend to look angry at him, it's never going to work of course...but I have to try. I repeat his fabled words back to him sarcastically.

'Let's have a break in Paris you said, it'll be romantic you said.'

"Aye, and it was, it was very romantic, I didn't hear you complaining at the time."

I childishly imitate him with my terrible attempt at a Scottish accent. 'Och, I dinnae hear you complaining at the time lassie.'

Callum laughs as he continues caressing my palms.

"I'm afraid I'm going to have to arrest you for that outburst, would you like me to get my handcuffs out again like last time?"

'Why?' I remain firmly petulant.

"It's a serious matter...impersonating a police officer."

I so love this man sat on the bed beside me, two years on, his voice still enchants me.

He continues gently soothing my head, all the while the excruciating contractions wash over me. In the hospital delivery suite a couple of young nurses and a couple of doctors are milling around, talking quietly amongst themselves. Casting discreet, but not *that* discreet, 'don't look now but' glances my way. I may be the size of a whale, but my ears are still fully functional!

'Callum, did you hear that?...geriatric...geriatric mother they said.' He chuckles at my indignation.

The two nurse's numbers are bolstered by the arrival of a stout, dour faced older woman, matronly looking in her pristine dark blue uniform. Tersely she looks towards Callum who is walking up and down stretching his legs near to my bed, equally tersely she barks at him.

"I don't approve of this modern parenting nonsense you know, the father being present at the birth indeed, your place is *outside*, outside in the waiting room."

"Och, I'm not the father," he says with a flash of his police warrant card, "I'm just here to make sure she doesn't escape from custody...again!"

The titters among the two young nurses were met with a brief scowl and venomous tut from the dowdy ward sister before she turns her scathing frosty edged attention back towards Callum.

"*When* things get messy and busy down there, and *they* will." She jabs an outstretched finger in the direction of my very much on display nether regions, "And you faint, don't imagine for a moment that we'll do anything about it, we'll leave you exactly where you fall, and we'll probably trample you underfoot repeatedly." Her aggressively gesturing finger takes aim towards the door this time, "You've been warned."

Our baby isn't due for another week, I had felt restless and unable to sleep at bedtime this evening. So with a mug of cocoa each, Callum and I had stayed up late watching a repeated episode of 'Cannon' on the telly. I felt an affinity with the grossly overweight TV detective as he struggled to catch the baddie. A kindredship, both of us with our huge bellies, him trying to catch an altogether younger and fitter criminal, chasing after him on foot across a piece of waste ground, me, munching my way through a large jar of pickled onions...my craving. Then Cannon and I both have to face up to grim and bitter disappointment. For the balding obese TV detective he knows the game is up as the baddie easily scales a six-foot-high wire fence and flees, while I, the beached whale in a nightie on the couch, well I have to confront the harsh reality that I had eaten *all* the pickled onions. No matter how optimistically I trawled around in the jar with my long fork all that remained was vinegar. Screwing the lid back on and uncomfortably stretching to place the jar on the coffee table hindered by my bloated carcass. I then had to confront something else, something entirely different, a surprising warm, soggy but not altogether new sensation.

'Jesus...Callum, my waters have just broken, the baby is coming...get me to the hospital, now!'

Guess who had left their little red Mini blocking the drive? Barely able to fit behind the steering wheel I'd just abandoned it there when I came home from meeting Kim at the Fox and Goose for an orange juice and no ciggie earlier this evening. Not wanting to waste time shuffling cars about, 'Tom Jones' was in the way of his Police Land Rover, Callum managed to sort of sympathetically fold me up and squeeze me into the Mini's passenger seat for the one-mile journey to Comberley hospital whilst I alternately groaned about the pain and his driving my little car too fast. Screeching to a halt outside the hospital he unfolded me and carried my quite considerable bulk inside.

The contractions are coming thick and fast now, I feel very reassured with Callum by my side, I always do, he has that effect on me. That self-assured half smile he always wears, that nothing is going to go wrong cute smile.

'I must look a fright.' Moaning between gasps of gas and air; I squeeze the blood out of his hand, telling him I feel horribly fat and unglamorous.

"You look beautiful sweetie, you always do, but your breath smells terrible...those pickled onions." He says wafting a hand in front of his face before glancing around and stealing a quick kiss from me while the dour faced sister, is distracted looking the other way.

There is much interest from the nurses, the frosty sister and the paediatricians all gathering around the business end, intently prodding and poking, all my modesty and dignity had abandoned me at the doors to the delivery room. My geriatric status seems to be garnering enough interest to ensure the delivery room has drawn a capacity crowd.

With several determined but painful pushes, some uncharacteristic verbal abuse from me aimed at Callum and some lovely encouragement from the two young nurses our baby arrives into the world...The until now frosty ward sister even managing a happy smile announcing to me,

"Congratulations Mrs Gilchrist, you have a beautiful baby girl." She concedes with a more muted and somewhat forced. "Mr Gilchrist, well done for not fainting."

Oh, did you catch that? sorry it's been a while, quite a few things have happened since we last spoke, sorry I forgot to say...Mrs Gilchrist. Callum and I were married in Edinburgh last summer, it was a lovely day. He...that man of mine...my husband looked fabulous in his Argyll jacket with his kilt and his sporran.

Kilt...I imagine you are wondering about the rumour? You must be saying go on Teresa...tell us, spill the beans we're dying to know is anything worn under the kilt?

Well, from my own personal experience I can say a resounding no...everything under Callum's kilt is in perfect working order! Sorry just my little joke. Seriously, as regards to what is worn under a kilt, well I know the answer to that particular conundrum now but unfortunately I couldn't possibly comment. You see I'm the very happy wife of a proud Scotsman and I'm sworn to secrecy.

Our wedding ceremony was held in a very pleasant register office after which we spent our special day in a beautiful hotel with friends and family. We honeymooned in Sorrento in Italy. I don't think I stopped smiling for the whole week.

So now, a result of that romantic break in Paris nine months ago we have been blessed with a healthy 8lb baby girl...Charlotte Teresa Gilchrist. I chose the first name; Callum is responsible for her middle name. It's something of a Gilchrist family tradition, the child's middle name passed on from the respective parent's Christian name.

He is walking around the room with her now...his daughter, lovingly cradling her in his arms, a very proud daddy intently gazing into her eyes. Look at him, chatting away to her. I think someone maybe totally smitten.

I notice one thing, his ever present half smile is missing at the moment; he isn't doing that now...no, he's absolutely beaming with delight. Beaming at her and beaming at me.

Now, if you'll excuse me, it really has been a bit of a day. Very constructive, but this particular geriatric, dappy, dozy, flirty, daft blond mare with an allegedly wrinkly forehead and too much energy just needs a little snooze.

~ooo~

Other novels by Edward Stringer.

Least Expected Fortune.(330 pages)
ISBN 978-1-7384485-0-0

An Unexpected Change of Fortune.(350 pages)
ISBN 978-1-7384485-2-4

Available from Amazon in paperback and Kindle e-book.
A series of two novels. Set in 1944, following the fortunes of four young men from very different walks of life thrown together to form a specialised covert unit three years previously, amidst the darkest days of WW2. On the run up to D-day, they take advantage of an opportunity that crosses their path, crossing the Rubicon in doing so. Fuelled by their ambition, they hatch a plan to amass a fortune to realise their dreams for the future.

*"We've done our duty, more than done it. Let's use this brief unique opportunity and our particular talents for ourselves. There is nothing we can't do if we put our minds to it. Let's build something together…something we can call our own."*
Sgt Luke Reynolds…3 Section, LSR.

Printed in Great Britain
by Amazon

51891607R00162